SUBVERTED

COAST GUARD RECON BOOK 4

LORI MATTHEWS

ABOUT THE BOOK

From the bestselling author of the Callahan Security Series.

Meet Finn Walsh of the U.S. Coast Guard's TEAM RECON. As in reconstructed. As in broken and needs fixing.

After an abandoned ship is found in international waters, Team RECON is summoned by Homeland Security to find answers. On their approach to the vessel, Finn Walsh has massive reservations about boarding the empty U.S. Navy ship. His worst fears come to life when they find all the navigation and electronics equipment disabled, smashed, or gone. But when Finn finds a hidden stash of dead bodies, and the boat begins to sink because of a violent storm, he can't get off the thing fast enough.

Homeland Security analyst Victory Stanhope evaluates foreign and domestic terrorist cells from the safety of a desk in Washington D.C. After a dangerous stint with the CIA, that's exactly how she likes it. But when a 'request' to investigate an abandoned ship comes from the Director himself, Tory heads back into the field as the reluctant leader of a

Coast Guard special operations team. Life becomes more interesting after she realizes that the unforgettable man she slept with once at a low point in her life is part of the team she's overseeing.

Although neither of them can fight the whirlpool of emotion between them, in the interest of national security, Tory sidelines her strong attraction to Finn and throws herself into the riddle of what happened to the crew of the *Oceanus Explorer* and who is selling government secrets to other nations.

The stakes get even higher when Tory realizes that the sinister mastermind of the treasonous plot is closer to home than she thought possible.

Subverted

Copyright © 2022 Lori Matthews

eBook License Notes:

You may not use, reproduce or transmit in any manner, any part of this book without written permission, except in the case of brief quotations used in critical articles and reviews, or in accordance with federal Fair Use laws. All rights are reserved.

This eBook is licensed for your personal enjoyment only; it may not be resold or given away to other people. If you would like to share this book with another person, please purchase an additional copy for each recipient. If you're reading this book and did not purchase it, or it was not purchased for your use only, please return to your eBook retailer and purchase your own copy. Thank you for respecting the hard work of this author.

Disclaimer: This is a work of fiction. Names, characters, places, and incidents are products of the author's imagination, or the author has used them fictitiously.

For Suzanne Burke. A true friend through it all. Thirty-eight years and counting. Here's to the next thirty-eight.

ACKNOWLEDGMENTS

Once again, a heartfelt thanks to Joseph D'Elia (Lieutenant, USCG) who is always willing to answer all my questions and then turn a blind eye when I manipulate the answers just a wee to suit my needs. I couldn't have created Team RECON without his help. Any mistakes are my own.

My deepest gratitude also goes out to my editors, Corinne DeMaagd and Heidi Senesac. They are truly the most patient and understanding people. The fact that they can take my ramblings and make them sound coherent, is truly a miracle. Thanks also go out to my cover artist, Llewellen Designs for making my story come alive: my virtual assistant, Susan Poirier and my FaceBook guru, Amanda Robinson. My personal cheer squad which I could not survive without: Janna MacGregor, Suzanne Burke, Stacey Wilk, Kimberley Ash and Tiara Inserto. My husband and my children who make my hair turn gray but also make me laugh. And to you, the reader. Your emails and posts mean the world to me. The fact that you read my stories is the greatest gift ever. Thank you.

PROLOGUE

"Are you sure?" He squinted intently at the screen.

The tech seated in front of the monitor nodded in a jerky motion and blinked rapidly.

He straightened his tall frame, still peering at the screen. He then turned, went over to a table in the middle of the small room, and grabbed a satellite phone. He stared down at it. If the tech was wrong, there would be hell to pay. On the other hand, if they'd found the correct spot, then they were ahead of schedule. It was good to be ahead of schedule.

He glanced at the tech again. The kid couldn't be older than mid-twenties. He was about five-feet-ten inches with bright orange hair and a ton of freckles. Danny, he thought the kid's name was. He was skinny, as though he hadn't filled out yet. He looked like a geeky teenager. He still had acne, for Christ's sake.

This whole thing made the man uneasy. His close-cropped hair made a rasping sound as he ran his hand over it. He thought he'd stopped caring about his assignments years ago, but this one… he couldn't put his finger on it, but it was BS and he knew. If there was any way, he'd abort the mission and disappear into the jungles of the Amazon or the mountains of Tibet. Somewhere no one would think to look for him. This mission had bothered him from the very beginning. It wasn't about the killing. He was used to that. It was the betrayal. He didn't care about his country anymore. It hadn't cared about him in a long while. But still. This was betrayal on a different level, a level that went against his personal moral code.

The titanium plates in his leg said he should make the call, but somewhere in his dark heart a smidgen of loyalty remained. Something he thought he'd stamped out long ago. The question was what to do about the lingering allegiance. He traced the scar on the left side of his throat. Another gift from his country. Once he made the call, there was no going back. If he didn't make the call, there'd be no going forward. He glanced at the screen again.

He'd signed away his life a long time ago. He wasn't afraid of dying, not in the least. But which hill did he *want* to die on? If he proceeded, then he would live a bit longer and go on to the next assignment. If he stopped, they would take him out, no question. He might, however, have just enough time to leave a small warning. Did he want to do that? Could he?

"What are you waiting for?" The harsh bark came from behind him.

He turned. Mr. Brown was standing at the entry point of the room. Danny, the freckled tech, was standing just behind him. He hadn't noticed that the boy had left his station. So, the little shit had ratted him out. No doubt he had been promised some sort of bonus if he got things done quickly, but the only bonus the kid, and everyone else on the ship, would get was a bullet in the back of the head when this was done. Too bad they didn't know that. Danny wouldn't have been so quick to spill his guts.

He pointed at the screen. "Look."

Mr. Brown stepped up and studied the screen for a long moment. "Jesus, I can't see a damn thing."

"Exactly," he confirmed. "Making the call without being one-hundred percent is not optimal."

Danny took a seat at the station and swiveled his chair around to face the monitor.

"Are you sure?" Mr. Brown growled at the tech as he stared at the screen. Mr. Brown wasn't the man's real name, just like he didn't go by his given name either. It was best to refer to each other by color, and he'd always been Mr. White, as in his hair color. No one wanted their real name known. Hell, they'd been doing this kind of work for so long, half of them didn't remember what their real name was.

"Yes, sir," Danny said.

Mr. Brown stared a while longer, but the picture on the screen did not get any clearer. He straightened. "Make the call."

With a muted sigh and a glare at Danny, he nodded and hit the button on the phone. The decision was out of his hands. He would just have to go along with it. The small part of him uncomfortable with the assignment was now screaming at him to stop, but there was nothing he could do. If he was going to survive, he'd have to crush the last bit of light in his dark soul.

The call was answered. "We've found it," he said.

"Good. Proceed." The line went dead.

"It's a go." He glanced at the screen again and then the tech. The kid smirked. He decided instantly that he'd enjoy physically erasing that smug look when he killed the man.

CHAPTER ONE

Finn Walsh stared at the origami crane in his hands. It was a delicate bird and had been a bit of a bitch to make, but he liked it. He set it down on the desk with the other paper animals. It was getting too crowded, he noted. There had to be hundreds of forms on the table. He needed a new hobby. Hell, he needed a life.

He ran his hands through his tousled brown hair, then stood up and walked out of the second bedroom he used as his office and into the main living room. The kitchen was situated in one corner. He grabbed a beer out of the fridge and opened it then leaned against the large island with the granite countertop. He looked out over the living area with its black leather couch and matching chairs to the large flat-screen TV on the wall. He took a long swig of the IPA.

Setting his beer down, he rolled his bad shoulder. The gunshot wound had healed nicely but his injured shoulder stiffened up a lot more than the other one. It was uncomfortable a lot of the time if he didn't do his exercises. It wasn't as strong as it had been either. The doctor said it would take a bit of time. Finn wondered if it would ever come back fully.

The announcer was reporting about a car race in Europe. Maybe he should take up racing. There was a track outside of Miami. He could learn to race. He loved to drive fast. It could be fun, but it would also require some sort of regular schedule. Being part of Team RECON, the Coast Guard special operations team he was assigned to, meant he never knew where he would be or when. He'd most likely end up having to withdraw from races too often.

He glanced out his patio doors off the living room. The others in the group liked to see the water, and he had to admit it was nice, but he preferred the Miami skyline. He liked to know the world was out there. It was a holdover from childhood. His dad would lock him in a closet when he misbehaved. The punishment terrified him, but not because of the dark. The darkness had never bothered him, but he never knew if anyone was still in the house with him. Was he all alone, or would his father come back? If someone were to ask him, he couldn't be sure which option he'd been more afraid of.

He took another swig, savoring the strong, heavy taste of the beer. It was Friday night, and he was home making origami animals. *Fuckin' pathetic*. He could have gone out on another date with Lucinda, or was her name Lucia? Whatever it was, she was keen and beautiful. He just wasn't interested in her. She was boring.

The only woman he really wanted to go out with again was Lady X. That wasn't her real name of course, just what he called her. She'd told him her name was Donna, but that was a lie. He knew it the moment it had come out of her mouth, but he didn't care. It was a one-night stand. What did it matter? That's what he'd thought at the time. The thing was, he didn't want it to be. Not then and not now, all this time later, but he had no way to track her down.

The night in question had happened years ago, when he'd

been stationed in Virginia. It had been spectacular in every way possible, but he got a callout first thing in the morning and had to leave before getting any of her information, not that she would have given it to him anyway. They'd met at a bar in D.C., and he'd gone back a couple of times, but she never showed up again. She was "the one that got away."

When his cell rang, he answered quickly. "Axe, what's up?"

There was laughter on the other end. "You're home, bored to tears with your zoo animals, aren't you?" Axe laughed again. "Carolina is in town so she, Sloan, and Andrea are all going out. We're left to our own devices. Elias said to call everyone and head to his place."

"Sounds good. I'll bring some beer and meet you there shortly." He clicked off the call. Well, that explained why Nick was in such a good mood lately. Carolina, his better half, was visiting from Morocco. He had no idea how his team leader and good friend managed a long-distance relationship like that, but he figured it was all about finding the right one.

He grabbed his car keys off the counter and started toward the door. He'd pick up some beer and some snacks. Elias's girlfriend, Andrea, loved Cheetos, so he'd grab some of those, too. Man, she could eat like a horse, yet was totally in shape. He liked a woman who could eat. All these women like Lucinda, or whatever her name was, picked at a salad and pretended they loved it. It gave him the creeps. Too thin and scary. He liked women who ate well and didn't worry so much about their figure. *Life is short. Eat cake.* He'd seen that sign outside of a coffee shop once, and it had stuck with him. There was much truth to those words.

Twenty minutes later, he walked into Elias's apartment after greeting Mrs. Jimenez in the hallway. She'd become much friendlier after it came out that Elias worked for the

Coast Guard. She and all the other retirees in the building loved having him around now. She was always bringing over food to him.

"Hey," Finn greeted everyone as he put the beer and snacks on the kitchen island in the middle of the loft space. "Mrs. Jimenez?" he asked, pointing to the stuffed peppers on the counter directly ahead by the stove.

"Yup." Elias grinned and patted his belly as he sat back on the couch in the living area. His dark brown hair was buzzed short, and his deep brown eyes were filled with mirth. "She's taking care of me, and it's a good thing 'cause Andrea doesn't cook, and I'm tired of making all the meals."

Finn laughed as he walked around the island and into the kitchen area. "I'm sure you'll survive. I'm stealing some peppers. Mrs. Jimenez is a great cook." He grabbed a plate out of the cupboard.

Nick walked down the hallway from the bathroom. "Hey, Finn. Are you getting peppers? Heat up some for me." Nick scratched the stubble on his jaw. His dark hair was also cut short, but not buzzed. He winked one of his blue eyes at Finn and pointed at Elias.

"Wait now! Those are my peppers. What am I going to do for dinner tomorrow?" Elias walked over to the kitchen island.

Nick chuckled. "You left them on the counter."

"You'll just have to cook, sunshine," Finn said as he put some stuffed peppers on a plate. "Besides, I brought Cheetos. You can claim you bought them for your girlfriend and make brownie points."

Elias grunted. "I hate that crap. She'll know one of you guys brought them."

The buzzer for the front door of the building went off, and Elias immediately went over and checked the camera. He buzzed the visitors in. Two minutes later, Cain and Axe were at the door.

Cain brought more beer and Axe had pizzas. "I thought you guys might be hungry. I stopped over at your guy's pizza truck and picked up a few pies. He's doing swift business." He set the pizzas on the counter and pushed a lock of dark blond hair out of his blue eyes.

Elias had gone into business with Miguel Gutierrez, who made amazing pizza out of a truck. Elias said, "Yeah, he's doing well. If it keeps going well, we'll look for some restaurant space."

Axe put the pizza on the island, and Finn handed out more plates. He pulled the peppers from the microwave and set them on the table, then went back to get some cutlery.

"Mrs. Jimenez," Cain said appreciatively. He grabbed some pizza and then went over and sat down at the dining table. He snagged a pepper off the plate. Cain's green eyes and black hair tied back in a man bun always made him a hit with the ladies. Finn was surprised he was free on a Friday night.

Finn grabbed some pizza on his way over to the table and pulled two peppers from the plate before he sat down. All the guys joined him, and the room was silent as they all dug into the food.

"If at all possible, save a slice or two for Sloan. She'll be desperate for greasy food once she gets home from a night out with your girlfriends," Axe said, giving a side-eye to Nick and Elias.

"I think Sloan's the instigator, so don't be complaining to me." Elias got up and went to the counter. He brought back a six-pack of beer and put it on the table.

"Agreed," said Nick as his cell phone went off.

Finn glanced at Nick's phone, and his stomach immediately knotted. Finn couldn't see who was calling because the phone was face down on the table, but he instinctively knew it was trouble. So did the rest of the team because everyone stopped eating and held their breath.

"Taggert," Nick answered the phone. "Yes, sir." There was a long pause while Nick listened to the officer on the other end.

Finn glanced down at his food, but he was no longer hungry.

He was just getting used to being in Miami. It was a different sort of gig for all of them, but he liked it. They weren't at sea all that much, and it was good to be with such a close-knit team on U.S. soil.

Somehow, he had the feeling this call was going to upset all that.

For over a week now, Finn had sensed something bad was heading their way; a niggling anxiety that he couldn't shake. He always got the feeling when things were about to turn to shit in his life. The last time he'd had the sensation, he'd gone ape-shit on his old boss just before he'd been shot. A trickle of sweat rolled down his back as he pushed his plate away.

"Yes, sir. They're with me now." There was another pause. "Yes, sir. Will do." There was another short period of silence and then one final, "Yes, sir," before Nick broke the connection. He put the phone down on the table and looked up at them.

"That was Admiral Bertrand. He has a new assignment for us." When his face grew serious, the knot in Finn's gut tightened. "Apparently, the Canadian Coast Guard found a ship, the *Oceanus Explorer*, floating off the coast of Nova Scotia in international waters after it was reported by a passing cargo ship. It appears to have been abandoned. It's registered to a shell company. They're looking to see who really owns it, but it's very convoluted."

Finn's heartbeat ticked upward.

"Bertrand wants us to go check it out. The Canadians are willing to hand this off to us, or at the very least, they have requested our assistance."

"What makes the Canadians think it's an American ship?" Finn asked.

Nick shook his head. "They didn't say they thought it was American, just that they were having trouble tracking down the owner."

Something didn't add up. "But why reach out then?" Finn asked.

Nick shrugged. "That's what we're supposed to find out. There's something going on, but no one wants to say what. Bertrand wants us up there ASAP. He wants us to fly into Maine and meet up with the Coast Guard cutter, *Robert Walton*, and they'll take us out to meet the Canadians."

Axe frowned. "Why don't they just bring it into port? Why do they want us to go out and meet the Canadians at the site?"

Nick shrugged. "Your guess is as good as mine."

Finn looked down at his plate. Whatever this was, his gut said it was going to be worse than eating three-day-old sushi.

CHAPTER TWO

Finn stared out over the ocean. It was hard to believe that twelve hours ago he was enjoying the balmy night air in Miami. Now, he was freezing his nuts off in the middle of the Atlantic. Okay, maybe not the middle, exactly, but they weren't close to anything civilized.

The weather was cold and gray. The clouds overhead dark and heavy with moisture. Finn wouldn't have been surprised if the heavens opened and dropped torrents of rain within the hour. He shivered as he stood on deck. When had he become so friggin' wimpy about the cold? He'd only been in Miami for four months or so. Had he really lost his tolerance to the cold that quickly? He sighed. They had been in Panama for a while before Miami, so maybe it was justified if he had, but still it sucked.

"Jesus, it's cold out here," Elias said as he came to stand beside Finn at the railing. "Why are we outside?"

"To prove we're not soft. That the move to Miami hasn't changed us in the least." Finn stuffed his hands in his uniform pockets in an effort to warm them up.

"Yeah, no." Elias shook his head. "That can't be the

reason we're out here. I've changed, and I hate the cold. So if that's why we're here, then I admit defeat. Now can we go inside and get warm?"

Nick came to a stop beside them. "We're out here because we're approaching the abandoned vessel. She'll come into view in the next couple of minutes. I want you all"—he turned to include Axe and Cain in the conversation as they joined the rest of them at the railing—"to take a hard look at her and see if anything jumps out at you. Bertrand has been damn tight-lipped about this, and I'm not sure why. I want first impressions and ideas on what we may be walking into. Eyes peeled; senses sharp. I don't like not having details, so let's make sure we're all focused on the task at hand."

"Easy for you to say," Axe grumbled, "you're wearing a down jacket over your uniform. We're all in windbreakers."

Nick grinned. "Not my fault you guys didn't read the weather. This part of the world has been unseasonably cold this spring."

"Now you tell us," Finn grumbled, curling his lip at his boss. He was already tired of being cold, not to mention he was hungry. The news last night had left him without an appetite, and they'd caught a ride on a military plane out of Miami at six a.m. He'd skipped breakfast to sleep longer, a decision he now regretted. It had just gone three p.m., but all he'd had was a power bar and some coffee.

"I know you're all hungry and tired," Nick said as he stuck his hands in his jacket pockets. "Me, too. As soon as we get a look at the ship, we can go inside and grab a quick bite and get some hot coffee. It's going to take a bit to coordinate with the Canadians on boarding the vessel."

There were a few more grumblings, but Finn remained quiet. His brain was already on the mystery that had just appeared on the horizon. All the horror movies about abandoned vessels pinged around in his head. He normally tried not to be too superstitious but boarding an abandoned ship in the middle of the ocean when no one knew what was going on freaked him right out. Shivers raced along his skin, and they weren't from the cold.

Nick raised his binoculars. "There she is. Take a look and tell me what you see."

Finn lifted his own field glasses and focused in on the abandoned ship. His heart stuttered in his chest. He recognized the lines of the vessel right away. His cousin had been posted on one as a civilian contractor. A thread of anxiety tensed within his gut as he lowered his binoculars "It looks like a—" He stopped when he saw there were other Coast Guard members up on deck.

Nick dropped his arms and looked at Finn, one brow arched. Finn tilted his head in the direction of the two other guys that were only about fifteen feet away. Nick nodded. Finn raised his binoculars once more.

Just because it looked like a former U.S. Navy vessel didn't mean it *was* one. He read the name on the hull. The *Oceanus Explorer*. Oceanus was the Latin word for ocean. Not exactly the most creative name and bound to have been used many times. He sure as hell hoped it wasn't a former Navy ship, nor would he express his suspicions out loud where he could be overheard. Maybe this was why Admiral Bertrand had been so tight-lipped.

Finn studied the ghost ship more carefully as the cutter he was on cruised toward the abandoned vessel. It was slightly over two hundred feet long. The pale gray paint job looked fresh and in good shape. There was rigging on the back most likely used to lower submersibles in the water and pull them out again.

"Anybody? Comments?" Nick asked.

"I can't see a reason to abandon her," Axe offered.

"Me either," Nick agreed.

"That rigging in the back," Elias commented, "I'm thinking it's for lowering submersibles, yeah?"

"Looks that way," Nick responded. "At least, it's definitely for lowering something."

Axe commented, "She's in good shape and made to withstand serious weather and water conditions. Makes no sense to abandon her."

Finn dropped his binoculars and looked around. The guys who had been there were gone. He leaned in so he was slightly closer to Nick. He kept his voice low. "It looks like a T-AGOS 22."

"What the fuck is a T-AGOS?" Cain growled.

Finn glanced around once more, reassuring himself they couldn't be overheard. "The T designation means that it was operated by civilian contractors. AGOS stands for Auxiliary General Ocean Surveillance. They were used in the 1980s by the Navy under civilian command to track down submarines using sonar. Then, later, they were modified and used to help with narcotics interdiction. Most were sold off or given to NOAA. You know, the National Oceanic and Atmospheric Administration. Some were transferred to other countries as part of deals."

"How do you know so much about it?" Axe demanded.

He shrugged. "My cousin worked on one for years. I took an interest."

Elias raised his binoculars again. "You think NOAA lost one of their ships?" He scanned the abandoned vessel.

"That ship doesn't belong to the agency," Cain stated. "If it did, they wouldn't have abandoned it, and if something had happened to the people on board, we'd all have heard about it and the National Oceanic folks would be all over the situation."

Finn nodded. "Cain's right. If this was one of the

NOAA's ships, they would be out here searching for it. Or calling the Navy for help."

Cain leaned on the railing. "The fact that Bertrand was not giving out details about it makes it more likely this was sold or given to another country, and he or someone else is afraid it's coming back to bite us on the ass."

"That makes more sense." Nick sighed. "It also means that not only will he want to know what's going on, but the higher-ups are going to be all over his ass about it, which means he's going to be all over *my* ass about it." He ran a hand over his chin. "Let's go in and grab some food and hot coffee. Then, once we make contact with the Canadians, we'll board the ship."

The guys all turned and headed inside. Finn was the last one through the door. The anxious feelings he'd had for the last week intensified painfully in his chest. His heart rate had ticked up and was staying there. They were walking into a really shitty situation. He knew it in his bones. No one abandoned a ship like that without good reason.

Once inside the mess hall, Finn grabbed a tray and got in line after the others. They were between meals, but the head cook had saved some food for them so, in no time, they were all tucking into some hot stew with warm crusty rolls.

"The Canadians said they couldn't trace the ship, right? And they asked for our assistance. Do you think it's because they recognized the class of ship?" Finn asked, then took a bite of his roll. The food was good, and he was hungry.

Nick swallowed. "Could be. That would certainly explain why they asked for help. It would also explain why Bertrand is being so close-mouthed with the information. On the other hand, it could be something altogether different. We're not going to know until we get on board." Nick's phone buzzed, and he glanced at the screen. "Eat up, gentleman. Our ride to the other ship leaves in fifteen minutes."

The ride over to the abandoned ship wasn't great. Rain that had held off finally started pouring down in sheets, and the wind had really picked up, whipping up the waves. Finn was thoroughly drenched by the time they boarded the vessel. There were also a lot more people on the launch than expected. He'd counted seventeen crew besides his teammates.

"What's up with all these guys? Why are they coming?" Finn asked.

"Skeleton crew to run the *Explorer* since we're taking over from the Canadians.

They came alongside the abandoned ship, and the transfer started. Nick was the first man up the ladder.

"Jack Williams," a voice said as Finn reached the top of the stairs. "Command Officer of the *Cape Fraser.*"

"Permission to come aboard, sir," Nick said as he turned up the collar on his jacket.

"Permission granted." The man gave a quick smile. "Although it's not my ship, so I'm not sure what that's worth." Williams was a tall man, somewhere in his late forties by the look of things. His blond hair was in a buzz cut. His brown eyes were friendly, but there was a wariness there as well. Finn didn't blame him one bit for being cautious. This situation warranted vigilance, for sure.

Nick introduced the team, and they all shook hands. He went on to introduce some of the others before Williams stopped him and motioned to the ensign next to him. "This is Grant Finley. He's going to take care of your guys and show them what's what on board so they can take over." Finley, with bright blond hair and light blue eyes, looked to be in his late twenties.

Williams continued, "Let's get inside. It's too damn cold and wet to stand about out here." He led everyone inside and through several halls to a small conference room. The others followed Finley deeper into the ship, presumably up to the bridge and wherever else they needed to be to keep the ship moving. Finn and the team entered the conference room.

Williams gestured to the chairs surrounding an oversize table. "Have a seat gentleman."

They all took off their wet jackets and hung them over the backs of the wooden chairs. Then they all sat down.

"I would offer you coffee, but we're not exactly making ourselves at home here. We're trying to limit our…interactions with the vessel. Finley will show your guys what to do to keep her afloat, but with the storm coming, I don't mind telling you, it's not going to be pretty."

Finn's gut churned. What the hell did that mean?

"Um… Why exactly is that? I mean, what is going on?" Nick asked. "We weren't given a lot of detail."

"Let's start with some background," Williams stated.

Nick nodded. "That would be helpful. To be honest, we're not quite sure why we're here."

Williams frowned. "There's not much we can tell you other than the *Oceanus Explorer* was spotted floating in the shipping lanes, without power, and several vessels tried to hail her when she veered into their path. They reported her as looking abandoned. We arrived yesterday morning and boarded her. She is, indeed, abandoned."

"Okay, but again, I'm not sure why we're here, nor do I understand why the U.S. Coast Guard is taking possession of her," Nick countered.

Williams cocked his head. "Probably better to show you." He stood up. "Follow me."

Nick stood, and the rest of the team followed suit. Finn's senses kicked into overdrive. He wanted to take in as many details as possible. Missing something could come back to haunt them later.

He glanced at the junior officer whose name tag read

Basden, M. He was a tall, gangly kid with big eyes and not a bit of meat on his bones. He was ushering them all out the door. It was obvious he wanted to be at the end of the line. Finn wasn't keen to have the kid behind him, but there wasn't much he could do without causing a fuss. The kid was Canadian, so he was probably friendly, or so Finn hoped.

Cain wasn't having it. When Finn approached the doorway, Cain was already there and gestured for the kid to go first. Basden started to refuse but took one look at Cain's face, shrugged, and then walked through the door.

Cain shook his head. "No little grunt is going to walk behind me on a freaking ghost ship," he growled.

Finn grinned. Leave it to Cain to put into words what everyone else was feeling. They followed Williams and Basden down into the bowels of the ship. In the engine room, Williams finally stopped and pulled aside the life jackets hanging on the wall. Imprinted into the iron wall was the name *USS Impenetrable.*

"Shit," Elias mumbled. It was low enough that Finn was probably the only one that heard it standing behind him, but he heartily agreed.

"That's why we called." Williams dropped the life jackets back in place. "We tried to trace the ship under her current name, *Oceanus Explorer,* but she appears to be owned by various shell corporations, or so I was told. When we discovered this, we called the Navy who told us they sold it off ten years ago and no one could help us. An hour or so later, I got word that you were on your way."

"I see." Nick's face remained impassive.

Finn frowned. It didn't make sense. Why send them to check out a ship the U.S. Navy had sold off years ago? What else was going on?

Nick crossed his arms over his chest. "I'm guessing there's more to this."

Williams nodded. "Come on. I'll show you."

They all followed Williams back to the main section of the ship. He stopped outside a closed door. "We have searched every inch of this ship but didn't find a single soul." He opened the door.

The first thing that hit Finn was the smell, copper mixed with stale water. He wanted to gag. The room itself was larger than he'd expected. It had oversize monitors mounted on the walls above a bank of computer equipment. There were eight chairs in front of different keyboards. This was the room where they would have tracked submarines in the past, but this equipment was state-of-the-art. Someone had refurbished this ship with the latest and greatest tech equipment.

It was too bad someone else had shot it all up. Every screen and piece of equipment had multiple bullet holes in it. There were pools of dried blood all over the room. If he had to guess, a dozen people might have died in this room. And this is why Team RECON was there. Someone had killed a lot of people on board a former U.S. Navy ship and then made the bodies disappear.

Nick grimaced. "This must have come as quite a shock."

Williams nodded. "Yeah. It wasn't what we were expecting and, to be honest, we didn't know what to think."

"I can see why." Nick moved into the room. Elias, Axe, and Cain followed.

Finn stood in the doorway. Adrenaline pumped hard through his veins. This was beyond creepy. Whatever went on here, it wasn't good. It looked like an execution.

"You didn't find any bodies?" Finn asked.

Williams shook his head. "Not a one. By the look of things, at least ten people were shot and killed in here. There are some blood pools in a few other rooms as well."

Nick glanced over at Williams. "How many?"

"Three more locations and about another eight blood pools. So at least eighteen people were shot here."

"Jesus," Axe muttered.

"Yeah," Basden said. "It's…" His voice faded out.

Finn didn't blame the kid. There were just no words to describe this.

Nick curled his fingers into a fist and he tapped on his chin, as if in thought. "What the hell happened?" he asked Williams. "Where are the ship's logs?"

Williams grunted. "Just as gone as the crew. With the equipment all shot to hell, we can't pin it down. No paper logs either."

"So there is no way of knowing if it's piracy, or they allowed themselves to be boarded, or if someone on the crew carried this out." Nick tipped his face up and stared at the ceiling.

"What do you think happened to the bodies?" Elias asked the question they were all wondering.

"Over the side?" Cain offered.

Williams shook his head. "No. Our current location is one of the major shipping lanes between Europe and North America. Halifax is a day closer to Europe than the US. A lot of ships stop in there before heading south. If someone had dropped that many bodies overboard, ships' personnel from the other vessels would have seen at least one, if not more."

Finn didn't necessarily agree, but he didn't want to antagonize Williams. "How long do you think she's been floating on her own?"

"It's hard to say." Williams leaned against the wall. "The food in the fridge is still good, so inside of a week. We've been looking at the currents to try and figure out where she came from, but really she could be from anywhere. We can go back up to the conference room, and I can show you what we've dug up on the currents and weather."

Nick nodded. "That sounds like a good place to start. You're okay with us taking the lead on this then?"

Williams' head jerked back. "Take the lead? You can have this mess. We'll help you any way we can, but the Canadian Navy doesn't want any part of this. There's just nothing good going to come from this."

Finn couldn't help but agree with Williams. His senses were screaming at him to get his ass off that ship. Whatever was going on was a shitstorm of major proportions, and they were headed right into the eye of it.

CHAPTER THREE

Victory Stanhope stood at her desk and stared at the man in front of her. "What do you mean I have to go, Steve? I'm an analyst. I don't do field work."

Steve Wiseman, her boss, grimaced and ran a hand through his thinning gray hair. His belly hung over his pants, and the blue shirt that had been clean this morning already had a coffee stain on the sleeve. "Tory, I know you usually like to stay behind a desk, but there's talk that this could become a big issue. You are the only one who specializes in this sort of thing."

"This sort of thing? Rogue men who make a big splash when they're supposed to be undercover? I don't recall writing that on my resumé." She put a hand to her temple. She'd pulled her long blond hair into a severe bun this morning, which was likely contributing to the intense throb in her head at the moment.

"Damage control. You're good at damage control. Hell, you're good at just about everything, but in this instance, we need you to ride shotgun with these guys so they don't go off the rails and start an international incident."

She sighed and plopped down onto the brown leather chair behind her desk. She tugged down the hem of her gray pencil skirt and scrutinized the sleeves of her white blouse. Not a coffee stain in sight. "What makes everyone so concerned about this team causing an international incident? From what I've read, they pretty much cause a ruckus wherever they go."

Steve shook his head and sat down in one of the visitor chairs across from Tory. "The top brass is in an uproar. The Canadian Coast Guard vessel that found the *Oceanus Explorer* reported they found blood on board. Eighteen spots, to be exact. They believe the crew may have been executed."

"Holy shit," she gasped.

"Yeah," Steve agreed. "It's battle stations up there. They specifically asked for you to go, Tory. They sent in their best team, but they want eyes and ears on these guys. With your background, they think you've got the best shot at not only keeping up with them but managing the fallout."

Tory ground her teeth. She'd left the CIA three years ago and was perfectly content to sit behind a desk at the Department of Homeland Security, where she now managed people and intel. Heading into the field again, ranked right up there with getting a root canal with no Novocain. She'd seen too much, and everything she'd witnessed had been brutal.

The desk meant safety to her. Her bosses had no idea what they were asking of her, but she understood from their perspective that it was a no-brainer. She was a field agent. She could handle seeing eighteen dead bodies and not fall apart. Well, at least in theory.

"Do I have a choice?" she asked. She hated the defeat already ringing in her ears.

Steve frowned. "Well, they said to ask but, in truth, no not really. They want you, and if you don't go, your career with DHS will be over. They won't fire you, but they'll give you a series of lateral moves and you'll end up like Cliff Bogart, in a closet down the hall, monitoring alien contact."

"It's called Non-mainstream Communications, and I would point out it was Cliff that brought that other matter to our attention." She sighed. "But I get your point."

Tory leaned back in her chair and closed her eyes for a second. She'd never talked about her time as a field officer for the CIA, and she never would, but that silence was costing her now, and she wasn't sure she wanted to pay the price. What choice did she have? If she didn't help the top brass in what they perceived to be their hour of need, she was signing her death warrant. She had no desire to jump ship again and start over at a new agency. She could only do that so many times before people would start asking questions—questions she wasn't prepared to answer.

"Where am I going?" she asked. When Steve gave her a sympathetic look, her stomach plummeted.

"Sorry, kiddo, they're on a ship in the middle of the North Atlantic."

"You've got to be kidding me." Her fingers curled around the arms of her chair. She hated being on the water with a passion. It made her violently ill. The seasickness pills that her doctor prescribed helped, but she just ended up feeling sick all the time. "Why haven't they towed the ship into shore yet?"

"Possibly because it would cause serious controversy if the press gets hold of it, but more likely because the Canadians want nothing to do with this and were just as happy to hand it over to us at sea than in one of their ports. You can't blame them for that."

"No, I guess not."

He glanced at his watch. "There's an airplane waiting to

take you to Portland, Maine, and from there you'll take a helicopter out to meet the Coast Guard cutter, *Robert Walton*."

"There's a plane waiting now? They want me to go tonight?" She tried to keep the panic from her voice. Nighttime at sea, God, she already felt ill.

He nodded. "They are deadly serious about this. There's a storm moving in, and they want you out there ASAP. If you miss the window, it could be a couple of days before you can make the trip again. Head home and pack a bag as quickly as possible and then get to the airport."

"Wait, bad weather means big waves." Her stomach rolled just thinking about it.

Steve shrugged. "Sorry. I am powerless to stop any of this. From what I understand, Admiral Bertrand of the Coast Guard is less than thrilled about this, too, but even he doesn't have a choice in the matter."

"Fabulous. The Admiral doesn't want me with his guys. This just gets better and better."

"Sorry about all this, but you really are the only one around here that has any idea how to survive with these guys. The rest of us have all been riding a desk for way too long. The game has changed, and we're all too out of touch and"—he patted his belly—"out of shape to be running around the North Atlantic with a pile of specially trained operators." He grinned. "I guess it doesn't always pay to shoot up the ladder at such a young age."

Tory narrowed her eyes at her boss and then promptly gave her boss the middle finger.

Steve laughed. "You'd better get a move on. You know they'll be watching to see when the jet lifts off. Best not keep the higher-ups waiting."

"Yeah, I guess."

Steve stood up. "Be safe out there and stay in touch. They're going to want constant updates. If I can't update them, it will be my ass, which in turn will be—"

"My ass. Yeah, I get it."

Steve nodded and walked over to the office door. He paused before he opened it and looked back at her. "Tory, I know you can handle yourself, but please be cautious with these guys. We all want you back in one piece."

She did, too. Being in one piece was definitely preferable. "Steve, do you think this has to do with the other thing?" she asked as dread filled her chest.

Her boss shook his head. "I have no idea, but I think that's what the big worry is. It's the elephant in the room no one wants to admit is there. They're all scrambling as it is." He sighed and then opened the door. "Just be very careful."

She nodded and watched her boss leave her office. He was trying to tell her to take it easy and not jump into anything. Think twice before making a move. Well, he needn't worry. She was well beyond the days of jumping into something like this with both feet. They'd be lucky if she waded in up to her ankles. If the other thing was involved, then she was now in a prime position to be a scapegoat. She needed to watch her back as well as her front.

She squared her shoulders. She would deal with the team members. She would get them to see things her way or, at the very least, get them to keep their mouths shut about whatever it is that they found. She was not damaging her career over this. She'd worked too hard to put the past behind her to let a bunch of overzealous Coast Guardsmen drag her down now. With any luck, this had nothing to do with the breach in the security that she was sure had happened.

Twenty minutes later, Tory was standing in front of her walk-in closet with a cup of tea in one hand and a shoe in the other. Should she bring dress shoes? And what about a suit? Would she need to appear official anywhere? Who knew, but it never hurt to be prepared.

She put the shoe next to the other one on her bed. Then she took a sip of her tea before she put the mug down on her dressing table. Walking back over to the closet, Tory decided to take a navy suit and another white blouse. That combination always looked professional.

She put both on the bed and turned back to the closet. She didn't want to face what was coming. She should be in a rush but big waves made her nervous. She looked around the room. It was her oasis of calm. Her place to regroup and recharge. The walls were a soft gray, the same color as her eyes, and the carpet was a lovely cream color. The duvet on the bed was white with matching curtains that hung on the window and pooled on the floor. The only splashes of color in the room were the red, green, and blue throw pillows she had on her bed. Just seeing it made her feel centered most days. Now, however, thoughts of big waves were agitating her and her sanctuary wasn't helping at all.

She knew she was running late and they were waiting on her. There was a car idling at the curb. Steve had sent it but, in reality, she knew it was his boss that directed him to get a car. They really wanted her to move quickly, but here she was; procrastinating. It wasn't just the big waves she wanted to avoid. She couldn't seem to bring herself to go into the closet and pick up her 'go' bag.

She'd thrown the damn thing in the back of her closet after the last catastrophe and hadn't seen it since. She'd need it now. Taking a deep breath, she smoothed her hair with one hand and then squared her shoulders. Tory crouched and grabbed the offending backpack from the far left corner.

She pulled it out and then sat down on the carpet and

opened it. It smelled like the desert and the sage tea she used to drink all the time. She pulled out the clothing she had inside, all clean, all packed and ready to go. Three pairs of cargo pants, three T-shirts, one beige, one gray, and one black. Underwear, bras, and her combat boots.

She pulled them out. They were all scuffed up and looked like they had seen better days. The dirt on them was sand from the desert, from the last day she'd been in Afghanistan. She let out a small sob as the memory of her best friend's smiling face came unbidden into her mind. Sara Wallingford Smith, Walli to her friends, was a bright light in the darkness. She made everyone laugh and always had a positive attitude. Tory missed her. They were sisters of the heart and Tory's soul ached for her loss.

No. She wasn't going to do this. Nope. She had work to do, and these were just boots. It didn't matter that the last time she'd seen her best friend alive she'd been wearing these boots. It didn't matter that the intel she was given and had passed on had gotten her best friend killed. Walli was dead and gone, and Tory had moved on with her life. She really had.

Admitting that she'd felt survivor's guilt had been a huge breakthrough in her therapy. It wasn't her fault the intel had been bad. She'd just passed it on. No, what had her feeling tremendous guilt, what made her leave the CIA was that *she* was supposed to be out there that day. It was *her* turn to go with a group of operators to check out the intel. Instead, Walli went because Tory was sick. She'd picked up some bug and had trouble being more than ten feet from the bathroom. Walli died because Tory had diarrhea. It was stupid and senseless and there was nothing she could do about it. She'd thought that she'd moved on so she hadn't expected the rush of memories that hit her when she saw the boots.

Tory stood up and grabbed her tea off the dressing table. She gulped half the mug, trying to swallow the lump building in her throat. She'd dealt with the past, goddammit. Hours spent in therapy to get over her friend's death, not to mention an abusive father and ghost-like mother. All that had come out in therapy as well.

She'd come out of it stronger, or so she told herself. At this moment, she didn't feel stronger. She glanced down at the mug in her hand. The liquid in it rippled from the slight tremor in her hand. She set the mug back down.

Triggers. That's all these were. Her therapist had told her this might happen from time to time and gave her some tricks to deal with the triggers. She could do some breathing exercises. She could look at her surroundings and remind herself that Afghanistan was the past and this… this was her present. One she had created to suit herself. Or she could just get her shit together and get moving.

"Fuck this," she mumbled as she picked up the bag and threw it on the bed. She hurried into her bathroom and gathered the necessary travel-sized essentials. She stuffed them in a toiletry bag and came out again. She dropped that bag on the bed as well.

As she passed her wall mirror, she realized she was still wearing her work suit. She should put on her cargo pants. It would make the most sense. But instead, she pulled off her skirt and reached for her jeans. She took off her blouse and dropped it in the laundry bag and then grabbed a light gray cashmere sweater. The color was an exact match for her eyes. It made her feel cozy. The spring weather hadn't cooperated yet. D.C. and the whole northeast were still having some cold days. No doubt the North Atlantic was freezing. It was probably always cold.

She checked her watch. It was the last birthday gift Walli had given her. It had been a bit of a joke since Tory was often late. The face was almost larger than her wrist, so she couldn't get the time wrong but she always wore it. It made her feel connected to Walli still. Right now, the clockface was a stark reminder that she was late.

Groaning, she pulled out her suitcase and started packing the various items inside. She repacked her go bag and stuffed it on one side of the suitcase. She put the boots in there as well. She also packed her heels. She glanced at her bag and then at her list. Everything was there except one last item.

She heaved a sigh. Moving out of her room, she walked down the hallway to her office. She went over to the picture of the ocean on the wall and took it down. She put in the combination of the safe and swung the door open.

There were various papers and some jewelry inside, but those weren't what she was after. She reached in and brought out a box. She spun the combination on the box and opened it.

The Glock was all cleaned and polished, so it gleamed in the light. She kept her weapon service-ready at all times like she'd been taught. She grabbed the gun, closed the box, and set it back in the safe.

The gun was heavy in her hand, but it also held a comforting feeling. It had been the thing that had kept her alive on several occasions. And although she wasn't happy to have to use it again, there was no way in hell she was going on an assignment like this without it. That's what the top brass expected. That's why they wanted her. Not just because she was good at spinning a story, but because she would do whatever had to be done.

She put the gun on her desk and rehung the picture. Then she grabbed the weapon and went back to her room. She opened the top drawer in her dresser and retrieved her shoulder holster. She put it on and then slid the gun into place.

She saw her reflection in the mirror. Here she was once again. Armed and dangerous. If only she could shoot the waves, so she didn't puke. She closed her eyes and said a small prayer that she wouldn't need to use her weapon on a human, that this adventure would be over shortly but, most importantly, she would not live to regret going on this assignment.

CHAPTER FOUR

Finn drummed his fingers on the table in the conference room. The situation was fast approaching shit-show proportions. After the Canadians received clearance to leave the *Oceanus Explorer,* they couldn't go fast enough. Finn didn't blame them. The situation seriously creeped him out. At least the *Cape Fraser* crew had promised to stay close in case the storm worsened, and their help was needed.

"What did Bertrand say?" Finn asked. He'd just returned from using the head and missed whatever Nick had said about his latest exchange with their boss.

Nick leaned back in his chair. "I was just saying that he wants us to search the ship."

"But the Canadians already did that," Axe protested.

"Yeah," Elias agreed. "It seems like it would be a waste of time."

Finn knew where Bertrand was going with the request. "Bertrand wants to dot his I's and cross his T's. He also wants to make damn sure we didn't miss anything vital that might be time-sensitive, something that might tell us where the ship came from or what they were actually doing on board before the blood bath. Saying the Canadians already searched it is not going to cut it with the higher-ups."

Nick nodded. "And to be fair to the Canadians, I am sure they were very thorough with their search, but they were looking for bodies. We're looking for something else."

Axe's eyebrows went up. "What are we looking for?"

"A reason the ship is still floating," Cain stated.

As soon as Cain said it, everything clicked into place for Finn. He should have thought of it sooner, but the creep factor had clouded his brain. "Shit. You're right. Why did they leave the ship floating and remove the bodies when they just could have left the bodies and scuttled the ship?"

Elias swore. "Jesus, you don't think they rigged it to blow, do you?"

Nick shrugged. "It's a very real possibility. Maybe they rigged it to blow and then ran into problems so they took the bodies and abandoned the ship."

"Meaning we could be sitting on a bomb." Finn fought to keep his emotions in check, but at this moment, all he wanted to do was get the hell off the ghost ship.

"Let's try and remain focused on the task at hand," Nick said. "Bertrand said to search the ship, so that's what we do. The Canadians have agreed to let us take it into Halifax once we've finished searching it. Since the engines are up and running, the skeleton crew we brought over with us has already set the course. We'll be leaving any minute."

Finn frowned. "Why aren't we taking it into Boston or Maine or something?"

"Optics," Cain grunted.

Nick nodded. "Cain's right. The fact that a former U.S. Navy ship, even if it was run by civilian contractors, was found with a lot of blood on board and no bodies will stir up a lot of attention. The longer they can avoid that news breaking, the better. Hiding it in Halifax will help keep the lid on things." He stood. "We'll split into two teams to speed the search. Finn, Axe, and Elias, you guys start up here. Search every office space and turn on every computer. See what you can find.

"Cain, you and I are going to start at the bottom in the engine room. We'll work our way up." He pulled out a case from his jacket pocket. "Here," he said as he opened the case. "Not sure if the earbuds will work with all this metal, but it's the best we've got. I want everyone to stay in touch. No wandering off on your own until we know what the hell is going on."

Finn took an earbud and then inserted it in his right ear. "Jesus, Nick. With all the equipment on the ship, the search will take all night. Wouldn't it be better to conduct the physical search and leave the computers to the techies?"

Nick hesitated. "I hear what you're saying, but my big worry is there could be something on the computers that sheds light on the whole thing. I'd rather know that now than later."

Elias installed his earbud. "I'd like to know what the hell they were doing out here. I mean, what could they possibly have been after? We're in the middle of the Atlantic Ocean."

"He's got a point," Cain said. "There's not a whole lot out here. Even if the ship was left to drift for a week, it was still in the middle of the Atlantic when whatever happened here went down."

Nick rubbed his forehead. "It's bugging me, too," he admitted. "I have no clue what the fuck they could have been doing out here. It's something I'm hoping you all can find out once you guys get into any computer equipment left on board. See if you can find a master list of what's supposed to be here in terms of equipment. Might give us a clue as to what's missing as well." He turned and picked up a box from the floor. "Here, put these on." He pulled out a pair of latex gloves, then passed the box to Axe. "We don't need our prints all over the ship. We've already contaminated this room and the bathroom on this floor."

Axe pulled on his gloves. "Our Guardsmen are already on the bridge. They have to be if we're on the way to Halifax, so I'm guessing the bridge and a few other areas are going to have their prints all over them before this is done."

"True, but we don't need to add to them," Nick said. "Okay, guys, stay in contact and keep your eyes open for anything out of the ordinary. We can't take this ship into port until we know for certain it's not going to blow up or kill people in some other way."

"Will do," Finn said.

"Cain." He turned, and Cain followed him out of the room.

Finn turned to Elias and Axe. "Where do you want to start?"

"The bridge is two decks up. We could start there and work down," Axe suggested. "I know the guys are up there working, but we need to at least give it the once over."

Finn shrugged. "Works for me." He started out of the room with Axe and Elias in his wake. He was doing his best to keep his mind off the fact that they could be sitting on a bomb, but there was just something ominous about the *Oceanus Explorer*. The waves tossed the ship around, and the groaning of the metal was getting on his nerves. The darkness was falling now, and he was getting hungry again.

They went up the stairs, not wanting to take the elevator. The power was on, but who knew if it would stay that way. They had no idea of the condition of the ship. Finn wasn't interested in being stuck in an elevator.

When they reached the bridge, they found three Guardsmen on watch. The one piloting the ship was a Commander named *Oliver, G*. He was in his forties with dark hair, graying at the temples. The other two were Lieutenants Junior Grade. They seemed to be struggling with the equipment. The ship wasn't reacting like it should. They kept cursing in hushed tones. The fact that their superior wasn't yelling at them for their language was telling. Finn's gut tightened. The ship was in trouble.

Pushing that thought aside, Finn addressed the Commander, "Sir, we need to take a quick look around, see if we can find anything about who was on the ship."

"Understood," Oliver replied. "I doubt you're going to find anything, however. There wasn't even a scrap of paper left up here."

"Sir, I can't get the GPS to function properly. I think we're off course, but I can't really tell," one of the other JGs said. The taller man's name read *Wickham, Q.* His young face was filled with worry. His brow was crinkled, and his throat worked convulsively, like he was swallowing hard, or fighting the need to hurl.

"I understand, Wickham. Call over to the *Walton* and tell her we're going to need guidance assistance."

"Sir." Wickham grabbed a satellite phone off the counter in front of him and made the call.

"I take it that means there is no way to see where the ship has been using the current GPS system," Finn said.

Oliver opened his mouth to respond when the shorter officer with bright blond hair called out, "Sir, I'm getting all kinds of weird readings from the engines." He blinked rapidly as his fingers flew over the keyboard in front of him.

"What sort of weird readings, Hastings?" Oliver barked.

"It says the engine power is fluctuating, but I don't know if that's true or not. The storm is too loud for me to hear anything, and I can't tell by feel because of all the waves."

"We might be able to help with this." Finn touched his

earbud. "Tag," he said. There was no response. "Nick Taggert," Finn tried again.

"Go for Taggert." Nick's voice sounded in his earbuds.

"Are the engines okay? Are they fluctuating power?"

After a few seconds of silence, Nick responded, "No. All appears normal down here."

"Thanks. They seem to be having problems with the equipment up here on the bridge."

"Copy that," Nick replied.

Finn turned to Oliver. "Engines appear to be normal. Why do you think the computer equipment is malfunctioning? Is there some sort of virus or something?"

Oliver shook his head. "No virus, or at least not that we know of. Take a look under the control panels."

Finn crouched down and peered into the shadows below the rack holding the equipment. "Aw—Fuck me!"

"What?" Axe demanded as he came and crouched down beside Finn.

"This." Finn pointed to all the wires. Every single one of them had been cut. Some had been repaired and were being held together by electrical tape.

Elias bent down and looked under the counter he was next to. "These assholes weren't playing," he said as he pulled out another bundle of taped wires.

"Son of a bitch. They were certainly thorough." Axe stood up.

Finn straightened. "Did you and your men tape these wires up?"

Oliver shook his head. "No. The Canadians did it, and a damn good thing. This storm is intensifying, and if we lose connection to the engines, we're dead."

Finn exchanged a look with Elias. *Great*. Just more fun on the ghost ship. Something else he didn't need to think about.

He turned to Oliver. "We'll get out of your hair. Let you get back to driving the ship. Good luck, sir." He nodded to Elias and Axe. "Let's head down a level and see what we can find." They all filed out of the bridge and went down the stairs.

When they reached the bottom, the passageway was long and narrow with a lot of doors off it. "I gotta say, this just keeps getting better and better. All those wires cut. Somebody really went to great lengths to make sure they weren't going to get caught."

Elias nodded. "Yeah, let's be on guard. Who knows what else we might come up against?"

"Agreed." Axe looked up and down the hallway. "You guys want to split up?"

"Sure," Elias said. "You and I can take the rooms on the left, and Finn, you take the other side." He pointed to the right. "We'll clear each room and meet at the other end of the hallway. Yell if you find anything interesting."

"Will do." Finn turned and opened the first door on his right. It was a storage room. The shelving units on each wall contained supplies like paper products and cleaning fluids. Finn took a quick look around, but there was nothing of any real interest.

He stood in front of the shelves and tapped his earbud. "There are a lot of cleaning products in here. Why didn't they use them?"

Elias's voice sounded in his ear. "That's a good question. Take a picture with your phone."

"Copy that." Finn took the picture and then headed out of the room. He moved down the passageway to the next room. It was someone's office judging by the single desk and chair in the space. There wasn't a scrap of paper or even a paper clip. The place was empty.

He walked out and went to the next door. It was the

same. So were the two after that one. At the fourth door, he paused. The door was locked. He frowned. If the Canadians had searched the ship, how could the door be locked? He tried the knob again and realized the door wasn't locked, just stuck. Finn pushed against it, but it didn't budge. He stepped back and put his shoulder into it. The door flew open, and Finn stumbled into the room.

It was empty. This one didn't even have a desk in it. It was just a white tile floor and four gray walls. Finn just stood there for a second and looked at the space. There was something about it that was niggling at him, but he couldn't place what it was.

"Hey, Finn." Axe's voice crackled in Finn's ear. "Come here. We're in the office two from the end on our side."

Finn turned and walked out of the room. He moved down the hall and entered the room Axe and Elias were in.

"What's up?" He stopped dead and stared. There were three more dried pools of blood. One on the desk and two on the floor. "Shit."

"Yeah." Elias nodded. "Have you found anything yet? 'Cause all we've found is bloodstains. There's not one laptop or desktop, not one piece of paper. Nothing."

Finn ran a hand through his hair. "I haven't found anything either. I think I have four more rooms on this level."

Axe crossed his arms over his chest. "Let's clear the last rooms quickly and glance at the deck below. If it's like this one, then I say we go help Nick and Cain. It will take longer to search all the equipment down there than it will for us to walk through empty offices. I don't know about you, but the sooner we're off this tub, the better I'll feel."

"Agreed." Finn turned and walked back to the next door on his side. Another storage closet. This one had more cleaning products and office supplies. So they must have done some sort of work that required paper. They just took every used scrap with them.

It only took a few minutes to clear the rest of the rooms on that deck and then they headed down to the one below. The rooms there were the same, just empty spaces. There was one more space with blood pools in it, but otherwise, there was just furniture. No papers. There was nothing left anywhere. Not a computer in sight.

Finn hit his earbud. "Nick, you want some help? There's nothing up here to find."

"Say again? You're breaking up." Nick responded.

"Where are you?" Finn asked.

"Forward ho—" Nick's voice cut out.

Axe frowned. "Forward hold, I think. Let's head there and regroup."

Finn nodded, and they made the trek to the forward hold. The ship was starting to really roll in the waves. Finn lurched as he walked, resorting to using the bulkheads at times so he wouldn't fall. If they lost engine power in these waves, it was going to be a big problem.

A few minutes later, they arrived in the forward hold area. "Hey," Finn said.

Nick looked up from examining the wall. "Hey. Did you find anything?"

"Not a fuckin' thing." Elias shook his head. "Not one piece of paper. Not a single laptop. Not even a desktop. There is nothing to find on this ship."

"Other than the rooms with blood. It's so fucking weird." Finn just couldn't get his brain around it.

Cain appeared from somewhere on their left and nodded at Nick. "They tried, but they didn't succeed."

"Tried what?" Axe asked.

"To blow a hole in the side," Cain said, then took a swig from a water bottle.

Axe's eyebrows hit his hairline. "Holy shit. Seriously?"

"Yeah," Cain said, "and it looks like it was sheer luck that it didn't work."

Finn frowned. That didn't make sense. "What do you mean?"

"It looks like they put a charge in a couple of spots, hoping to blow a hole in the ship. But either the charges weren't strong enough or they weren't set right. You can see the burn marks there on the hull." Cain pointed to the side of the ship with his flashlight. The black marks across the hull were evident.

The ship rolled and groaned in the waves.

"It might be time to get off this tub." Finn pointed to the scorch marks. "The explosives might not have been strong enough to knock a hole in the hull, but they would've weakened it, and all this rolling around in the waves is not going to help the situation."

Nick frowned. "You think the hull could give way?" he asked Cain. As their resident explosives expert, Cain would have the best understanding of the situation.

Cain shrugged. "I think given the right set of circumstances, the stress on the damaged hull might be enough to cause a leak or two. It might even be enough to finish the job the explosives started."

Finn did his best to appear calm and levelheaded, but every last nerve in his body screamed at him to get the hell off that ship. Staying on board smelled like catastrophe to him.

"He's got a point," Elias said. There was a loud groan and a deep roll, and the guys all had to steady themselves on the bulkheads.

"Okay, let's go." Nick took the lead as they all exited the forward hold area. Finn was bringing up the rear. He moved up the stairs as quickly as possible.

They all had to be thinking the same thing. Being dumped in the North Atlantic during a storm was a recipe for disaster. It didn't matter how many ships were around to help rescue them. A few minutes in the frigid water would be enough to induce hypothermia, and it would quickly go downhill from there.

Nick spoke with Commander Oliver and then called the *Robert Walton* and requested the launch come get all of them. The captain, Greg Gerhart, put up some resistance. "I understand the weather is bad, Captain, but the integrity of the hull is in question." There was a long silence as Nick listened to whatever Gerhart was saying.

Finn ground his teeth. They needed to get to safety ASAP.

Nick sighed. "No, there doesn't appear to be any more explosives on board, but the hull integrity is questionable," he repeated. "It looks like they tried to scuttle her with explosives but botched the job. The hull could crack under the stress of the storm surge. I wouldn't suggest risking anyone's life by having a crew stay on board this ship. If she goes down, then she goes down. I would rather not be on her when that happens."

There was more silence. Finn glanced at Cain, who shook his head. It was stupid. They knew Gerhart was just covering his own ass. He was following orders. Also, the risk of coming to get everyone was not insignificant, just that the risk of a hull breach was greater.

"Yes, sir." Nick clicked off the call. "He's going to check the weather and check with his crew and get back to us. I would imagine he'll also reach out to his commanding officer."

"You've got to be shitting me," Axe exclaimed.

"No. He's serious. I get where he's coming from, but he's not the one inside a damaged tin can in a bad storm." Nick punched a number into his satellite phone. The reception wouldn't be great, but it was better than nothing out here.

"Admiral Bertrand, sir, we have a problem," Nick started and then proceeded to fill Bertrand in on their current circumstances.

Finn smiled slightly. That was the thing about Nick. He wasn't above calling in the big guns when it was necessary. Nor did he care how it looked to outsiders. It was one of the things that Finn loved about being part of Team RECON. They could cut through a lot of the bullshit. Bertrand would tell Gerhart to get his guys over here and pick them up. Gerhart's nose might get out of joint, but he'd do it. It was nice to have backup.

CHAPTER FIVE

If she'd thought the plane ride to Maine was bumpy, it was nothing compared to the Coast Guard helicopter she was currently in. The aircraft, and its passengers, bounced violently. Tory bit her lip as they dropped suddenly. She'd taken motion sickness tablets, but she wasn't sure they were going to be enough. She was nauseous as hell and doing her best not to puke all over the back of the pilot's seat.

She said a small prayer as she stared out into the darkness. Great sheets of rain came in sideways at times. When the chopper surged upward, she was thankful she was strapped in. With all the ups and downs, she probably would have broken her neck by now if she wasn't.

"Lady, someone must really want you out here to have us flying in this." The co-pilot's voice was crackly through the headset. He swore when the chopper bounced once again.

"Sorry you have to make the trip, gentlemen." She tried to sound calm and professional, but in the next instant, the drop was so dramatic she let out a small scream.

"Shit," the pilot said as he battled with the controls

against the elements. "We're almost there, but I gotta tell you, I'm not sure I can land on the ship."

Tory's stomach did an extra flip. "Does that mean we have to fly all the way back?"

"No." The co-pilot took over since the pilot was now talking to someone else on a different channel. "It means we might have to use the equipment to drop you to the deck. It will be ugly, but it might be the only way to get you down there."

Tory looked over to the winch and other paraphernalia tucked into the side of the helicopter. "No way in hell," she muttered.

"What?" the co-pilot said. The wind outside buffeted the chopper so that they seemed to move sideways.

Tory didn't bother to respond since both men were busy controlling the chopper. There was not a chance in hell she was going to be dangled from the helicopter in a storm like this. Nope. No way. She was a Tom Clancy fan, but she was no Jack Ryan.

She stared out into the darkness once more and started praying. She hadn't done that in years. Not since Walli was killed. She figured since God hadn't saved her friend, He wasn't listening to her, so why bother? But she sure as hell hoped someone was listening now because it seemed to her like the ride was getting choppier and more dangerous.

When lightning lit up the sky, both pilots swore. The co-pilot said, "Ma'am, we're looking at our fuel gauges, and it's taking more fuel than it normally would to get out here. We're gonna have to turn back in the next five minutes or so if we don't connect up with the *Robert Walton*."

Tory's stomach clenched. The ride out had taken so much longer than she'd expected, and it had been hell. The thought of going all the way back through the storm made her stomach heave. She coughed and then did her best to hold down the chips and coffee that had passed as dinner. "Um, why wouldn't we connect with the *Robert Walton?* Didn't she send coordinates?"

The co-pilot laughed. "Those coordinates are where they thought they'd be. It's all just an estimate. You know, like in school, the math problems. They are traveling at a certain rate of speed in a certain direction. We plot our course to intercept them." The helicopter dropped again.

Tory grabbed the seat and prayed, this time that she wouldn't puke all over herself.

"Anyway, we should be at the interception point in five minutes, but with this storm, we have no idea if they managed to stay on course or if they managed to maintain their speed."

She gritted her teeth. "Can't you just radio them and ask?"

The co-pilot frowned at her over his shoulder. "We've been trying to reach them for the last ten minutes."

He didn't growl exactly, but she immediately realized how stupid and disrespectful she sounded. "I'm sorry. That was stupid. This ride is…just more than I bargained for." The helicopter turned sideways in the wind.

The co-pilot turned back to her and grinned. "Yeah, it's not our usual run. It's kinda like a ride at the fair."

She gave him a quick smile but remained silent. If she opened her mouth now, she was afraid he'd wear her last meal. *Ride at the fucking fair.* She hated carnival rides, and this was the longest one ever.

The sky lit up, and there was a loud crash. Tory screamed. She was sure the helicopter had been struck by lightning. This was it. She was going to die in a metal contraption over the North Atlantic.

There seemed to be a flurry of activity in the front. Both pilots were tapping gauges, jabbing buttons and chattering furiously into their headsets. Thank God at least there were no alarms blaring. Tory clamped her jaw and gripped her seat in a death grip. What had they said about the life jackets? Were they under the seat? No, that was an airplane. Where the hell were they?

She started looking around wildly, but then drew in a deep breath and let it out to calm herself. She tried to do the breathing exercises her shrink had taught her. *Her shrink.* She'd stopped seeing Doctor Fleming last year. She was ready to move on, and Fleming had agreed. She'd faced her survivor's guilt and dealt with the fact her father had been abusive. She had good friends, new and old, in place of a family. They were her support system. She'd been ready to take on the world again.

Tory was also over her reckless phase. She'd made some colossal mistakes, Josh Hargate being the biggest. She still had a hard time believing she'd crossed that line, but he'd hit on her on a day when her father had called and she'd spun out. A shudder went through her.

She did miss some of the bad old days, though. One-night stands, extreme sports, all kinds of risky behaviors. Anything that would take her to the edge, make her actually feel something again, instead of just being numb.

Well, not really.

Because right now, she was feeling all kinds of things... mostly terror. She glanced out into the storm again. This was craziness. Her bosses were insane for sending her. On the other hand, if the ship was part of the other issue, it would be worth the trip.

She rubbed the tension from the back of her neck. The only regret she actually had from her bad old days was not giving Blue Eyes her real name and number. They'd had the most amazing night together. It was the best sex she'd ever had, but it was also more. They'd connected somehow, in some real way that still stuck with her.

Of course, back then she hadn't been ready for any kind of relationship, and even if he had called, she would have screwed things up. She'd been a mess, but she still found herself looking for him whenever she went to a bar. She knew he was in the Coast Guard, and for one long minute when she realized she'd been assigned to work with a Coast Guard team, she let herself dream that he would be the one flying the helicopter, or maybe he was on the ship. Ridiculous.

She needed to get her head out of the clouds. There was another flash and then a loud crash as the thunder rolled over them.

Then, in the next instant, it all stopped. The rain and the wind were gone. The chopper was steady. Tory blinked. Had they all died, and she didn't realize it? What the hell happened? "Uh…" What was the co-pilot's name? Rick something. Rick Jonas. "Lieutenant Jonas, what's going on?"

He glanced back at her. "We're in the eye of the storm."

"You don't sound happy about it."

"Well"—he paused—"it's good in that we're not battling the storm so much, but it's bad in the sense that no matter what direction we go, we're going back into that mess. We're now in the center of it."

"Oh." Why the hell had she asked? She looked out the window. She couldn't see much. The running lights of the helicopter didn't pierce the darkness, but at least she was safe and steady for a few minutes.

When the helicopter banked hard to the right unexpectedly, Tory clutched the seat once again. She was about to ask what was going on when she saw lights in the distance. It had to be the *Robert Walton*. Relief flooded her veins. She was almost done with this ride from hell.

She stared out through the windscreen and realized there

were actually three ships out there. The *Walton,* the *Oceanus Explorer,* and the last one must be the Canadians, or so she assumed. "So how's the transfer going to work?"

Jonas didn't respond. He seemed to be totally engrossed in whatever it was he was doing. She stared out the window as the ships got closer. The ones on the right and left were well-lit and seemed to illuminate the ocean around them. The ship in the middle, which must have been the *Oceanus Explorer,* was darker. There were only a few lights visible on deck. The ships were bigger than she'd thought they'd be. That was good. But so were the waves. She couldn't be sure of the size of the swells, maybe ten or fifteen feet at a guess. At least they'd found the *Walton.* That meant they were carrying some speed. Maybe it wouldn't take too long to get to Halifax. Who was she kidding? In this storm, it was going to be a long, nightmarish sail.

As the helicopter dropped altitude, she could see more clearly. The front of the *Walton* dipped low in the trough of a wave, and water broke over her bow. Then she came back up again like a top. How the hell were they going to land on that? She stared out the window until they flew past the ships. They banked right again and then came back around. She realized that they were going to land on the back of the cutter. This was not going to be easy. She glanced at the pilot. She couldn't for the life of her remember his name, but she fervently hoped he knew what he was doing. He'd gotten them this far, she reminded herself.

"Okay, I want you to prepare for a hard landing. Brace yourself in the position we talked about at the beginning of the flight," the co-pilot directed her.

Her heart hammered against her ribs. "Are we going to crash?"

He shook his head. "No, but it's better to be prepared

just in case. This is a bitch—er…excuse me, ma'am. This is a difficult landing, and it might not be smooth."

She nodded. "I understand."

Jonas turned back, and he and the pilot focused on putting the helicopter safely on deck. She glanced out the window beside her. The only plus was they were still in the eye of the storm. There was no way in hell they would have made the landing if the wind was blowing hard.

She watched out the window as the deck of the *Walton* got closer. They were about twenty feet away when suddenly the pilot pulled up hard. Tory stared out the window as the ship below almost came up to meet them. The wave beneath was monstrous.

"Jesus," she muttered. Suddenly the helicopter ride didn't seem so bad. She wanted to stay on board and go back to solid land.

The pilot hovered for a minute and then moved forward once again, coming up from behind the *Walton*. This time he waited until the back of the ship was almost on top of the wave, and then he moved the chopper down only slightly and the ship came up to meet them. He immediately put the chopper on the deck and secured it as best he could.

"Okay, time for you to go," Jonas said.

Someone opened the door beside her and climbed in. She couldn't tell a thing about them. Survival gear obscured every human aspect of the person, except for the basic form. Even the individual's hands were covered as they unfastened her harness. After grabbing her luggage, a gloved hand waved in front of her, an invitation to grab it and step free of the chopper. She slid forward in her seat and then remembered that she still had her headset on. She looked over at the pilot, but he seemed busy speaking into his headset mic. "Lieutenant Jonas." When he turned and looked over at her, she continued, "Please send a message to the ship when you land safely back in Maine. I want to know you're okay."

He gave her a quick smile and a thumbs up.

She stood and almost fell. Her shaking knees were not the best foundation for holding her upright. The rocking of the deck under the waves didn't help. The person in the survival gear offered her a hand and helped her from under the rotor. Big fat raindrops hit her in the face as they made their way across the deck. She was no longer in the eye of the storm. She was back in the fray.

CHAPTER SIX

Finn stared at his reflection in the mirror. The lines etched into his face proved just how tired and stressed he was. He sighed. His doctor warned him that stress was bad for him. It made all of his anger fester inside of him until he blew. He was a pressure cooker. Origami was a way to relieve that stress, a way to be in the moment.

Anger management. It was all a crock of shit. He snorted. He'd had to complete the classes and the extra sessions with the doctor as a condition of his remaining in the Coast Guard, but it had been long and painful for him. The only good thing he got out of it was the origami. Surprisingly, he really enjoyed making things out of paper. He did find the folding very soothing. He'd always liked to work with his hands. Someone told him he'd probably enjoy knitting, too.

He washed his hands and threw some water on his face, then he reached for some paper towels from the dispenser to dry everything. He pulled, but they were stuck like someone had pushed too many in and now he couldn't get one out. He reached over with both hands this time and yanked. A chunk of paper towels came out, but a scrap of paper also fell out and hit the floor.

He dried his face and hands and then reached down and picked up the paper. It was white and folded a couple of times. He unfolded it and read *Praetorian is active. ME.* He turned the paper over, but it was blank on the other side. What the hell did it mean? What was Praetorian? Was it important, or was the note just some stupid thing that got shoved into the paper towel dispenser by accident? He shook his head and shoved the paper into his pocket. *Whatever.* Just another mystery on the ship from hell. He headed back to the boardroom.

"How long until the launch from the *Walton* arrives?" Finn asked as he walked back into the room.

Nick shook his head. "Not sure. They're sending one, but Gerhart is trying to determine who should stay on board and get the *Oceanus Explorer* through the storm."

"Are they fuckin' nuts? This thing could go down at any moment. Why do they want to save it that much? You would think they'd rather let it go to the bottom of the Atlantic. Then they don't have to worry about bad publicity." He dropped into one of the god-awful chairs.

"That would make more sense," Nick agreed as he sat back down at the boardroom table.

"We're missing something." Cain took a swig from his water bottle.

"What? On board the ship you mean?" Axe asked.

Cain shook his head. "The higher-ups know something we don't, and they aren't sharing. Whatever it is, it's important enough for them to risk lives to keep this tub afloat."

Cain had a point. There was more going on than they were being told. Even Bertrand was reticent. It made him uneasy. He stared at the gloves on the table. "Maybe it's as simple as they want to process the ship and see who was on it."

"Maybe," Nick allowed, "but I think Cain is right and there's more to this than we're being told. I think there's even a possibility that they have an idea of where she's been and what the crew were up to. I'm guessing they don't want to let her go until they can determine one way or the other what this ship was involved in."

Made sense on one hand to Finn. "That makes me worry that whatever they think happened is pretty damn important to them, which scares the shit out of me."

"Agreed," Nick said.

As Elias walked into the boardroom, Finn caught a whiff of bleach. Something triggered in his brain again, but stayed out of grasp. "Where'd you come from? You smell like bleach."

Elias's eyebrows rose. "Um, I was in the kitchen. I cleaned some cups with bleach and then washed them so we can make coffee." He pointed to the coffee maker in the corner. "I couldn't find any paper cups, and by the sound of things, it's still going to be a bit before we get off this tub. It's going to be a cold, wet ride over to the *Walton*, and I want something warm inside me before we go out there."

"Yeah," Finn said, but he was distracted. *Bleach*. Where had he smelled bleach? The room with the stuck door. "I gotta check something." He shot to his feet and left the boardroom. He took the stairs two at a time and then came out in the passageway one deck below the bridge.

He heard footsteps on the stairs, and soon the whole team was walking down the passageway with him.

"What's going on?" Nick asked.

Finn walked into the room with the stuck door, and the others crowded in behind him. He stood there in the empty room and took a big breath. "Do you smell that?"

"Bleach," Axe agreed as he went over and stood by the wall on the left, "but what's so special about the smell of bleach?"

"They had enough cleaning products to clean the entire ship, but whoever did this only cleaned this room. Why? Why only clean this room and leave blood pools everywhere else?'

Cain leaned against the doorframe. "They ran out of time?"

"Even if that's the case, what the hell happened in this room that they took the time to clean it before the others?" Finn questioned. "These aren't amateurs. We know that from how empty the place is. They left nothing behind that could identify them. These guys are pros. So as a pro, where do you start on a job like this? The room that's going to take the longest or the one that could cause you the most problems?"

Elias walked around the room. "I get what you're saying. If it was us and we needed to clean up and abandon ship, we'd wipe out whatever would lead back to us first."

Axe folded his arms across his chest. "What do you think happened in here that they wanted to clean up?"

Finn shook his head. "No fucking clue."

Nick stood off to the right. "I'm not sure we're going to find any answers here, but it sure as shit adds to the mystery." He shook his head. "This whole ship is just one big mystery."

As if listening, the ship rolled hard to the port side. The guys all stumbled and grabbed for a bulkhead. There was a lot of creaking and groaning coming from the old ship, but then there was another sound, a solid thump like something fell.

As the ship righted itself, Finn asked, "Did anyone else hear that thump?"

There were general murmurs of agreement. "It sounded

like it came from behind that wall." Cain pointed to the wall across from where he stood in the doorway.

"Agreed," Elias said.

They all stared at the bulkhead, but it was just that, a wall.

"What's on the other side of it?" Nick asked just as the satellite phone went off. He turned and walked out into the passageway to take the call.

"Let's go see," Finn said as he strode past Cain out of the room.

He glanced back to see Elias and Axe coming with him. Cain lingered with Nick, which was the right call. No one should be on their own on this ship. Finn ground his teeth. The sooner they were out of there, the better he'd feel.

They walked to the end of the hallway, but it was a dead end. They hadn't missed anything from their first pass earlier.

"I don't get it. That thump couldn't have come from outside the ship, could it?" Finn stared at the wall in front of him.

"No. It was definitely an inside sound. Let's try the floor below. Maybe there's access from there." Axe turned and led the way down the stairs. They came out on the deck below and went to the end of the hallway. It was another dead end.

"Let's look through the rooms and check the other end," Elias suggested. "We only took a quick glance last time. Maybe we missed something."

They looked in every room but came up empty until they hit the other end of the hall. There was a narrow door that looked like it was a closet. Finn almost passed it by, but then he shrugged and pulled open the door. They all stared down a narrow passageway.

"If this were a horror movie, one of us would die some sort of horrific death in the next few minutes," Axe said with a macabre grin.

"Thanks for that, asshole." Elias shook his head. He started down the passage with Axe behind him.

Great. Finn grimaced as he brought up the rear. "Isn't it always the guy at the back that dies? Either one of you want to change spots?"

There was general laughter, a thread of nervousness ran through the sound. They rounded a corner and then came out in what looked like the kitchen.

"What the hell?" Finn said as they entered the food prep area. There were boxes of foodstuffs scattered on the floor. "Why would they have created a back hall into the kitchen?"

"Supply storage?" Axe was standing next to the semi-stocked shelves. He studied the foodstuffs. "After the Navy sold it, maybe whoever bought it thought it was better to bring in supplies from the back."

"It's a possibility," Elias agreed. "Do you think one of these boxes falling was the thump we heard?"

"Couldn't be. We were a deck higher. It wouldn't have been loud enough."

They walked around the kitchen, opening all the doors, but found nothing. Finn opened the freezer and walked in. There were shelves with lots of frozen meats and veggies. There were a few shelves of what looked like spices as well. He had started to leave when he caught a whiff of bleach again and stopped.

There was no way they cleaned the freezer with bleach. "Guys," he called.

Axe and Elias came into the freezer.

"Is this where we all get locked in the freezer by some serial killer that's here and we don't know?" Axe's grin was back.

Elias shook his head again. "Axe, I'd lay off if I were you. Finn doesn't look like he's in the mood for serial killer jokes."

"Hey"—Axe held up his hands—"just trying to lighten the mood."

"Do you smell bleach?" Finn broke into their banter.

Elias frowned but Axe cocked his head. "Yeah," he said. "Now that you mention it, I do." He paused. "And something else."

Finn agreed. There was another smell, but he couldn't quite put his finger on it. It had been too faint in the room upstairs, but here it was stronger. It was hard to discern since they were standing next to a bunch of spices.

Finn moved toward the back of the freezer. Boxes had been stacked against the wall, floor to ceiling. His gut tightened. This was not good. He knew it in his bones. "Help me move these boxes."

Axe grabbed a small step stool that had been out in the kitchen area and started handing boxes to Elias and Finn. On the second trip, Axe swore. "There's a door behind here."

The smell of bleach and something else was getting stronger. By the time they'd finished moving all the boxes from blocking the doorway, Finn had identified the smell. "Roadkill," he murmured.

"Huh?" Elias demanded.

"It smells like roadkill. Meat left to rot." Finn nodded toward the door. "I think we've found the dead bodies."

"Fuck." Elias stood and stared at the door. "No wonder the Canadians didn't find them. It's not like they were going to take apart the freezer."

Finn narrowed his eyes as he studied the door. "Clever really. I bet there's some sort of storage area back there."

Axe grimaced. "We should go back and tell Nick and Cain. They're probably looking for us. We didn't leave breadcrumbs." He glanced at his watch as the ship rolled steeply again. Some of the jars fell off the shelves, smashing on the floor. "The launch is probably on the way or already here."

Finn nodded as the ship righted itself. "You two go. I'll check this out."

Axe shook his head. "This is going to be nasty. You don't need to see it on your own. We'll all go."

Finn frowned. "We—"

"I'm with Axe. We go as a team." Elias set his jaw and crossed his arms over his chest.

Finn nodded. He'd wanted to save his buddies from seeing this, but he appreciated that they wouldn't let him shoulder this one alone. "Okay then. Let's find something to cover our noses and mouths, and if it can block the smell, even better."

They looked around in the freezer and then went back into the kitchen. On the floor in front of one of the sets of shelves was a box of N95 masks. Next to it was a bunch of medical supplies. Bandages, gauze, unused syringes. Elias walked over and picked up the box of masks. "Eureka!"

He handed out the masks, and they put them on. "Save the rest," Finn said. "Chances are good we're going to have to go in more than once."

Elias nodded and put the box on the lowest shelf. They walked back into the freezer.

"Ready?" Finn asked. His gut knotted and his heart began a steady slam against his ribcage. He had no clue what they were going to find behind the door, but he knew it wasn't going to be good.

Axe and Elias nodded.

Finn reached out and opened the door. The smell hit him like a wall, the mask not thick enough to filter the rancid odor. His gut heaved, and his throat worked to hold back his gag reflex. Keeping his breaths shallow, he stared at the space in front of him. It didn't matter how many times Finn saw a dead body; the smell was the thing that got to him most. And this was a hundred-fold of anything he'd faced before.

A set of stairs led up, but it was dark. The light from the freezer only illuminated the first few steps. He found a light switch on the wall to his left. As soon as he turned on the lights, he immediately regretted it.

Blood smears stained the walls all the way up the narrow stairwell. At the top of the stairs a huge splash of red covered the wall, as though someone had tossed a can of red paint on the bulkhead.

Finn's eyes burned from the stench of bleach and decomposing bodies. The ship rolled hard again, which caused a weird sound and then a sort of thump. It was what they'd heard in the other room.

Wanting more visibility on the steps, he pulled out his phone and turned on the flashlight. He started up the stairs, careful not to touch any of the smears. He had to turn slightly sideways because the stairwell was narrow, and he didn't want to touch the walls on either side. He made it to the top of the stairs and stopped dead. Axe and Elias stopped behind him.

"What is it?" Elias asked.

Finn swallowed. The smell made him want to puke but didn't bother him nearly as much as the sight of eighteen dead bodies strewn around the room. The storm had knocked over what looked like buckets of bleach so the floor was slick, and with the level of decomposition that had occurred, the bodies slid side to side in the room with the rocking of the ship. The thumps had been the bodies hitting the walls.

"I…" Finn was speechless. How did he describe this? He moved out of the way so the other two could get out of the stairwell.

"Jesus, Mary, and Joseph," Elias growled as the ship rolled on a large wave and the bodies slid toward the other side of the room. He made the sign of the cross.

"I think I'm gonna puke." Axe turned and hurried down the stairs.

Finn closed his eyes. "I need to take pictures."

"Fuck no," Elias snarled. "Nobody needs to see this."

"Agreed, but if the ship goes down, we need proof of what happened, and maybe we can identify these people. Bertrand is going to want to see this."

Elias shook his head. "No one wants to see this."

"You know what I mean."

"Fuck yeah, I do. Just get it done so we can get the fuck off this hell hole."

Finn turned off the flashlight on his phone and opened the camera to snap pictures to preserve the evidence as much as possible. He tried to avoid looking at the details too closely, focusing his gaze on the area right above the bodies as he aimed the camera and fired the shutter. Elias was right. No one needed to see this. Without looking at them, he tried to get the faces but they were distended and bloated, some were turned away. He swallowed convulsively as he worked, fighting back the bile rising in his throat. He knew he should go over and turn their heads, but he just didn't have it in him to wade through the goop covering the floor between him and the corpses.

He saw one with bright red hair and what looked like a tattoo on his left arm. He made sure to get pictures of it. He kept working robotically, taking pictures of any distinguishing marks. He found it easier to dissociate from the horror and focus on just snapping the next picture. Another body had white hair and what looked like a large scar down his neck. He had blue eyes or at least Finn thought they were probably blue when he was alive. Now he wasn't sure. It was hard to tell. They had a sort of opaque fog over them which means these people had been dead for a couple of days at least.

He spent another few minutes trying to take as many pictures as possible. He was finishing up when the ship rolled suddenly which sent the bodies toward him and Elias.

"Jesus," Elias yelled and backed down the stairs. Finn went down a couple of steps from the landing and waited. The white-haired man slid through the doorway until his torso caught on the doorjamb and he stopped. His right arm was flung out to the side. Finn took a picture and then realized that the goo that was on the floor was now cascading down the steps and coating his shoes. He quickly retraced his steps to the bottom of the stairs and went back into the freezer. He slammed the door behind him. He couldn't process what he'd just seen. His heart hammered. He was sweating profusely. A numbness set in. His mind's way of creating distance but he knew the full horror of that room would eventually haunt him.

He quickly took off the mask, but the smell had seeped into the freezer. He went out into the kitchen, paused, then grabbed a sandwich bag off the shelf. He put the phone in it and then shrugged and added the note he'd found. What the hell, it might mean something. Then he sealed it and put it into the pocket of his windbreaker. He went back down the hall where he found Elias and Axe.

He shuddered. "Damn, that smell makes me want to hurl."

Elias nodded. "Nothing is going to block that smell, man. There's nothing strong enough. I feel like it's on my clothes and my skin. Even in my sinuses."

Axe coughed and then so did Finn. "We need to get out of here." He started down the hallway and turned the corner, almost bumping into Nick and Cain.

Nick frowned and squinted. "You found bodies. There's nothing else that smells like that."

"Yeah, and it's worse than you can possibly imagine," Finn responded.

"Worse than Panama?"

Elias snorted. "Panama was a picnic compared to this."

Finn shuddered at the memory of the pile of bodies a group of mercenaries had left for the team to find when they were trying to secure a life-saving vaccine that had been hijacked. Elias was right. The scene he'd just meticulously photographed was much, much worse than the gruesome discovery they'd made in the jungle.

Cain grunted. "Shit."

Nick ran a hand through his hair. "The launch is here, but now that you've discovered the bodies, I know Bertrand is not going to want us to leave. Maybe I should go take a look."

"No." Axe shook his head. "I had to leave because I thought I was gonna puke. I don't know how these two stuck it out, but it was brutal. Even with N95 masks on."

"It was," Finn agreed. "We can't get in there without air tanks. The smell, Nick, it's unbearable. We can't spend any major time in there without throwing up all over the place and there's no point going for a cursory look."

Nick blinked. "It's really that bad?"

"A bunch of bodies left in a room for at least a week with no air circulation whatsoever? Yeah, it's that bad."

"What about the bleach?" Nick asked.

"To cover the smell," Finn said. "They wanted to buy time would be my guess. Since they couldn't sink her, it would be a long while before anyone twigged to where the bodies were when the ship was found but what they didn't count on was the storm. The bleach spilled on the floor. That thump we heard, yeah, well, the bodies are sliding across the floor with each wave. It's—" Finn stopped talking. Just the thought of it had him swallowing hard. He might get sick yet. His entire body had broken out into a sweat, and he was having a hard time regulating his breathing. He needed a shower and clean clothes, but first he needed off this ship.

Just then, the ship tilted drastically to the port side. They all braced themselves against the bulkhead. This time, it didn't stop rolling. Finn ground his teeth. This was going to be a close one. If the ship rolled too far, it wouldn't be able to right itself and they'd capsize. Finn said a quick prayer. He glanced around at his teammates. If he had to go down, this was the group he wanted to do it with.

The ship continued to roll so that they were laying on the wall. There were all kinds of crashes and bangs coming from the kitchen area. Finn held his breath.

There was a pause, and then the metal groaned long and loud before the ship rotated back upright and they were standing on their feet again.

"Jesus, that was close." Axe blew out a long breath while getting his footing.

"No wonder Gerhart didn't want to send the launch. That thing must be being tossed around like a toy in this storm."

"Okay, I'm calling it," Nick said. "We're done here. Bertrand is just going to have to live with us leaving. If the ship doesn't make it, then you'll just have to describe what you saw to him. It will have to be enough."

Finn nodded. The image of all those bodies and what the last wave had probably done to them was locked in his mind. "I have pictures," he managed to grit out from between clenched teeth. "I thought it might help with identification."

Nick tapped him on the arm. "Smart. Good work. Now let's get the fuck off this tub."

CHAPTER SEVEN

Tory wiped the water off her face as best she could and then had to offer her wet hand to the captain.

"Captain Gerhart, I'm Tory Stanhope."

The captain shook her hand gingerly. "You made it. It must have been a hell of a ride."

She managed a small smile. "You have no idea." When the ship started into a deep dive, Tory looked around for something to grab. They were standing just inside the door from the deck. There was a long hallway in front of them. She reached out and leaned on the wall, hoping that would help if she started sliding.

Gerhart did not look too pleased that she was there. She couldn't blame the man. DHS probably hadn't given him much detail on what was going on. "If you could maybe show me to my bunk and a bathroom, I'd really appreciate it." She shot him a bigger smile, hoping to soften him up a bit.

His face remained impassive. "Talco, show Ms. Stanhope her quarters."

Who the hell was he talking to? She glanced around to see a young guy standing in a doorway down the hall a bit.

"Yes, sir." Seaman Talco came out of the room and nodded to her. The thin red-headed sailor didn't look a day over sixteen, but she knew he had to be somewhere in his early twenties. "If you'll follow me." He turned and started down the hallway.

"Captain," she excused herself, nodding, and then hurried to catch up to the young man.

They walked along a hallway and then turned right and went down a set of stairs. At the bottom, they took a left. About halfway along that hallway, the seaman stopped and opened a door. Then he stepped back. "Ma'am."

"Thank you, Mr. Talco." He nodded again and started to leave, but she stopped him by asking, "Um, sorry, but can you tell me how to get to the bridge?"

Talco stared at her for a beat and then provided directions.

"Also, is the team back from the *Explorer*? I need to speak with them."

"Not yet, ma'am. They should be on their way shortly."

Tory nodded. "Can you have someone let me know as soon as they arrive?"

"I will let the captain know of your wishes." He tipped his chin down and then turned and moved swiftly away from her. So much for being nice. Her room was small with a single bunk and a small desk with a lamp. That was all she really needed. Except a bathroom. She looked around. There was none attached to the room. Well, she was just going to have to find it and fast. The rolling of the waves was already getting to her.

She pulled her luggage into the room and then returned to the hallway. She looked left and then right. She had a fifty-

fifty shot at getting it right. She turned right. She got almost all the way down to the end of the hallway before seeing a *Ladies* sign on a door. "Hallelujah," she said and quickly went inside.

It was basic, but it had toilets, sinks, and shower stalls. It would do. She took a minute to throw some water on her face. She really wanted to brush her teeth, but it would have to wait. She needed to understand what the lay of the land was aboard the ship.

Tory made her way back to her quarters. She had to brace herself on the wall when the ship rolled at a steep angle. She closed her eyes but that made it worse. Her stomach heaved and she gagged. She didn't want to throw up in the hallway. She looked back at the bathroom. Should she go back or just go and sit down on her bunk? She chose the bunk and made her way back to her room. She closed the door and sat on the bed.

The room was a dingy gray color, not like the calming neutral grays in her apartment. This was institutional greige, a yawn-inducing combination of gray and beige. The bunk and the desk had both seen better days, but at least she had her own space. Sitting there, with the ship in constant motion was not helping her upset stomach.

She needed something to do. She needed a distraction. Maybe she should go connect with the captain and see what he knew. He probably wouldn't want to talk to her since she was forced on him, but it was worth a try. Maybe it would make her feel better if she could see the outside. Didn't they say it was better to be able to see the horizon?

Tory got up and headed out of her quarters. She recalled the directions Talco had given her perfectly. She made it to the bridge in good time.

"Captain Gerhart," she said as she entered the bridge. He

turned and stared at her. "Er, permission to enter the bridge?" she asked in a quiet voice.

A muscle in Gerhart's jaw pulsed. "Ms. Stanhope, let's go to my office. Massey, you have the bridge."

"Sir," said the man that had been standing next to him.

Gerhart strode out of the room and down the stairs she had just come up. She cursed silently. She'd hoped being on the bridge would make her feel better but now she had to go back down into the ship.

She followed but stumbled when the ship lurched and whacked her knee on the handrail. "Fuck," she mumbled and then limped down the rest of the stairs. She managed to get to the bottom and turn into the hallway just in time to see Gerhart disappear into the last room on the right. At least the pain had taken the edge off her nausea. She moved down the hallway and then stopped just short of the doorway. She took a deep breath and squared her shoulders. Then she proceeded inside.

Gerhart stood behind his desk, hands on hips. "Ms. Stanhope, let me be clear. This is a very difficult situation, and I do not need you underfoot. I am not sure why you are here, nor who thought it necessary to risk those men's lives to fly you out here, but I do not have time to waste making small talk. Now, I need you to go back down to your quarters and remain there until further notice."

Tory stared at Gerhart. She'd dealt with military types many times, and he wasn't wrong. From his perspective, it was a waste of time for her to be on board, but he didn't have the whole picture.

"Captain Gerhart, I appreciate that this is a difficult situation for you and your people. I have no desire to be underfoot or cause you distress. However, I am here at the behest of Ronald Zucker, Deputy Secretary of Homeland Security.

The situation with the *Oceanus Explorer* could very well be part of a much larger, much more dangerous, set of circumstances. I am not at liberty to read you in on all of the details, but suffice it to say, I did not risk my ass or the lives of those chopper pilots coming out here for shits and giggles. I'm here because I have to be. The sooner you brief me on what's going on with the *Explorer*, the sooner I can be out of your hair." She held the captain's gaze and refused to give an inch.

He narrowed his eyes and then finally huffed out a breath. "Have a seat." He motioned to one of the chairs in front of the metal desk before he sat down in his own chair. "What's the last update you had?"

She settled opposite of him. "I was told the team was over on the ship, and there were blood stains. The supposition was that approximately eighteen people were possibly killed on board, and some equipment was shot up as well."

Gerhart nodded. "The only equipment left was the stuff that *was* shot up. The buggers even cut the wires to the electronics in the bridge. The Canadians patched them together as best they could, and my crew completed the job, but the whole ship could falter at any minute."

"The team found—"

"Captain Gerhart." A youngish seaman stood in the doorway. "Sorry to interrupt, sir, but the XO needs you on the bridge."

Gerhart immediately rose. "Tell Massey I'm on my way." He turned to Tory. "We'll have to pick this up later." With that, he left the room.

Tory followed. The look on Gerhart's face said that Massey rarely called him to the bridge, so this had to be some sort of emergency. Tory's knee screamed with each step she ran up, trying to keep up with Gerhart. She entered the bridge a few seconds after he did and immediately regretted her decision.

She had to grab the edge of a control panel to stop from falling face-first into the glass window of the bridge. The officer standing next to her grabbed her arm, hauling her over so she could brace herself against the panel better. When she gasped, Gerhart glanced over at her but continued to give instructions and rally information from his crew.

A gigantic wave crashed over the bow, water spraying against the windows of the cutter. Tory broke out into a cold sweat. Whoever said it was better to see the horizon when on a ship had obviously never been in this situation. All she could see was a wall of water. One terrifying wave after another crashed over the front of the vessel. She swallowed convulsively.

She turned to look at the *Oceanus Explorer*. It was hard to see the ship through the rain and the waves. The hull popped in and out of view.

"She's going down, Captain. Her hull is breached." Massey, who Tory surmised was the second in command, said it in a calm voice, but his face showed distress.

"Abandon ship. Get everyone off it immediately and back onto the launch."

"Yes, sir."

Gerhart turned to the young officer next to him. "Van Zandt, get crews ready to go out and scoop up anyone that falls in."

"Yes, sir." Ensign Van Zandt leaned over and hit a button on the panel in front of him. An alarm squalled to life.

Gerhart turned to Tory. "Go back to your quarters until we get everyone back on board. I need to know —"

"I understand, Captain." And she did. He needed to know she was safe.

Tory turned and started down the stairs. This time she held on tightly and went slowly back down to the deck below. The captain needed to know the location of everyone on the ship. If everyone who wasn't needed was in their quarters, then he didn't need to worry about them. He only had to worry about the crew performing their assigned tasks and, at this point, she was damn glad to be going back to her room.

It took her a bit longer, but she finally made it to her room. First thing, she went to her pack and dug in it for the dimenhydrinate tablets she'd packed. Without a sink in the room, she had to dry swallow two pills. Throat still working, she collapsed on the bunk. The wall of water out there, wave after wave—that had to be the most terrifying sight to those men who were getting off the *Explorer*. She closed her eyes and mumbled a prayer or two. They were going to need all the help they could get.

She glanced at her watch, not because she needed to know the time, but because she needed the comfort her best friend's watch brought. Walli had been an only child. Tory kept in touch with Walli's parents because it seemed like a nice thing to do but, deep down, it was the guilt that had her sustaining the relationship.

She also thought about moving forward. About finding someone else maybe. About tossing it all in and running away to Europe. Missions like this made her wonder why the hell she worked for DHS. She could do anything else. Why stay?

Reluctantly, she admitted to herself it was because the work gave her a sense of belonging. She was part of a team, and she needed that connection. Otherwise, she would just float away, or at least that's what it felt like. She needed something to ground her, and her job was it. Without that, she would be lost.

She rubbed her hands over her face and sighed. Since Steve had told her back at the office, she had to come to the North Atlantic, she'd been sort of wishy-washy about everything. Grabbing her gear, her gun, coming out here, it had brought up all those old memories. Walli wasn't the only soldier killed in action. Three members of the SEAL team she was with also died. Tory had thought it was all behind her but this circumstance was proving her wrong.

When the ship lurched, she gripped the edge of her bed to keep from falling to the floor. What the fuck had she gotten herself into this time? Her father would sneer at her for being scared and then sneer at her for getting herself into this position in the first place. If she'd listened to him, she would be a lawyer and running for Congress now. Both sounded like a death sentence to her, not that the situation she was in now was that much better, but at least she didn't have to deal with her father.

Being around him was a torture like no other. She hated him. He was her abuser, and yet she couldn't get rid of him completely. Try as she might, as long as she lived in the same city, he would drop by unannounced whenever he felt like it.

Last time, she'd been doing her laps in the pool at her gym when her father had suddenly appeared at the end of her lane. He was there to invite her to his birthday party, he'd said. She didn't buy his excuse. There had to be an ulterior motive. There always was with him, but she was damned if she could figure it out that day. She had politely declined his offer, and he left. It still made her feel uneasy, even now. And that had happened two months ago.

The ship rolled again and made some horrible groaning noises. *Dear God, how did the Coasties manage to be calm through a storm like this?* She glanced around her cabin. Was there a life jacket? What was she supposed to do if the ship capsized? And where the hell was the garbage can? She did not want to puke on the floor.

She could swim thanks to her hours at the gym pool, but the icy North Atlantic was nothing like doing laps in a heated pool. The frigid water was a game-changer. On the other hand, if she had to be on a ship that capsized, being on a Coast Guard cutter was probably the best place possible. It was kind of like winning the lottery, provided she didn't die of course.

CHAPTER EIGHT

When the alarm sounded on the bridge, Oliver yelled he didn't know if it was real or not so he asked Nick to check it out. Finn went below with Nick to discover that one of the spots where the explosives had been had given way. The small crack was getting bigger by the minute.

They were going down.

Finn cursed. They'd waited too long, and now it was going to be a shit show, and it was his fault. If he'd gone back to find Nick before going to check out the bodies, then maybe they would have gotten off the ship in time and he wouldn't have had to see that horror. But the skeleton crew would've still been on board, he reminded himself.

"Where are the lifeboats? Do we know?" Finn asked an ensign named Crosby. They were standing just inside the forecastle doorway.

Crosby pointed. "Halfway down the deck on the port side. We're listing to port so it's gonna be tough getting to them."

"Understood." Finn turned to Nick. "I'll go with Crosby."

Nick cocked his head. "Cain, Elias, and Axe are getting the skeleton crew down here. Once we get them organized, we'll meet you on the deck by the lifeboats."

Finn's heart crashed against his ribcage. Of all the time he spent in the Coast Guard, it never occurred to him that he would be on a sinking ship. Stupid now that he thought about it, but there it was.

He made sure his life jacket was secure and then touched Crosby on the shoulder. They headed out from the relative safety of just inside the forecastle doorway. The ship groaned as the bow went under another wave. Finn knew that one of these times the bow wasn't going to come back up again. He grasped the railing in a death grip and tried to focus on the task at hand. Freaking out wouldn't help and would probably get him, or someone else, killed.

Finn worked his way along the railing. He did not want to get washed overboard in this storm. The rain battered him like little pellets of ice. He was shivering before he and Crosby had made it even halfway to the life raft. His fingers were getting stiff from the cold water washing over them both from the rain and the spray.

The ship groaned again and pitched forward at an awkward angle. Crosby fell and started to slide under the railing and off the edge of the deck. He yelled and tried to grab frantically at the bottom of the railing. Finn grabbed at him and managed to get a hold of the back of his life jacket, stopping Crosby's slide. He pulled Crosby back under the rail and then helped him back to a standing position.

"Thanks," Crosby yelled as he got to his feet. He held on to the railing with both hands and took a few tentative steps.

This wasn't going to work. That had been too close. Crosby was afraid of falling again. Finn didn't blame the guy but they just didn't have the time. The list toward port was getting more pronounced by the minute. The crew and his team were waiting on them for the life raft. The launch couldn't get close enough. It was smarter to get into the lifeboat and have the launch tow the lifeboat over to the cutter.

Finn wiped the rain out of his eyes and then tapped Crosby on the shoulder. "Go back. Get a rope or something," Finn yelled above the howling wind. "We're going to have to tie a rope along the railing so the guys can have something less slippery to hang on to in order for them to get out to the life raft. Make sure everyone has their life jackets on. I'll deal with the raft."

Crosby hesitated for a second and then nodded. Finn quickly went around him on the rail and made sure Crosby was heading back before turning and proceeding to the raft. He wasn't sure he could manage it on his own, but he was damn sure Crosby was not going to be much help.

He put one hand in front of the other on the rail and just kept moving forward. The wind buffeted him and made the going much harder. The rain and the spray made it hard to see. Salt stung his eyes. A mantra struck up in his head: *Hand over hand. Foot in front of foot. Breathe in, breathe out.*

Rescue was not something Finn knew much about, which seemed ironic since he was with the Coast Guard, but they did so many different things beyond rescues that it had just never been part of his job. Now he regretted that. When he got back to Miami, he was going to make sure someone taught him more about how to deal in these situations.

He looked up. He was only a few feet from the raft now. He had just started to relax a bit when a large wave hit. He got slammed by the water against the railing and lost his footing. He slid under the bottom of the railing and was hanging on by one hand, dangling above the water. Unfortunately, it was the hand attached to his bad shoulder, the one with the bullet wound. The pain was intense. He couldn't breathe. The salt made his eyes sting. He could barely keep them open. He was not dying like this. No fucking way. He groped around until he managed to grab the railing where it was soldered to the deck and pulled himself back up until he was prone on the surface. His breath heaved in and sawed out in great gasps. He struggled to get onto all fours.

Finally, he pulled himself to his feet. Agonizing pain seared his arm muscles. He wasn't sure he could manage the raft on his own, but he was going to do his best. He took the last few steps and reached the raft. Now he just had to find the release.

As Finn turned, he saw Axe approaching. The entire crew lined up behind him. Everyone had a life jacket on.

"You okay?" Axe asked. Concern written all over his face.

Finn nodded and glanced at the crew. "Everyone ready?"

Axe nodded.

"Load them up then," Finn instructed. He held tight to the railing as Axe got everyone on board. Nick, Elias and Cain were the last ones. "Get in," Finn said.

"You first," Nick argued.

Finn shook his head. "We've got to launch this from the outside. I don't trust that these fuckers didn't do something to the lifeboats. If we're all inside and it doesn't release, we're fucked."

"I'll stay and do it," Axe offered.

Finn shook his head "I've got it. You guys go in and I'll lower you. If it works I'll slide down the rope and lower myself into the boat."

Nick shook his head. "Negative. Too dangerous."

"Look, we need to get all these guys off the ship before it goes down. We don't have time to argue. Just go."

Nick stared at Finn and then got all the team members on board.

The orange boat reminded Finn of a toy only much

larger. He released the three securing pins that held it in place and then he hit the button releasing the cradle arms and lowered the boat into the water. Relief swamped him when the raft reacted in the expected manner. Thank God the fuckers who destroyed this ship hadn't thought to mess with the lifeboats. They didn't think anyone on board was alive and would need them. He let out the breath he'd been holding. Now all he had to do was lower himself with the rope ladder over the side. Easier said than done.

Finn threw the ladder over the side and made sure it was secured tightly to the railing. The climb down was agonizing on his arm. Just the act of hanging on was a bitch. He got near the level of the lifeboat and realized it was floating away.

Nick appeared at the hatch. They had the diesel engine going but it was no match for the waves. He was yelling but his words were lost to the wind. Finn closed his eyes. Nick was telling him to jump. He let loose a string of curses and then signaled his understanding with an awkward thumbs-up. He could jump in or die.

"Looks like I'm going for a swim," he grumbled.

Finn took several fortifying breaths and then leaped into the waves. The shock was intense. Icy water closed over his head. Because he was already stiff and he had to fight the waves, it took him longer to get back to the surface. His lungs were screaming by the time he pushed his head above the water and looked around.

The life raft was off to his left. He looked up at the side of the ship and found the rope. He swam towards it and grabbed it with one hand. His shoulder was killing him but the coldness of the water was numbing the pain along with the rest of his body. It took him a bit longer than he'd thought but he finally got to the ladder. Nick reached out and helped pull him inside the life raft.

"Jesus, you just have to be the hero, don't you?" Nick said.

Finn laughed as he spluttered out seawater. He gasped. "Don't worry…I've got it…out of my system now… Your turn next time." Nick helped him to a seat. "All seventeen members of the skeleton crew and my team are all on board, sir," Nick said into the radio.

Finn leaned back against the gunwale. Now all they had to do was wait for the other Coasties to rescue them.

The *Oceanus Explorer* let out a loud groan, and the sound of metal rivets popping screeched over the roar of the storm.

"Oh, shit," Finn swore.

The bow of *Explorer* sank under the waves and didn't come back up. They needed to be away from her so they weren't pulled under. Cain was working the engine. He gave her all she had and the little lifeboat chugged away from the Explorer at an excruciatingly slow pace. It seemed like hours before they heard the voices of the men on the *Walton* but finally they were being pulled out of the lifeboat.

Forty minutes later, they were all safely aboard the *Walton* and sitting in the mess hall. They were drinking hot drinks and snacking on some French fries and nachos. Finn had never been so happy to be back on a cutter in all his life.

Captain Gerhart of the *Walton* entered, and everyone surged wearily to their feet. He addressed his crew members, patting them on the back. "You all have been through a lot. You did a fine job over on the *Explorer*. She went down through no fault of your own. You should be proud of the work you did today." There were a few "Thank you, sir," but most were too tired to say much of anything.

"Go get some sleep. See medical if you have any injuries. Dismissed."

To their credit, they all left with their heads held high and no grumbling. Finn was impressed. Gerhart must be a good captain. Just the fact that he came to speak with them instead of sending his XO was a sign that he took his leadership responsibilities seriously.

Finn leaned back against the bulkhead as the ship rolled in the waves. He was exhausted, and his shoulder was killing him. He'd ripped the scar tissue again. It had happened once before, while working out too hard just after he'd been shot. He remembered that pain, and it was exactly what he was experiencing now. Then, his doctor had told him to do more stretches to help keep it loose. Well, he'd stretched the hell out of it today.

"Gentlemen," Captain Gerhart said, "I appreciate the help you gave my people over on the *Explorer*. I know you had your own mission, but you stepped up, and I thank you for that. We do, however, have a few things to discuss."

Finn wanted to groan. He knew everyone else felt the same way. It was after midnight, and he was exhausted. Their position on the *Walton* was a weird situation. The captain technically outranked them, but Team RECON had a special designation as a team that answered directly to Admiral Bertrand. Under normal circumstances, Gerhart would just order them about, but he was respecting their special status. And they had to respect his status as a superior officer in return.

Nick, who also was leaning on a bulkhead, straightened. "Of course, Captain. We were happy to help, and we also have some things to discuss, but could we do it in the morning? My team is exhausted."

"I appreciate that, Taggert, but I'm getting pushback from headquarters about what's going on. Homeland Security is very invested in your mission, and I'm getting requests for information every hour on the hour. As a matter of fact, they even flew one of their analysts out here in the storm."

Nick blinked. "They did what?"

Gerhart scowled. "It was a nightmare for the helicopter pilots, but they did it. People are very interested in your findings. I understand how exhausted you all must be, but I'm afraid I will have to insist we discuss things tonight."

Nick slouched. "Of course. It might be advisable for us to grab showers and get changed first, though."

"Agreed." Gerhart nodded. "Be in the conference room across from my office in thirty minutes." With that declaration, he turned and strode off down the hallway.

"Fuck me," Axe growled. "I need serious sleep. and now we gotta talk to the higher-ups?"

"Don't forget the analyst. Jesus, flying someone out here in this mess, DHS must really have their balls in a twist about something."

Finn rubbed his face. "After what we saw? I'm pretty sure we know what they're upset about."

Cain straightened. "The question is what do they know that we don't? They had to know there was an issue with the ship to send out an analyst because we haven't said what we found and the analyst is already here."

"Shit," Finn grunted.

"Yeah," Nick agreed. "Well, boys, time to get showered and prettied up for the brass." He started out of the mess and then turned back. "Finn, how's the shoulder? I saw you lose your footing." Finn started to shrug but winced. Nick commiserated, "That good, huh?"

Finn sighed. "I pulled the scar tissue so it hurts like an SOB, but I don't think I did any major damage. A few strained muscles maybe."

"But because of the scar tissue, it's worse." Nick knew all about scar tissue thanks to some asshole who hacked his back with a machete.

Finn nodded. "Yeah."

"Okay, well, take something for the pain and get it

checked out." Nick turned and left the mess. Axe and Elias followed. Finn stood and followed at a slower pace, Cain walking close behind him.

"You sure you're good?" Cain asked, keeping his voice quiet.

Finn sighed. "I don't know about good, but my shoulder will be okay. Some ibuprofen and a hot shower will help."

"Let me know if it gets worse," Cain said and then stopped talking as they entered their quarters.

Finn appreciated Cain's offer. It was nice to know the team cared, but at this point, there was nothing anyone could do about his shoulder. Truth be told, he was more concerned about the mental fallout from seeing all those bodies. That shit was the stuff nightmares were made of and it was going to haunt him for a long time.

Twenty minutes later, Finn entered the room across from Gerhart's office. He was the last one to arrive. It had taken him slightly longer to shower because of his shoulder. It had also taken him longer to get his uniform on. He nodded to his teammates and took a seat.

The room was done in fake wood paneling with beige floor tiles. The table was laminate but large enough to seat a dozen people comfortably, more if necessary. Currently, only his team and Seaman Proctor were occupying the space. Proctor had set out coffee.

The temperature in the room was too high, and Finn was thinking he would be asleep in minutes if he didn't drink some, but Elias handed him a cup before he could get up and get one himself. "Thanks," he said with a grateful smile.

"Gentlemen," Gerhart said as he entered the room. They all immediately got to their feet but he waved them back into their chairs. "Washington is waiting on this, so let's not dawdle. Tell me about the bodies and anything else you found."

Nick started to speak. "Well sir, we found—"

Gerhart held up his hand. "Sorry, I'm going to stop you for a second. I just realized the analyst is not here. Proctor, go see what's keeping her."

"Yes, sir," said the short, stocky seaman before he left the room. He returned almost instantly. "She's here, sir." Proctor went back to stand against the wall, and all heads turned to the doorway and waited.

Ten seconds later, Finn's Lady X walked in.

CHAPTER NINE

"Captain Gerhart." Tory acknowledged the commanding officer as she entered the room and then turned to introduce herself to the rest of the occupants. "Gentlemen, I'm—" Her ability to speak vanished when her gaze hit on the man at the end of the table. *Blue Eyes*?

She blinked. No fucking way. It couldn't be. She wanted to pinch herself to make sure she wasn't hallucinating.

"Ms. Stanhope, is something wrong?" Gerhart demanded.

"Er, no. Sorry." She set her laptop down on the table and swallowed hard. Her stomach was in knots. "I'm Tory Stanhope. I'm an analyst with Homeland Security, and we're very interested in what you found on the *Oceanus Explorer*. I'm going to need you to go over it in great detail, but we'll hit the broad strokes first." She took a seat. Collapsed into it was more accurate.

Gerhart frowned. "Taggert, why don't you introduce your team and then tell us what you found."

Nick nodded. "I'm Master Chief Nick Taggert." He pointed around the table. "Chief Petty Officer Elias Mason,

Chief Petty Officer Cain Maddox, Chief Petty Officer Finn Walsh, and Chief Petty Officer Axel Cantor."

Tory nodded at everyone. *Finn Walsh*. So that was Blue Eyes' name. Now she knew it. She also knew all about him. She'd read their files on the flight up to Maine but hadn't bothered to download their pictures because bandwidth was so limited it would have taken forever. At the time, she hadn't thought it was important, but she wouldn't make that mistake again.

Oh, God. Finn Walsh. She could pick 'em, couldn't she? Finn Walsh was the one who was almost kicked out of the Coast Guard for severely beating his senior officer. 'To a pulp' was the description in the incident report if she remembered correctly. If he hadn't gotten shot while the investigation was taking place, they would have turfed him for sure. It was bad form to kick out someone who'd been shot in the line of duty. The whole fighting and insubordination issue had been swept under the rug. But her trepidation came down to the fact that Finn Walsh had anger issues just like her father.

She took a breath and then counted. It was another trick her shrink taught her to refocus. There was a job to do, and that had to be her priority right now. She could deal with the personal stuff later. Still, Finn Walsh was now up there with Josh Hargate. God, she needed to work on making better choices.

"So…" She cleared her throat. "Um…please tell me what you saw over on the other ship."

Nick hesitated. "Could you be more specific? I'm not trying to be difficult, but it was a good-sized vessel. Besides the bodies, are you looking for any specific information?"

It was a fair question. After what she'd read in his file, and his initial, clarifying question, she immediately liked Taggert. Intelligent but also personable. She poised her hands on the laptop's keyboard. "What I'm really looking for are your impressions of the ship. What did you see, and what did that mean to you? What didn't you see, and was that significant in some way?"

Nick nodded. "Okay." He looked around the room. "And feel free to jump in, guys, at any time." He turned back to Tory. "I would say that whoever was running it were professionals, probably ex-military."

Tory was doing her damnedest to keep her gaze on Nick, but it was hard. She wanted to stare at Finn. It was so good to put a name to his face, and she loved the name. Finn. It suited him to a T.

She cleared her throat. "What makes you think so?" she asked. She really needed to get her shit together. This was ridiculous.

"The ship was clean," the man sitting on the end next to Finn said.

Maddox, that was his name. "Clean how, Chief Maddox?"

"If we were going to do something on that ship and didn't want it traced back to us, we would do certain things, like removing all the computer equipment, getting rid of all the papers. That's what they did. They knew what they were doing like we would know what to do. That comes from military training."

Made sense. She tapped her fingers lightly on the keys. "Did they make any mistakes? Was there anything that might be a lead as to who they were or what they were doing?"

Nick shook his head. "Unfortunately, the ship sank before we could do more than give it a cursory once-over. But like Cain said, it was clean. Professional-level clean."

"They did make one mistake," Elias leaned forward in his chair.

Axe nodded. "The explosives."

Tory frowned. "Explosives? Explain." She took a few notes but really, so far, they hadn't said anything that would rule this ship in or out as being part of the security breach.

Finn spoke, "It looked like they had tried to blow holes in the hull, but they botched the job." He traced a finger around the rim of his coffee cup.

Tory looked up from her notes, and their gazes locked. Heat bloomed in her cheeks and then in other parts as she remembered their night together. *Damn, he was fine.* "So, ah, Chief Walsh, how did they botch the job?" At least he was taking her mind off her seasickness.

There was a slight tremor in the corner of his mouth. It looked like he was trying not to smile. Was he laughing at her? Did he know that she couldn't concentrate with him in the room? She missed what he'd just said. "I'm sorry, can you repeat that?" she asked while staring firmly at her laptop.

"I said it looked to me like they probably wanted her to sink fast. Instead of putting all of the explosives in one location and blowing a hole, they spread it out over three areas. Three holes would be better than one. My guess is whoever did it might not have realized that the *Explorer* was a former U.S. Navy ship, and as such, has a very thick steel-plated hull. The three charges weren't enough to blow through it. If they'd left it all in one spot, they would have been successful."

Tory frowned. "So, not professional then?"

Nick cleared his throat. "It's a bit of a mystery. Our thinking is that they didn't have an explosives expert on board, or perhaps something happened to him or her."

"Like a bullet to the head," Cain drawled.

Tory nodded. "Makes sense." She made another note. "What else can you tell me?"

Nick looked at Finn and nodded. Finn shifted in his seat. "When they realized they couldn't scuttle the ship, they went to great lengths to hide the bodies. I mean, they would have been found eventually if the ship had made it to port, but hiding the bodies bought them some time. In the end, it was enough time, too. The charges weakened the hull enough that eventually it gave way under the pressure of the storm."

There was a reluctance to discuss the bodies. Tory could sense it in Finn. He didn't want to talk about it, but was it because of what he saw, or because he wanted to save everyone else the details? Meaning, he didn't want to hear if it was gruesome. Was he worried about her sensibilities?

Tory got up and poured herself a cup of coffee as a stall tactic. "Captain, did the helicopter pilots make it back safely?" she asked.

Gerhart grunted. "Yes."

"That's a relief." She was hoping that exchange illustrated that she was not just a pencil pusher. She needed these men to trust her and tell her everything down to the smallest detail. Were they hesitating because she was a woman, or for some other reason?

"Captain Gerhart, perhaps you could dismiss your man. The things discussed in this room require a high-level security clearance."

Gerhart frowned but nodded to Proctor, and the man left the room, closing the door behind him.

Tory started again. "Gentlemen, I am sensing hesitation from you in speaking about finding the bodies. I'm not sure what your reluctance stems from. If you are worried about upsetting me, please don't." She decided to be honest. "Eight years as a field agent for the CIA and two as an analyst at DHS has exposed me to just about every depravity humankind can offer up. You won't upset me with details."

Nick hesitated. "Fair enough." He turned to Finn. "Do you want to explain?"

Finn nodded slowly. He was still reluctant. Now that he

knew her background, it had to be something else. Was it that horrific? Oh, God, and she was making them relive it.

"It all started because I smelled bleach. Otherwise, I doubt we would've found the bodies before the ship sank." He continued in a very precise and careful manner. Like he was reading the ingredients on a bottle of laundry soap. Distancing himself from the memory. It was obvious he did not want to have to go through this again, none of them did by the looks on their faces. And she couldn't blame them.

"There were eighteen blood pools found on the ship. I think that roughly correlates to the number of bodies I saw. It was hard to get an exact count due to the state of decomposition and the fact that the bodies were being tossed around by the storm."

He paled as he spoke, and she knew just how much it was costing him to continue. Human beings had the capacity to perform some heinous things. It was hard to get over that sometimes.

"What were they wearing?" she asked hoping to dehumanize the retelling to allow some relief for Finn.

"They had on civilian clothing. Jeans and T-shirts. Some had button-down shirts. All males as far as I saw but again the lighting wasn't great and the circumstances made it very difficult to get an accurate assessment of the situation."

"Did you notice any tattoos or distinguishing marks that might identify them?"

Finn nodded. "A few but nothing that would identify them as a whole. I didn't see the same tattoo on multiple people."

Tory glanced up from her computer as Finn finished speaking. It truly was horrific. Gerhart had put a hand to his mouth. She glanced at him. He was pale, and he suddenly looked ten years older than he had earlier in the day. She had thought about turfing him, too, asking him to leave with the seaman earlier but, in reality, she might need him. If this was indeed somehow part of the security breach, then it would be all-hands-on-deck.

Tory took a sip of her cold coffee. Not helpful to her stomach. She grimaced. "I'm so sorry you gentlemen had to see that and even sorrier that now you need to relive it…but I do have a few more questions. Do you think you can continue?" She looked directly at Finn. He was exhausted, and his shoulder was hurting judging by the way he was digging his fingers into it. Maybe the bullet hole hadn't healed properly. She remembered running her fingers over the scar.

Finn shifted in his chair. "Let's get this over with."

She nodded. "Was it possible to recognize any of the faces?"

"I didn't know any of them, but it was possible to make out some of their features," Axel Cantor reported.

"Did any of you recognize any of them?"

Finn and Chief Mason shook their heads.

"You mentioned tattoos. Any other distinguishing marks?" Tory asked.

Mason frowned. "One guy had a pretty gnarly scar on his neck."

"A scar? Could you describe it?" Tory fingers were poised to type in more notes.

"I took pictures." Finn's voice was quiet. "I wasn't sure the ship would make it, and I knew someone would want to identify these people."

She stared at him. In the midst of all that horror, he had the presence of mind to take pictures. Impressed wasn't the word. She was floored. She also had an overwhelming desire to get up and hug him. Hard.

"That's—" She had to clear her throat. "That's incredible work. May I see them?"

Finn leaned forward and took what looked like a sandwich bag from his back pocket. He opened it up and removed the phone. He unlocked it and handed it to Nick, who handed it to Tory.

"Thanks. I'm going to want to study these photos. Do you mind if I keep the phone for a bit?" She knew she could have sent them to herself or even airdropped them but the reality was she couldn't let him keep them on the off chance he decided to send them to anyone else. Not that it seemed likely but still she had to make sure.

"That's fine." He rattled off his security code.

"Again, thank you. These pictures could make all the difference."

Nick cocked his head. "The difference to what?"

Tory looked up. "Sorry?"

"You said the pictures could make all the difference. Difference to what? Why are you here? A DHS analyst is flown through one of the worst storms on record to get out here, and that's all before we found the bodies. Why? What's going on?"

Tory frowned. She really didn't want to get into anything. She couldn't. "Unfortunately, I cannot answer your questions." She winced and, in that moment, decided to be honest. "I know you've all been through a lot, and you deserve answers, but I'm not allowed to give them. I wish I could."

She wouldn't categorize the stares as hostile, but they weren't friendly, and she didn't blame them one bit. "Why don't we call it a night? It's after two a.m. I know you're all exhausted. We can pick this up tomorrow." She got up from her seat and glanced down at the table. "Is that piece of paper something you found on the ship?"

Finn nodded. "Yeah, it was shoved into the paper towel dispenser in the men's room." He pushed the bag down the table toward her. Tory picked it up and gingerly pulled out the piece of paper, holding it by the very corners. Maybe they could get some prints off it.

She opened it. *Praetorian is active.* Blood drained from her head, and she swayed on her feet. Her knees then gave out, and she crashed back into the chair. Her worst nightmare had just come true. It was real. The thing she'd been dreading for months had just turned into a real monster. How the hell was she going to fight it?

CHAPTER TEN

Finn thought she might pass out. Whatever was going on, Tory Stanhope knew a lot more about it than she was letting on. The words on that slip of paper meant something to her, something not good.

"Are you okay?" he asked as he hurried around the table to her chair. He had to admit, seeing her walk in the door had been a shock, but now he couldn't help but think it was a nice surprise. He finally had a name for his Lady X.

"Um, yeah. I…just…that is..." She stared at the note as if hoping the words would change.

Finn had the urge to sweep her up into his arms and hold her tightly. He wanted to feel her against him. Not just because he wanted her physically, but because he wanted to comfort her, and he wanted the comfort that holding her would give him.

Instead, he stood behind her chair and waited for her to get herself together.

Tory stood up again. "Um, sorry, gentlemen, I must make some calls. If you'll excuse me." She slipped the note back into the bag and sealed it. Then she picked up Finn's phone and her laptop. She tucked them under her arm and walked out of the room without a backward glance.

"What the fuck was that about?" Cain demanded. "Er, sorry sir." He nodded at Gerhart.

"Don't apologize, son. I was wondering the same thing. What did the paper say?"

Finn shrugged. "It made no sense to me. Something about a war council being active."

Gerhart shook his head. "Okay then, you men get some sleep." He started to leave and then stopped. "After hearing what you all went through, I just want to say again how much I appreciate you stepping up and helping my crew. You make the Coast Guard proud." He gave them a tight-lipped smile and then left.

Nick said, "I want to second what he said. Today was rough. More than that, this assignment was fucking brutal, and you all were aces. I am proud to serve with every one of you."

Finn swallowed. "The feeling is mutual."

Everyone else murmured their agreement.

"Get some rest," Nick said. "I'll call Bertrand and fill him in. Finn, what exactly did the paper say? Bertrand is gonna want details."

"It said, '*Praetorian is active.*' With two letters after it. Capital M capital E."

"Okay, thanks." Nick glanced around the room. "I don't expect any of you to be up and moving any time before ten-hundred hours. That's an order."

"I like the sound of that," Axe said through a yawn. They all filed out of the room and went back to their assigned quarters. It took no time at all to climb into their bunks.

Finn lay there in the darkness. He was exhausted, but his mind was racing. His Lady X, a woman he never truly expected to see again, but hadn't stopped searching for, was on board the *Walton*. Tory Stanhope. He mouthed her name in the darkness. He liked it. It suited her. Her long blond hair had been down when he'd met her but he liked the cool professional styling of having it in a bun. Her eyes were as he remembered them. There was a hidden sadness there but when she smiled, they lit up. She'd gained a couple pounds and it looked good on her. She'd been too thin when they'd met. Not that her curves weren't nice but now they were… extraordinary. He wanted to run his hands over her body again. He smiled. It was like winning the lottery after the day he'd had.

Ex-CIA she'd said. Tough for sure. But he already knew that from their one night together. He should have realized she wasn't just a pencil pusher. She'd recognized his scar as a bullet wound right away. She also hadn't asked him how he got it, like it was no big deal.

Maybe when all this was over, they could go out on a real date. He'd missed those big gray eyes. He'd love to make them light up again. He yawned. Yeah, he'd definitely ask her out this time. He dropped off to sleep, dreaming of Tory.

The next morning the team was seated in the mess hall, eating a late breakfast, when Tory walked in. Finn immediately noted the dark circles under her eyes and the fine lines around her mouth. She hadn't slept, or at least not much.

She came and stood at the foot of their table. "Morning," she said. "Hope you got some rest."

There were a few murmurs of greeting. Everyone had stopped eating and were waiting for her to speak. She gave them a quick smile. "When you've finished your breakfast, meet me in the same room we met in earlier." She nodded at them and then turned on her heel and walked out of the mess.

"What the fuck was that about?" Cain asked. "And why is that the first question that comes to my mind every time she's in the room?"

Nick grinned. "She's definitely big on playing things close to her chest."

"It's a need-to-know thing, and you don't need to know," Axe said with a mouth full of food. He finished chewing. "I think that's a good thing. After yesterday, I don't want to be involved in whatever mess she's dealing with. Ain't nothing good gonna come out of it."

Finn's gut was in knots. He had to agree with Axe. He wanted to spend time with Tory, but not like this. Whatever the bigger picture was, he knew on a fundamental level that it was bad.

He ate the last bite of his eggs and put his knife and fork on his plate. "What did Bertrand say when you spoke to him last night, Nick?"

Nick set aside his coffee cup. "Not much. He was incredibly tight-lipped. He did say that alarm bells were ringing all over Washington, not just with DHS, so whatever this is, it's big. He said he'd let us know our next moves later today. He wasn't sure if we should stay on board the *Walton* or head back to Miami. Now that the storm is over, it should be no problem getting us back to Maine and then home."

"I vote for home," Elias said. "I don't like the North Atlantic so much. Too effin' cold."

"Agreed," Axe said and then forked the last bite of his cinnamon roll into his mouth.

Finn wanted to go back to Miami too. Rest his shoulder in the warmth of the sun. On the other hand, Tory was here. He'd love to connect with her again in oh so many ways.

Nick stood. "If you boys are finished, let's go meet Ms.

Stanhope. Maybe grab some coffee to go. This could end up being a long day."

Ten minutes later, Finn walked into the room to find Tory there by herself, standing at the head of the table. Her computer in front of her, and a notepad next to it. She seemed lost in thought and didn't appear to hear him come in, which was fine by him. It gave him a moment to study her in all her hotness. The woman was gorgeous. She'd been wearing a suit the night they met, and he'd thought that was sexy, but today's outfit somehow seemed even sexier.

She was wearing black cargo pants and a gray T-shirt. He was pretty sure she would be wearing army boots, too. He had no idea why that made him think of sex, but it did. Everything about her made him think of sex. Sex and, oddly enough, comfort. Her presence brought him comfort somehow. *Weird.*

The weight she'd put on since he'd last seen her looked good on her. Generally speaking, she looked healthier, albeit tired and a bit green around the gills. Seasickness was a tough one and not surprising with the size of the waves from the storm. She also seemed to be more controlled. She'd been wild when they'd been together. Her energy had been electric. It had fueled their animalistic sex. He'd reveled in it, but he liked this calmer Tory, too. It made him want to hug her and curl up with her in his lap on a rainy Sunday.

Her blond hair was pulled back into a tight bun again this morning. He remembered what it was like to run his fingers through her hair. It was soft like silk. He shut down that line of thinking. It wasn't going to help in this situation. They wouldn't have much time before the others showed up, but he wanted to…what? Reconnect was really what he was thinking.

"Hey," he called the greeting softly.

Tory looked up from her laptop. This close, it was easy to

see she'd definitely been up all night. It took all his willpower to not go over and immediately hug her. She looked like she could use one in the worst way.

"Hey, yourself," she said and then offered him a shy smile. "I have to say it was a bit of a shock to see you last night."

"Yeah, for me too, Tory." He grinned, and she had the grace to blush.

"Look, about that—"

"Hey, no worries. I understand. I could have been anyone. Why give me your real name? I get it. Best to be safe."

"Well, yes"—she nodded—"but that wasn't what I was going to say. I was about to say that we're going to have to work closely together. Can you handle that without things getting awkward?" Gone was the soft smile. Now she was all business.

Finn hesitated for a second. "Er, yeah, no problem but, ah, I was kind of hoping that maybe we could—"

"No." She shook her head. "Sorry, but no. This"—she tapped her computer—"is the number one priority. Nothing else matters at this point, and there can be nothing but a working relationship between us. Are you good with that Chief Walsh?"

Finn ground his teeth. There was no need to be a bitch about it. "Absolutely, Ms. Stanhope," he growled. He walked to the other end of the table and took a seat just as Nick and the others filed in.

Tory still stood at the head of the table, and everyone took their same places from last night. Nick and Axe on the right, Finn at the end, and Cain and Elias on the left.

Tory was reading something on her phone. Finn waited in silence. He was royally pissed off. What the hell? She didn't have to be so cold about it. He needed to fold some origami. It would calm his brain. Right now it was going a mile a minute and not in a good way. He clasped his hands on the table.

"Sorry for the delay, guys." She looked up and put her phone down. "I was waiting for confirmation before I proceeded. I just received it."

She took a deep breath. "What I am about to tell you is of the highest level of security clearance. Normally, you would never be read in on something like this, but I am going to need your help. Admiral Bertrand has already given it his okay. To be clear, he didn't have a choice. This comes from the top, the Director of Homeland himself."

She looked each man in the eye in turn and then said, "You are now all under my command."

Finn's gut churned. Working on the same project was one thing, but under her command? She wasn't even in the Coast Guard. He glanced over at Nick whose eyes were narrowed.

RECON's team leader spoke up, "Perhaps you could be a bit clearer. You mean we're working with you for the duration, or we're now permanently assigned to you?"

"You are now assigned to work *for* me until this crisis is solved. I do not have a timeline on that. Let's hope this wraps up sooner rather than later. The longer it goes on, the worse it will be."

"For whom?" Finn ground out.

Her gaze met his. "For the United States of America."

Axe snorted. "Dramatic much?"

Finn couldn't help it; he grinned. Leave it to Axe to lighten the moment.

Tory turned to Axe with a cold smile. "Yes, it's dramatic, but warranted in this situation."

"And what situation is that?" Nick asked.

She took a deep breath. "I was at a conference in Brussels about six weeks ago where a diplomat from a Middle

Eastern country made a joke about the U.S. running out of toilet paper in the Federal buildings and someone had to use their department's quarterly report to wipe their ass instead. I laughed it off, as did all my colleagues but, in truth, that did actually happen, and I wondered how they knew. It wasn't common knowledge. Gossip, I figured, at the time.

"Later, at that same conference, one of the representatives from an African country we have been working with to help create more stability wondered out loud to me how we could justify spending so much money on border security. He named the exact figure To. The. Penny." She frowned. "Who were we to tell them what to do about gun control with our own spending elsewhere?

"I started asking around. Did anyone else have any strange encounters with other diplomats? Did they run into anyone who knew some detail, some factoid, that they probably shouldn't? I immediately heard back from multiple people regarding quite a few incidents. It's worth noting the diplomats were from various countries, not just one."

Cain cocked his head. "Are you saying that someone was leaking information?"

She nodded. "That's what I thought at first. I went back to DHS and told my boss and my boss's boss what was going on. They told me to poke around and see what I could find out without drawing attention to anything. It's not normal for DHS to be involved in something like this, but my career with the CIA and the fact that it wasn't something we handled made me uniquely qualified to do it discreetly without raising an alarm.

"After two weeks of looking, I couldn't find a pattern. It wasn't just one department that had information leaked; it was many. It wasn't one country using these leaked facts; it was a dozen or more and they weren't even in the same area of the globe. I couldn't get my brain around it until an agent in my office mentioned something to me."

Finn leaned forward as Tory shifted uncomfortably and drummed her fingers on the table.

She continued, "Several months ago, somewhere in the middle of the Atlantic, a male voice said the following words over an emergency radio frequency: *Praetorian is ready for phase two.*"

Finn's gut tightened when she repeated the name from the paper he'd found.

"What does that mean?" Elias asked.

Tory crossed her arms. "We had no clue. As a matter of fact, we never would have paid any attention to it except that it *was* broadcast over the emergency frequency. Several ships in the area asked the speaker to repeat what they said. They asked if that was a call for help. Were they in trouble? Nothing. Zero response. They informed the Coast Guard. It was written off as one of those crazy things, and no one thought any more about it.

"Fast forward a month, and suddenly the Pentagon loses communication with Europe."

Nick cocked an eyebrow. "Wait, what do you mean 'loses communication'?"

Tory sighed. "Perhaps you could all save your questions until I've finished. It will go a lot faster that way." She took a beat and smoothed a hand over her hair. "Okay, let's start at the beginning. You know about the submarine communication cables, yes?"

The room remained silent, and Finn had a spasm of guilt. They knew what she was talking about, but her attitude about questions had pissed them off. He was pissed off, too, but if he actually did the adult thing and took a moment to put himself in her shoes as his shrink had suggested, he could totally see where she was coming from. It couldn't be easy being a woman in this environment. And coming up against a one-night stand at work had to be her worst nightmare. No wonder she rebuffed him. He was the asshole for being pissed off. He sighed to himself. He really needed to pack up his bruised ego and work on curbing his temper more quickly.

Tory gamely continued. "There are a series of cables that connect all of the continents around the world except Antarctica. These fiber optic cables run along the ocean floor and are very strong. They run ninety-nine percent of all data traffic around the globe."

She took a sip of coffee and then set her mug back down on the table. It slid slightly, and she reached out to stop it. "I should say here that the government has their own cables…" Her voice faded out as she watched her coffee mug slide again and gather speed this time, careening toward the edge of the table. She grabbed it and then steadied herself with the table edge as the floor pitched to a forty-five-degree angle.

"Shit!" Nick leaped out of the chair. "Rogue wave!"

CHAPTER ELEVEN

The men scrambled to their feet and braced themselves against the room's bulkheads. Tory just stood there, looking stunned. Finn crossed the room and pinned her to the far wall with his body. He knew from experience things were going to fly. He and Tory were in a bad position, but there wasn't time to move.

The room continued to tilt upward. Finn and Tory were on the downside, which meant things were going to fall in their direction. He kept Tory cocooned between his chest and the bulkhead. He rested his forearms on either side of her head and made sure his body totally covered hers so she wouldn't get hit with flying debris. His shoulder twinged but he froze, refused to move to alleviate the pain.

The table was bolted in place but the rest of the furniture in the room slid across the floor and crashed into the wall beside them. He leaned in so his mouth was next to Tory's ear. "It will be over in a minute. Just stay where you are."

He grunted when a chair hit him in the legs. The coffee pot flew off the table and shattered next to Tory's head. A few shards got embedded in Finn's arm, but he managed to keep her from getting cut.

The ship still seemed to be rising. This had to be one hell of a wave. He glanced down. Tory's gaze locked with his. Her eyes were open wide, and her fingers clutched in his uniform shirt. He was so tempted to kiss her, he almost did it. She looked terrified, and he wanted to take her mind off it. Ease her fear. Hell, he just wanted to hold her close, but the smell of her shampoo was getting to him. Even with his adrenaline pumping, or maybe because of it, he was getting hard. Not good. Being this close to her was doing funny things to his equilibrium.

Suddenly, the floor started to even out, but then pitched in the other direction. Finn kept Tory pinned to the wall by bracing his feet. The length of her was pressed against him, which did not help his situation at all both with his shoulder and other things.

"I'm sorry," she breathed.

He smiled at her. "Don't be. I'm not." There was no point in lying. She had to be able to feel his hard-on through her cargo pants. She looked up, startled, but then a small smile tugged at the corners of her mouth.

Everything slid in the opposite direction and smashed into the far wall. A few moments later, the ship leveled out again.

"Everyone okay?" Nick asked.

There was a general chorus of yeahs, and Finn took a step back from Tory.

"You're bleeding," she said as she glanced down at his arm.

"Just a few bits of glass. I'll see one of the EMTs in a bit. They're probably dealing with a lot of casualties at the moment."

Tory stepped out from behind him. "Why don't we take a small break so everyone can regroup and get cleaned up."

Cain bent down and picked up her notepad. He handed it to her.

"Thanks." She gave him a quick smile. "I'm also going to see if I can track down more coffee. I could use some." She turned and left the room.

"Finn, you okay?" Cain asked.

He watched her go out the door. "Yeah," he said but kept his body turned away from the guys. It was gonna take him a minute to calm down. He needed a cold shower a lot more than hot coffee. "I'm gonna go get the glass shards pulled out of my arm. I'll be back in a bit." He walked out of the room and went in search of the EMTs.

A half-hour later, they were all back in the room. Finn had come back with a bandage on his arm to find the guys had cleaned up the mess and were sitting around chatting.

"How's the rest of the ship look? Any major casualties?" Nick asked.

"The ship's a bit of a mess but no major injuries. One dislocated shoulder and a broken toe are the worst of it. Mostly glass shards, like me."

Tory walked back into the room, carrying a tray of coffee and upside-down mugs. She took in Finn's bandage. "Just a few more scars to add to that arm." She shook her head and then proceeded to hand out the coffee cups.

Finn shrugged. Not much he could do about that. He turned, and Nick cocked an eyebrow at him. *Shit.* He didn't want to talk about his one-night stand with their new lady boss. He kept his face neutral but glanced around the room, looking for paper.

Elias slid a few sheets over to him. "Thought you might need this," he murmured.

Finn readily accepted them. "Thanks." He then buried his nose in the paper stack.

"So," Tory said, "where were we?"

Nick cleared his throat. "You were saying about the government having their own separate cables."

"Right." She smiled her thanks. "So, as I said, a few months ago, the Pentagon lost communications with Europe. The cables were out. It's rare, but it happens occasionally. A fishing trawler catches one in its net or an underwater earthquake causes a rock fall or some such. No one thought much of the reason it happened but focused on getting them back up asap.

"The weird thing was that they came back online by themselves a couple of hours later. It was assumed at the time that there must have been some sort of seismic event underwater that caused a rockfall or whatever, and then maybe aftershocks cleared the debris from the cable so they started working again." She paused. "Are you with me so far?

"I'm a bit confused on the timeline," Finn said. "How much time passed between the transmission and the cable going out?" He didn't really care, but he was throwing her a bone. Plus, he wanted to clear the air between them. She avoided looking at him just as much as he was avoiding looking at her. It was noticeable. He forced himself to focus on her as she answered.

Tory looked over at him. "Three weeks and two days to be exact. And it was four weeks after that I went to the conference, and another three until I put it all together. Once I looked at the fact that countries around the world had information they shouldn't and that information was from many sources going to just as many sources, it became obvious what had happened."

"You mean the cables were tapped?" Elias asked.

She nodded. "Yeah, that was the conclusion I'd come to. I told my boss and, in turn, he spoke with the top brass of multiple departments and the White House. An investigation was to be launched on how this could have happened and where. And then the Canadians called and said there was a ghost ship with lots of blood and no bodies."

Nick leaned back in his chair. "So, they sent you immediately to see if it was connected."

She nodded. "And thanks to Finn finding that note, we now know it was."

Finn kept working on his origami elephant. Too much eye contact wasn't helpful either.

"So what does all this mean?" Axe took a sip of his coffee.

"It means that someone out there has hacked the governmental data cables connecting us to Europe, and they've been selling off little bits of data to interested parties."

"Do we have an idea who's behind it? Is it the Chinese or the Russians?" Elias asked.

Tory shook her head. "No, it's not them."

Finn spoke up. "It's not a country. It's a company." All heads turned to him, and he set his origami elephant aside.

Tory nodded. "Finn's right."

He continued. "If multiple countries have the information, then it can't be a single country selling to everyone because they'd want to keep all the details to themselves. It makes them stronger. The fact that little bits of data are spread out across many countries makes it more likely some group did it. A group with money. If it was a militant group, they would have shouted it from the rooftops and only sold it to their allies. So what's left? A group with the money and expertise to do it but no ideology to espouse. Has to be a company."

Tory added, "We think that it's probably some sort of

paramilitary or former military group. Quite possibly a company involving military contracts overseas, but you're right, Chief Walsh, they'd have to have money and the skills to do it. It's not easy to tap into one of these cables."

Finn glanced over at Tory. That was a lot of stress to handle. Tracking down the leaks. Figuring out the cables had been tapped. Did that mean she needed stress relief? Was she out in bars picking up men? Finn crushed the zebra he'd been making. The thought of Tory with another man was…maddening.

"So *Praetorian* is the name of the project then, I take it," Nick said. "Coming from the idea of the Praetorian Guard who were supposed to protect the Roman Emperors, but more often than not, overthrew them and handpicked who would succeed them. You think they're trying to overthrow the U.S. government?"

Tory shrugged. "That's what you're going to help me find out."

CHAPTER TWELVE

Tory looked at the shell-shocked men. She couldn't blame them. Her stomach hadn't quit rolling since she'd read the note that Finn had found about Praetorian being active. And it wasn't just due to seasickness. It was a hard nut to swallow. Finding out someone was selling their country's secrets was devastating. Finding out that no one had one fucking clue who was behind it made it scary as hell.

She avoided looking at Finn on principle, but she kept finding her gaze straying to his. She'd been cold on purpose. She needed him focused on the task at hand. And then there'd been the rogue wave, and any coldness had melted between them faster than marshmallows in hot chocolate.

Still, there could be no distractions. If he thought she was open to another night of amazing sex, that might cloud his judgment, make him lose focus. Oh, who was she kidding? It would cloud *her* judgment. *She* would lose focus. She was already struggling. She needed to stay far away from Finn Walsh. Her desire to throw herself into the safety of his arms was almost overwhelming.

She straightened her shoulders. "I know I've thrown a lot

at you, but I'm going to add to it. So far, it's all been innocuous bits of information that have come to light, stuff that might give a country a bit more bargaining power or a shot at embarrassing the US. But, and this is huge, whoever they are, they have access to a lot of highly classified data. I cannot stress this enough. The Pentagon has been breached. Anything sent to our embassies, other governments…it's all been tapped. Eventually, all that information will come up for sale. Time is of the essence. We need to find out who has the information and stop them before they give away all our secrets."

"What do you want us to do?" Elias asked. "Are we going to search for the point in the cable that's been tapped?"

"The Navy is taking care of that. The *Walton* is going from here to join some of the T-AGOS to track down the breach in the cable. They've already checked some distance of it, but there's a lot of ground to cover"

"But we're not going with her," Nick stated.

"No, you're not." Tory frowned. "Due to the nature of this investigation…" She had pissed the guys off in the beginning, and although they'd warmed up a bit, they still weren't totally on board with this. Best thing to do was tell them the whole truth.

"Here's the thing. Everyone in Washington is up in arms over this. And I mean *everyone*. It starts at the executive level, and trickles to every three-letter agency or department. They're having trouble keeping it under wraps. The last thing anyone wants is for the press to find out. So, since I put everything together, and you guys were on site, the White House decided that we should continue to work on this as a team.

"You guys have impressed people at the most senior levels of government. They like what they hear. They also don't want territorial disputes between agencies. So the CIA is going to work it from the outside, see if they can figure out who the seller is by using their contacts in the countries we know have some information.

"Our job is to come at it from the point of the *Oceanus Explorer*."

"But the ship sank," Axe protested.

"Yes, but Finn took pictures. And you guys were on board. We're going to go over all the details and see if we can glean anything helpful. It would have been ideal if we had the bodies or even some DNA, but we have pictures, so it's a place to start."

Finn looked uncomfortable. She raised an eyebrow at him. He was hiding something.

Finn sighed. "We may have DNA."

"What do you mean?"

"I mean some of the…goo from the floor with the bodies dripped all over my boots and possibly got inside. I didn't look too closely. I did end up in the ocean and had to swim to the life raft but there's a possibility that all the…goo didn't get washed off."

She wanted to simultaneously kill and hug Finn. "It might have been helpful to know this sooner," was all she said. "But better late than never. Please put your boots and socks into a bag, and I will have them delivered to the lab in Quantico when we get off the ship."

She glanced at her watch. The chat had taken longer than she'd thought. "Okay, guys, you have twenty minutes to get your gear and meet me on deck. There's a chopper about to touch down and it will take us to Maine. From there we will get on a military flight to Virginia. I will give you the address of our new office space. I expect everyone to report in right after you've all gone shopping."

"Wait, we're not staying here to work on this?" Finn asked.

She shook her head. "We have more resources down in Virginia and more flexibility to move around."

"I'm sorry, shopping?" Nick cocked an eyebrow.

"No uniforms. We want to keep a low profile. If you have enough clothes with you then great, but my understanding is that you guys are now based out of Miami. So, if you need civilian clothes, pick some up. You'll be reimbursed." She held up a finger. "Do not, however, buy super expensive clothing or crazy watches or anything beyond the basics. You won't get the money for them."

"Noted," Nick said and then stood up. "Are we good to get our gear?"

Tory nodded once. "See you on deck in fifteen." Once they all filed out of the room, she collapsed onto a chair. That had taken more out of her than she thought it would. She was exhausted. She'd been up all night talking with her boss, Steve, and those calls had escalated up the chain of command at DHS. They wanted answers pronto, and she didn't have any to give. They were very upset the ship went down. Well, what the fuck did they expect her to do about that?

She rubbed her face. They wanted the pictures, but she couldn't send those either because they were in the middle of the Atlantic. As it was, they were talking on secured satellite phones, and that still made her nervous. They were just going to have to wait until she was back in Virginia to see the pictures, not that it would do much good. Her bosses weren't field operatives. She doubted they'd seen anything like this before. Seeing those images wouldn't do anything but give them bad dreams.

She inhaled a deep breath and then exhaled gustily. This whole thing was a nightmare for the U.S. and for her, compounded by the fact that Finn was now on her team. *Of all the gin joints*, as Humphrey Bogart said. She looked at her notepad. Why did he have to be the violent type? That was so…disappointing.

She got up from the table and moved over to grab her luggage from the corner. It was time to make her way up on deck. When she stepped out of the room, she saw that Gerhart was at his desk in the office opposite. She walked across the hall. "Captain Gerhart, I just wanted to thank you for having me on board. I know I was foisted on you in the worst possible moment in the worst possible conditions, but I appreciate you helping me and keeping me in the loop."

Gerhart smiled and stood. "Ms. Stanhope…" He paused, then, "What is going on is truly catastrophic. I'm sorry I wasn't more helpful when you first arrived. You have my apologies and my sincerest wishes for this all to come to a conclusion sooner rather than later. If there's anything I can do to aid you, please don't hesitate to ask."

Tory walked across the room and offered her hand. "Thanks, Captain. Let's hope we can all work together to get this situation under control. Good luck with your search."

Gerhart shook her hand then released it. She turned and walked out, grabbing her luggage and pulling it along behind her. She made her way up on deck. If she hadn't made a friend of Gerhart, at least she'd made an ally, and sometimes that was all she could ask for.

She exited and walked across to the chopper, idling on the deck. It was bigger than the one she came out on, but it would be since there were six of them heading back.

The co-pilot took her bag and stowed it in the large helicopter. Then he helped her up. As she stepped in, she realized the whole team was already inside. *Shit.* She should have known they would be quick. There was one seat left next to Finn. There was more room in the next row back, but it would look silly if she squeezed herself back there instead of taking the open seat.

Sitting down, she tipped her head toward Finn and strapped herself in. She was glad the rotors were going so she didn't have to talk to him. She grabbed a headset and pulled it on. This was going to be a long flight. The heat from his leg pressing against hers was already igniting fires in other areas.

This was ridiculous. Maybe she just needed to get laid. She snorted softly to herself. It wasn't that. No, it was touching the sexiest man she'd ever been with; that was the problem. She could, and had, relived every second of their time together in excruciating detail. Even the smell of him made her crazy. She remembered it well. Something woodsy mixed with something all male. It ticked her heartbeat up a notch or two.

She leaned her head back against the seat and closed her eyes. She'd gotten no sleep last night. She might as well sleep now. It wasn't like they were going to get much rest until the situation was contained. "Sleep while you can" was what her boss at the CIA had always said to her. He'd been right.

Tory opened her eyes and blinked. Right. The helicopter. She glanced out the window. They were setting down in Maine. That had gone by in the blink of an eye. She drew in a deep breath. Then let it out again. Next up was the flight to Virginia. She would work during that one.

When the pilot gave them the signal, she took off her headset. She tried to undo her five-point harness, but it just wouldn't let go. Finn reached over and got it unstuck for her. When the back of his hand brushed against her right breast, she felt the light touch to the tips of her toes.

She mumbled her thanks and then shot to her feet, but she stumbled, not fully comprehending her foot was asleep not to mention she wasn't moving for the first time in what felt like years. Was it possible to have land sickness?

Finn reached out and caught her. Holding her arm, he captured her gaze. "Are you okay?"

"Um, yeah."

His blue eyes looked stormy, as if he was wrestling with some emotion. Well, he wasn't the only one. Heat bloomed in her nether regions, and her breast tingled where his hand had brushed her. She'd damn near kissed him when he'd been pressed against her during the rogue wave. She really wanted to. Badly. *Violent,* she reminded herself. He could be violent.

She cleared her throat. "Sorry. Pins and needles. My foot." *Great.* Now she couldn't even speak in complete sentences. She straightened and limped from the chopper. Her foot was killing her, but she was determined not to give in to the unexpected weakness. Not in front of Team RECON. Head held high, she grabbed her roller bag and her shoulder bag and hurried across the tarmac to the waiting jet.

"We're going on that?" Axel asked.

Tory nodded. "Yes, DHS sent the jet for us to use."

"Is it fully stocked? I'm starving." Axel rubbed his belly.

"You're always hungry," Finn replied with a snort.

Axel smacked his good arm. "And you're not?"

Finn grinned. "I didn't say that."

Tory walked up the stairs and boarded the jet. The guys all boarded behind her. The jet was all decked out in shades of cream to brown. The brown leather seats were super comfy, and Tory was looking forward to the flight even though she knew she would have to work the whole way. It was just nice to be off the damn ship. Dry land had never looked so good. She'd survived it without puking her guts up. Score one for her.

Tory took a seat at the back. The table in front of it and the electrical outlet on the wall meant she could set up her laptop and notepad, which she did quick-time. The great thing about traveling private was no one was going to tell her to put her electronics away. There was also no one to make any food or drinks. She hadn't wanted to be the bearer of bad news, so she hadn't mentioned it, but the guys were just going to have to wait to eat.

Within minutes, they were airborne, and she was already on her satellite phone, filling Steve in on their next steps. "I do have the boots and socks bagged that the Chief Petty Officer had been wearing when he took the pictures. It's a long shot, but if you can have someone meet the plane, they can take them for DNA testing immediately."

Steve sighed. "We need some luck on this one."

"You're telling me." She toyed with her pen. "We are a couple of months behind on this. I can't even bring myself to think about what's out there."

"I know. We've got people going over it now."

"Wait. What do you mean?"

"I mean, we have people, lots of them, going over every email that has been sent, every text, every bit of data we can scrape together to figure out what these people might have. There's a lot of innocuous stuff, and some other stuff that will be embarrassing when it gets out, but there's also some serious information that could alter our relationships with other nations if it gets released."

Tory ran a hand over her forehead. "What are we doing about that?"

"There's not much we can do. We're trying to get ahead of some of it, and the rest we'll just have to pray doesn't see the light of day."

She grimaced. "How likely do you think that is?"

Steve's chair squeaked, and she knew he'd just leaned back. "I think, Tory, that you need to do all you can to figure out who is behind all this because if we don't stop some secrets from getting out, our goose is cooked."

She closed her eyes and swore.

"Yeah, you said it. Anyway, I have to go tell the higher-ups what's going on. Your office space is all set up and ready to go as requested. It's well-equipped."

"Any chance you can have pizza delivered? It's well past lunchtime, and these guys are hungry. The ship ran into a rogue wave before we lifted off so the kitchen was out of commission when we left."

"Pizza, huh? I'll see what I can do." Steve hung up.

Tory put the phone down on the table and leaned her head back on the seat. Her mind was racing. She needed a thread. One tiny thread. That's all it ever took. When she'd been with the CIA, all her cases started with a thread. The more she pulled, the more it unraveled until there was nothing left of the terrorist network or whatever else she'd been working on.

So what was the thread in this case? Would it be the DNA? She hoped so, but there had to be something else. The pictures maybe. But with the bloated faces and the bad lighting, it was unlikely facial recognition software would work.

She had to find that one thread.

An hour later, her eyes jerked open as the plane hit the runway. She blinked. They'd landed. She must have dozed off. She glanced around the airplane, but the guys were all half asleep as well. She packed away her stuff and got ready to deplane just as her satellite phone rang.

"Stanhope," she answered.

"Victory. How are you? I hear you just set down outside of Richmond in Virginia."

Tory swore silently. "Jeff. What is it you want?"

"Come now, Victory. That's no way to greet your father."

"I'm busy. What do you want?" How the fuck had he

known they literally just touched down at a private airstrip west of Richmond, Virginia? The man's resources were extraordinary.

"I heard all about what you're busy doing. You make sure you do a good job. You need to uphold the family name."

"Is that it?" Tory's patience was stretched thin. This man, who the world thought of as debonaire and urbane, was a sadistic abuser. He was also a U.S. Senator.

"I want you to keep me in the loop just like your boss."

"No."

"Victory, I am a sitting U.S. Senator. I need access to the most current information to do my job properly."

"No, I will not share anything with you. If you want to know something, call my boss." She clicked off the call and looked up. Her gaze locked with Finn's. Heat rose in her cheeks. She was horrified that she'd been overheard. She hated her father. Speaking to him always made her ill. But no matter how hard she tried to cut him out of her life, like a fucking bad penny, he kept popping back up.

She let out a breath and looked away. What she really wanted to do was scream and then throw herself into Finn's arms and spend the next forty-eight hours screwing his brains out so she didn't have to think. But that was destructive behavior, and she wasn't going to do that anymore.

As she gathered herself and then her things, she felt the weight of Finn's stare. He knew she was upset. Somehow, he knew. It wasn't like they'd spent a ton of time together, but they had a connection. At this moment, she fervently wished they didn't. She wanted to suffer her humiliation alone. She finally looked up and said, "Alright, boys, it's time to go."

They all filed out of the plane. A young guy, a civilian, stood on the tarmac. "Ms. Stanhope?"

"Yes?" she asked, trying to figure out what was going on.

The guys spread out around her and immediately went on alert.

"Um, I'm Craig Winslow. I, uh… I was told to pick up some boots from you?" He looked at her and then the guys. He shifted his weight from foot to foot. He couldn't have been more than twenty-five. There was a distinct glint of nerves in his big brown eyes, which looked even larger due to his glasses.

The tech. She'd forgotten all about him. Damn her father. "Yes, of course." She pulled the bag with the boots and socks out of her luggage. "Please process them as quickly as possible." She signed the bag and handed it to him.

"Um, yeah. I'll let them know." He took the bag. "Um, thanks." He turned and walked over to an old red Toyota. The door squeaked as he got in, and a minute later, he drove away.

Tory sighed and moved over to the three waiting SUVs. The guys closed in around her. Nick pointed at Finn and said, "You okay to drive?"

He tipped up his chin.

"Okay, you take Tory with you in the first SUV. Axe, you're with me in the second. Cain and Elias, you two are in the third." He turned to Tory. "I assume you know where we're going so why don't you text it to Finn and he'll send it to the rest of us? We all have enough clothing to last the next few days. We can pick some up once we're settled. We'll figure out phones and methods of staying in touch once we're at the office."

Nonplussed, Tory stared at Nick. *She* was supposed to be in charge. *She* was the one to decide things. Except that her father's call had left her all discombobulated.

Nick started walking toward the SUV and then glanced over at her and stopped. "Sorry. Habit. Did you want to do something different?"

She clenched her teeth so hard her jaw hurt. It wasn't him she was mad at. It was her father, or more accurately, herself, for letting him get under her skin. She would look like an idiot if she changed the assignments now. She made a conscious effort to relax her jaw. "No, that's fine." She grabbed the handle of her bag and headed to the first SUV. She handed her bag to the airport valet who put it in the back for her, and then she walked around and got into the passenger seat.

Finn climbed into the driver's seat and spent the next few moments getting the seat and mirrors set up the way he wanted. Finally, he turned and stared at her.

"What?"

"I need the address." He gestured to the screen on the dash.

"Shit," she mumbled to herself and dug out her phone. She tried to will the heat out of her cheeks, but it wasn't working. "I have your cell so there's no point in texting it to you.

"I have a burner."

"Already?" She was impressed.

"We always travel with a few extras."

Tory nodded. "What's the number?"

Finn rattled off his digits and then waited for her text to show up. He immediately forwarded it to the rest of the guys. Then he plugged the address into the SUV's GPS. It said the ride would take thirty-nine minutes.

Good. Thirty-nine minutes of silence where she could get her shit together after her father's call and be on her game when they arrived at the office space. Thirty-nine minutes of torture because she was in the SUV with Finn Walsh. Was it torture because he had a temper and that scared her, or was it because she wanted him? Badly. Very badly. Deciding that didn't bear close inspection, she leaned her head back on the seat and closed her eyes.

Finn pulled out of the airport and made for the highway. "So, do you want to talk about it?"

Her eyes flew open. "Talk about what?" She willed the color out of her cheeks. Did he know she was still attracted to him?

"That phone call."

Her stomach relaxed just a little. He was trying to be helpful, but she didn't need his assistance. "No," she said through clenched teeth.

Finn sent her a quick glance and then went back to studying the road ahead of him. "It might help to talk about it."

She closed her eyes and took a deep breath. A scream had climbed its way into her throat, and she was afraid if she opened her mouth, it would escape. Her father always set her off. She was seriously discombobulated. She wanted to pull the trigger and drop him. She was two parts terrified of him and ten parts enraged by him. No, that wasn't true. She was angry with herself for still being even the slightest bit scared of him.

She let out the breath she'd been holding. "No, it won't help. Nothing can help when dealing with that man."

Finn turned on the windshield wipers as a light mist began to fall. "Are you sure?"

"Yes!" she snapped and then immediately felt bad. Finn had no idea of the inner battle she was having. It was her problem, not his. He had done nothing wrong. "I appreciate the offer but I would rather talk about something else." She glanced down and realized that she was clutching the door handle so hard her knuckles were white.

"So, what's your favorite kind of pizza?" Finn asked.

"What?" She blinked. The switch was out of left field.

"Pizza. On these types of ops, we usually eat quite a bit of pizza. I was just wondering if you have a favorite."

She rubbed her face with both hands for a second. "I appreciate what you're trying to do, Finn, but it's unnecessary."

Finn glanced at her again, this time with a frown marring his forehead. "Er, you don't want to eat your favorite kind of pizza?"

She blinked and then gave him a long look. Was he being serious about the pizza? She couldn't actually tell. "Hawaiian."

"No." Finn shook his head.

"I'm sorry. What do you mean no?"

"Fruit does not belong on a pizza. It's just fundamentally wrong." Finn shook his head again.

Tory cocked one eyebrow. "I hate to break it to you, but ninety-nine percent of the time, pizza is made with fruit on top."

"Are you crazy? No. Just no. No one puts fruit on their pizza. No one. Fruit does not belong on pizza." Finn was adamant.

"Tomatoes are fruit."

"What?" Finn turned to stare at her for a second.

"Tomatoes," she said again, "are fruit. Botanically speaking, anything you eat with seeds inside is actually fruit. So, peppers, eggplants, and tomatoes are all fruits. Those things are often on pizza, so fruit on pizza is the standard."

Finn's brow was all puckered. "Okay, now you're just making shit up."

He looked so shocked Tory burst out laughing. "I'm really not."

"But I don't understand. How can they all be fruit? Wait. Does that mean a strawberry is not a fruit?"

"Strawberries are aggregate or accessory fruit, meaning

the flesh of the strawberry actually comes from the flower. The seeds are the tiny things on the outside."

"I…just…wow. Fruits. Who knew it was so complicated?"

Tory started laughing again. It felt good to laugh.

Finn grinned. "Pineapple, fruit or vegetable, I don't care, does not belong on pizza. End of story. If you want fruit on your pizza besides tomatoes, add some eggplant 'cause we're not getting pizza with pineapple on it."

"We'll see," was all she said, but she was smiling as she glanced out the window at the passing greenery. The tension had eased from her jaw. Her stomach had settled, and her nerves weren't so jangling. Finn had done that. He'd made her relax and helped her settle down. She glanced over at him. He knew just how upset she was, and he'd done his best to help her out.

A warm feeling spread in her chest. Maybe he wasn't so bad. Maybe almost killing his old boss was a mistake or had an explanation at the very least. Shit, now she was making excuses for him.

She sighed to herself. She wanted to date him. Like *in the marrow of her bones wanted to date him.* She would really like that. But maybe she'd like it too much.

CHAPTER THIRTEEN

Forty minutes later, they pulled up in front of a one-story bland office building in the middle of an industrial park. It was built like a strip mall with what looked like three distinct office spaces. Each entry door was glass, but it was impossible to see the inside from their angle. There were big windows in the front of each space, but it looked like the blinds were down in all three.

Finn stared at the ugly building. "What is it with DHS and their crappy office spaces?"

Tory raised her eyebrows and smiled. "Why do I sense there's a story behind that question?"

Finn snorted. "They put us in an office building in Miami. Us! Makes no fuckin' sense. We need a warehouse space. We need gun safes and places to store explosives. We need a gym to stay in shape and a place to practice hand-to-hand combat. We do office work, but not like you do. It's ridiculous to have us in this kind of setup, not to mention the fact that the people we often deal with are violent. We worry that one day someone might come after us and end up hurting or killing some poor office worker."

She tipped her head and lifted her brows, a smirk flirting with her lips.

He suddenly realized she had been kidding, and here he was ranting on. "I'm sorry. It's just that it's a worry," he finished lamely.

The smile had slid off her face. "No, don't apologize." She reached out and touched his arm. "I get it. You're right. It doesn't make sense. And your worry is legitimate. When this is over, I will bring it up with the appropriate people."

He smiled at her. "Thanks." It was nice to sit and talk to her. It made him feel…connected. He hadn't felt that in a long time other than with his teammates. They were a connection, but he needed more. Tory was like a soft breeze knocking out the cobwebs. He'd like to spend more time just hanging out with her. He'd like to do other things with her, too. A smack on the SUV's window beside his head had him jumping and reaching for his gun, which wasn't there.

Elias stood grinning at him. "You coming?" he asked through the glass.

Finn flipped him off and then turned to Tory, but she was already getting out of the SUV. So much for their quiet moment. He sighed and got out as well. He grabbed his bag and Tory's luggage from the back of the SUV and followed the group to the boring brick building.

"Finn was just telling me that you guys are in an office building in Miami." Tory unlocked the glass front door that was on the right side of the building. She pulled it open and then stepped inside. Reaching over to her left, she turned on all the light switches. The florescent overhead lights came on with a hum.

They all filed in and assessed their surroundings. The walls were a yellowy-beige with a medium gray threadbare carpet on the floor. The large space was pretty beat up. It had obviously been used quite a bit but had a stale smell to it.

A half dozen battered desks with chairs were all pushed together in the middle of the room to form a rectangle. On the desks were a bunch of laptops. Cords dangling from the ceiling connected to the computers. Someone from DHS had been busy.

On the right-side wall, there was a whiteboard with markers and an eraser. On the opposite side of the room, Finn noted a solid door that was closed. Bathroom was his guess, but it could be anything. There was another door at the back of the room. It, too, was closed. Kitchen maybe.

Axe went over and opened up the door on the left side of the room. "Bathroom," he said.

Elias opened the door at the back of the room and disappeared through it. Finn glanced at Tory, but her focus was on her phone, so he followed Elias through the rear door.

"Well, this is a surprise," Finn said. It was a second room that was larger than the first. There was a kitchen area along the right wall that included an island, which was currently stacked with pizzas and cartons of soda. In front of the island were four stools.

Off to the left side, there were four sets of bunk beds running along the wall. A rolled-up sleeping bag rested on each bed, along with a pillow. On the far wall, there was a bank of computers with large monitors hung on the wall above. These were all hardwired just like the ones out front. A sitting area complete with a leather couch and coffee table were located against the rear wall. It wasn't the Ritz, but they'd stayed in worse.

Finn rolled Tory's luggage over to the first set of bunk beds. He figured she would want a lower bunk. He went to the next set of bunks and put his bag on the lower bunk as well. He didn't want to have to climb up to the top bed with his shoulder still aching. He turned around just as the rest of the guys filed in.

"Pizza!" Axe grinned. He opened the top box and tore off a slice. "Still warm, too."

Nick shook his head. "Did you even look for plates?"

"Why bother? These pizzas won't be around long enough to need a plate." Axe took a big bite of his slice.

"Is that pepperoni?" Elias asked as he grabbed one for himself.

Tory finally came through the doorway. "Good, the pizza's here."

"You ordered it?" Finn asked as he leaned against a bunk bed.

She shook her head. "No, I told my boss and he took care of it." She went over and lifted the lid on the top pizza box. Then she moved it off the stack and set it on the counter. She opened the next one.

Finn grinned. "Your boss knows your horrific taste in pizza, huh?"

She glanced up at him as she shifted the next box over. "He better if he knows what's good for him." She lifted the lid on the last box and smiled. Pulling out a piece of pizza, she took a big bite.

"Is that pineapple?" Elias asked.

"Yeah," Finn confirmed. "Sacrilege."

Nick closed the pineapple pizza box and moved the other boxes back on top of it. He grabbed a slice of pepperoni for himself. Axe and Elias grabbed another slice as well.

"Finn, you better get in here while there's still pizza left, otherwise you'll be eating pineapple pizza." Tory winked at him.

"Yeah, no." He walked over and went around the island to the kitchen area. He opened the cabinets until he found some paper plates and took them down. He put the stack on the island but handed one to Tory.

She took it with a nod and plunked her slice on it. "You need to eat quickly," she said, pointing at Finn.

He frowned. "Why?"

"Because you have a doctor's appointment."

He cocked an eyebrow. "Come again?"

She reached for a can of soda. "You have to get your shoulder checked out. I made an appointment with one of our guys. I will send you the address."

He let out a long breath in an effort to keep his frustration to himself. "Look, my shoulder is fine. It's not necessary."

"I agree with Tory," Nick said. "Go. Get it checked."

Finn opened his mouth to protest, but the look on Nick's face stopped him. There was no point in arguing. Nick was his teammate, but also his boss. If Nick said "go," he had to go, but he didn't have to like it. He closed his mouth and grabbed a slice of pizza. He wolfed it down in a couple of bites and then did the same thing with a second slice. Then he guzzled a can of soda.

This mission was really starting to suck. If the doctor said he needed to do PT or some such, then they were going to send him home. He didn't want to be back in Miami by himself with nothing to do all day. Worse, if the doctor said it wasn't going to heal properly, then life as he knew it was over. He crushed the soda can. *Don't panic. Think positively.* That's what the therapist had told him. He needed to see that things could go his way and stop thinking the worst. Easy to say when you were sitting in a cushy office all day and didn't actually see the worst on a regular basis.

He turned to Tory. "So where am I going?"

"I already sent you the address. You need to change, though."

"What? Why?" What the fuck kind of doctor was she sending him to?

She took a swig from her soda and swallowed. "This goes for all of you. No uniforms, remember? We don't want to attract too much attention. People notice uniforms." She grimaced. "I should have had you change before this, but it's after five, so hopefully no one noticed us coming in. The rest of the offices in this building are empty so we should be fine. Just change out of your uniforms."

"There are probably a few other things we should review while we're discussing things." Nick pulled out a stool and sat down.

"Yes," Tory agreed. "There are some ground rules, but let's finish eating first and then we'll go over everything." She turned to him. "Finn, get a move on."

"Yes ma'am." He walked over to his bunk and pulled out some street clothes. He quickly reached over his head with his left hand, grabbed the back of his uniform shirt, and pulled it over his head. Then he snatched the medium blue T-shirt from the bunk and tugged it on. He winced as he put his hand through the sleeve. His shoulder really did hurt. Damn.

He toed off his boots, then unbuckled his pants and took them off. It didn't occur to him until that moment that Tory was in the room. He should have probably gone to the other room to change. Well, too late now. Besides, it wasn't like she hadn't seen him naked. If they were all going to live in this room together for a while, then she'd just have to get used to seeing the team change.

That thought stopped him short. Seeing him in his skivvies was fine, but he wasn't so keen on her seeing the rest of the team half naked. And what about her? Was she going to go to the bathroom to change? She probably would. Even though he wouldn't be able to see that beautiful body of hers, which he'd really like to see, no one else could either, and that made him happy.

He gripped the edge of the top bunk. He needed to calm the fuck down and focus. This was what happened when he got worked up about something. The thoughts came faster and faster until it was all a jumble, and if he was angry, he just saw red.

He did a couple of quick breathing exercises as he pulled a pair of faded jeans over his black boxer briefs and did them up. He pulled on his boots again and then straightened. He grabbed a light jacket out of his bag and the keys for the SUV from his uniform pants pocket. He was good to go, and his brain was back in gear. Sometimes he just needed to take a minute. *And that was okay*, he reminded himself.

He turned and started out of the room. "I'll catch you later. Call me if anything comes up."

"Will do," Nick and Tory said at the same time, and then they both laughed.

It was good to see her laugh. The sound kindled a warm feeling in his chest. Now, if she was only laughing with him instead of Nick.

As he climbed into the SUV and pulled away from the curb, he realized it rankled him a little that he had to leave. She was just starting to relax. She'd loosened up over the whole pizza conversation and had given her a chance to regroup.

Whoever was on that phone call, Finn would cheerfully have strangled them. As soon as she'd answered the phone, he had known something was wrong. He happened to be looking her way and saw her knuckles turn white where she gripped her cell phone. All the color had left her face, too. Her eyes had darted around like she was some sort of caged animal. It set off alarm bells for him in a major way. Reminded him of the panic on his mother's face when his father would come home drunk.

He pulled himself up abruptly. He wasn't going down that road.

He glanced at the GPS. The trip had only taken twenty minutes. The doctor was just up on the left. He felt a pang in the pit of his stomach. The pizza suddenly wasn't sitting well. He wasn't prepared for the doctor to tell him he'd done something serious to his shoulder. He couldn't deal with having to sit at home, doing nothing. There were only so many origami creatures he could fold. To compensate, he'd probably have to take up crochet or knitting, or some other shitty hobby.

He parked the vehicle and made his way into the doctor's office. He had no choice. He had to do this. He sighed as he opened the door. His future was riding on this appointment. It just had to go his way.

CHAPTER FOURTEEN

Thirty minutes later, everyone was finished eating. Nick and Elias were cleaning up the kitchen. "No, we've got it, Axe. No need for you to help," Elias said, sarcasm dripping off every word.

Axe lounged on the couch. "I thought you had it well in hand, but if you really need help, ask Cain."

Nick snorted a laugh.

"So—" Tory said just as her cell phone went off. "Sorry." She answered, "Stanhope."

"Tory," Steve said. "Have you logged in yet?"

"No. I was just getting to it." She crossed the room and flicked on the bank of computers one after the other. "They're booting up."

"Okay. Listen, I have a bit of bad news."

When Steve said he had bad news, it was never an exaggeration. "What is it?" She stood still in front of the computers and braced herself.

"The tech who collected the boots and socks from the airplane had some sort of car accident. He went off the highway and went down a steep embankment, rolling his car several times. He's dead."

"Oh, God!" she breathed. "That's awful. What about the boots or socks?"

"That's the thing. We can't find them. They must have been thrown from the car. We're still searching but, honestly, it happened in a wooded area and the chances of finding them are slim. We can call in dogs for the search but that would call more attention to it and I'm not sure it's worth the risk. You said the guy went swimming with them on."

"Fuck." She closed her eyes. One of her threads had just disappeared. "Well, let me know if they find anything." She bent over and logged into one of the computers. "Okay, I'm in."

"Check your email."

She pulled up the email and saw one from him. She opened it. "What's this?" It was a satellite picture of something in the ocean.

"We pulled some images off the satellite that was passing over that part of the North Atlantic last week. We *think* this is the *Oceanus Explorer*. We don't think the ship was stationary when these images were captured, but we've sent the Navy to check out the location anyway. Our people are studying them, but we want the Coast Guard team to look at the images and see if they see anything we've missed."

"Okay. I'll get them on it. I'll keep you in the loop if we come up with anything."

"Sounds good." Steve clicked off.

Tory turned to find the guys all standing behind her, staring at the images that were on the large screens above her head. "Anything stand out to you?"

Nick narrowed his eyes but said nothing. Axe just shook his head. Cain and Elias remained silent as well. She turned back and looked at the images. She didn't see anything that would help them either. She knew in her bones that they would need another lead for this to make sense.

Her phone went off again. "Stanhope."

"Tory, it's Daphne Colburn. I got a hit on one of your pictures. I'm sending you the information now. You can log in to the system if you want to see the match yourself."

"Yes!" Finally, they might catch a break. "Thanks, Daphne."

"No worries. You're buying next time we have a girl's night."

"Deal," she said and rang off. She opened the email, and a picture of a bloated face filled the screen. It was the man with the silver hair and the scar. Next to it was a picture of the same man looking younger and in military dress. "Miles Eckert," she read aloud. She scanned the rest of the document.

"Former Army Ranger. Sniper," Nick read. "He was hurt in Afghanistan when an IED exploded and took out the convoy he was in. He was discharged."

"That's not good," Axe said.

"What do you mean?" Tory asked.

"Normally, if you get hurt in battle, you get *honorably* discharged, and you might even get a medal. To just be 'discharged' means something happened." Axe's mouth was set in a firm line.

Tory looked to Nick, who nodded in confirmation. She read the screen again. "Do you know anyone you can call and ask about this, Nick? I can go through official channels, but it might take longer under the circumstances. The Army is notoriously closemouthed about personnel records."

Nick commented, "I can make a few calls."

"Thanks." She refocused on the screen.

"Look at the rest of the file," Nick commented. "The bit the CIA added."

Tory sighed. "Quite the laundry list of malfeasances, stealing weapons, gun running. He's worked for some of the worst people in the business. No wonder the CIA kept tabs on him. He was a gun for hire, and a good one by the looks of this report."

Cain moved over to stand next to Nick. "Who was his former employer?"

Nick grimaced. "Silverstone."

Cain nodded. "Puts it in perspective. Now we have a feel for the guy."

"But if he left Silverstone, who was he working for when he died?" Tory asked.

Axe asked her, "Tory, what do you know about Silverstone?"

"Only that they're a black ops group for hire, dressed up to look like private security contractors. They have friends in high places, but as far as I'm concerned, they're a bunch of thugs. I ran into their guys a few times in my CIA days. Always bad news. And I agree with Cain. Knowing he worked for Silverstone gives us an idea of just what kind of lowlife he was. Leaving Silverstone to work elsewhere means he just went further down the gun for hire black hole."

"Not big on redemption stories?" Axe asked. "Maybe he quit because he was disgusted with what Silverstone did as far as jobs were concerned."

"I believe in redemption, Axe," Tory said. "I just don't believe in fairy tales. Anyway, he has a daughter. She lives in Virginia about a half hour from here. She might know something."

Nick folded his arms across his chest. "I don't think it's a good idea to go by yourself. We don't know enough about this guy, or his daughter, to know if it's safe."

Tory frowned as she glanced at her watch. She wanted to be moving now. Taking one of the guys meant a delay as they had to get changed. *That* she didn't want to see. The image of Finn in his tight boxer briefs was already haunting her brain. She took a deep breath and willed the heat from her cheeks.

Tory stored the daughter's address in her phone and then started toward the door. "I'm okay on my own. You guys look at the satellite pictures and see if you can see anything interesting."

"Tory, you shouldn't go alone," Nick called out.

Tory waved her hand as she approached the door, only to have it open in front of her. Finn was back.

She stopped in front of him. "That was fast. What did the doctor say?"

"He said it's strained, but it will heal in the next couple of days. No permanent damage."

"Great." She started to walk around him, but Finn shifted so he was blocking her way. She looked up at him puzzled, but he was looking at someone over her shoulder. She turned and met Nick's gaze. "What?"

"It's too dangerous to go by yourself. We don't know what's going on. I wouldn't let any of my team members go alone at this point."

She was prepared to argue with him but then, at the last second, thought the better of it. If she was going to burn any positive credit she'd earned with the team, it better be for something more important than whether she went alone or not. "Fine. Finn, you're with me." She turned and walked out the door.

Tory glanced down and frowned. She was still in her cargos and T-shirt, but at least she'd thrown on a brown sweater. Not the best outfit to see the daughter in, but it would have to do. She always liked to be wearing a business suit when doing a formal interview. It lent weight to her presence. Cargo pants and a brown sweater were definitely less than ideal, but what she lacked in sartorial authority, she would have to make up in attitude.

Finn drove through the streets with skill. She was totally at ease with his driving. The daughter didn't live far but the little town was out by the national forests. Lots of deer roaming around. It was the one thing she was always wary of when she was out this way.

Tory tried to reason that bringing Finn had been the best plan because he was there and ready to go. She would have had to wait if she took one of the others with her. It was not at all because he looked just as good in his jeans as he did out of them. "I'm glad things worked out with the doctor."

"Me, too." The relief in his voice was pronounced. He'd been worried.

He must be in more pain than he was letting on. Good to know. It was probably true about all of Team RECON. They weren't going to say they were in pain unless they were on death's door. She sighed. That was not going to be helpful.

"We discovered that the white-haired man with the scar is named Miles Eckert. He was discharged from the Army without any distinction, which apparently is a bad thing. Nick is following up." She filled him in on the rest of Eckert's past, including working for Silverstone.

Finn made a right turn. "Nick was right. You shouldn't do this on your own. None of us should be on our own at any time during this operation. Silverstone is a scary bunch. Even if Eckert doesn't work for them anymore, you know…'cause he's dead, it's an indicator of what he was into."

Tory did her best to not sound peevish. She wasn't a moron. She got it. "I understand what you're saying. I brought you. We'll make sure to be on our toes, but we don't know enough to make any assumptions at this point." Maybe Axe had been right, and it was a redemption story.

Nah. She just couldn't buy it.

Fifteen minutes later, they got out of the SUV in front of a little white house with, literally, a white picket fence. It was adorable. Someone had obviously gone to a lot of trouble to turn this little house into a home. Colorful flowers planted in the garden scented the evening air. Tory had always wanted a garden but knew nothing about flowers. Her mother wasn't into gardening. Her mother hadn't been into anything, and then she just up and died.

There was a green minivan in the driveway pulled off on the far right. A child's blue tricycle was parked behind it. A black helmet with red rubber spikes down the middle was resting on the bike seat. There was also a skipping rope and a pink backpack on the grass next to the house.

They went up the driveway and down the walk to the front door where a *Welcome* mat was on the front step. She rang the bell. The door opened, and a woman of about thirty stood there. Her shoulder-length brown hair was tucked behind her ears, and she had a fork in her right hand.

"Mrs. Ginger Hollister?"

"Yes," the woman said, her brow pinched as if confused.

"I'm Tory Stanhope with Homeland Security." She flashed her credentials. "Do you mind if we come in and speak with you for a minute?"

"Homeland Security? Why would you want— If this is about my father, I have nothing to say to you." Her mouth compressed into a straight line, and she started to fold her arms across her chest until she almost stabbed herself with the fork. She frowned at it like she had no memory of picking it up.

"Mrs. Hollister, we really need to speak to you. It would be better for you if we did it inside. I'm sure you don't want your neighbors to hear everything we have to say."

Mrs. Hollister looked around her street before she opened the door wider and stepped back to let them in.

"Thank you," Tory said as she stepped inside. Finn followed her in. The door opened directly into a small living area, which was filled with toys. There was a dining area on the left at the back of the house. It had patio doors that led to what looked like a back deck. The kitchen was next to the dining area, but it was closed off so Tory couldn't see much.

"Have a seat," Mrs. Hollister said and sat down on one end of the brown microfiber sofa. There was a brown wooden coffee table in front of it. The floor was carpeted, but the dark gold carpet was threadbare in spots.

Tory perched on the other end of the sofa. Finn leaned against the wall by the door. "Is anyone else in the house?" he asked in a quiet voice. Mrs. Hollister's eyes went wide for a second, and the knuckles on the hand holding the fork turned white.

Finn raised a placating hand. "I only ask because I don't want your children to be left unattended." Finn kept his voice low and soothing. "Did you need to get them?"

She shook her head. "No. They're fine at the moment. They're downstairs playing video games. And my husband is on his way home from work."

Finn nodded.

Tory leaned forward. "Mrs. Hollister, what can you tell me about your father?"

"My father?" With a sigh, the fight seemed to drain out of her. "He was a good man at one point."

Tory found the woman's sadness palpable. She steeled herself against the flood of emotion that emanated off the other woman.

Mrs. Hollister offered a sad smile. "He loved me and my brother. We used to play catch and go to the park. He taught us to ride bikes and fish. He was a typical father. Then my brother was killed by a drunk driver, and something changed in him. Dad went to Afghanistan and came back a different man. He was cold and calculating. He was impatient and no longer wanted to have anything to do with me. He and my mom divorced not long after that, and I haven't seen him since."

Tory tried not to grind her teeth. This wasn't helping. She needed a thread. "Did you hear anything about him? Did he have siblings?"

"He was an only child." She paused. "My mother said that he got into some trouble with the military. Something to do with stealing weapons. I do know he got hurt in some kind of explosion. My mom said he had a big scar across his neck."

Tory frowned. "Is your mother around? Maybe we could speak to her."

Mrs. Hollister shook her head. "My mom passed away two years ago."

"I am so sorry for your loss." That was a blow. She regrouped. "Do you remember anything else about your father?"

The woman looked slightly guilty, as if she was hiding something.

"Mrs. Hollister, I'm sorry to tell you that your father was found dead yesterday." She let her words sink in and saw the shock and dismay register on the other woman's face. So, Ginger Hollister still loved her father no matter what she said. She reached out and gave the woman's hand a squeeze. "I am truly sorry for your loss."

Mrs. Hollister quickly brushed a tear off her cheek. "You know, he was so mean to Mom and me, and he didn't help us at all when I was still growing up. I should hate him, but…"

"He's still family." Tory knew that tug of war. She hated her father, but there was that tiny bit of her that still wanted his love and respect no matter how crazy or stupid that need was. "Mrs. Hollister, is there anything you can tell us about him more recently? Do you know who he was working for or what his job was? Where he lived?"

She shook her head and bit her lip. "We weren't in touch. He didn't want to be. He called me when Mom died, and I told him about his grandkids, but he said it was better if we stayed away from him." There was that guilty look again.

"But?" Tory prodded.

"I don't know where he lives or who he works—worked —for. I can't help you with that."

"But you do know something." It was a statement. Tory knew the woman was holding back.

Mrs. Hollister nodded slowly. "Yes." It was barely a whisper. She swallowed and shot a quick look at Finn. Then she met Tory's gaze. "He started sending me money."

"Money?"

"Once a month, he transferred money into my account."

An electric zing went through Tory's belly. *This was it.* The thread. The thing that would get the ball rolling. "How did that come about?"

Mrs. Hollister swallowed. "He called me about a month after Mom died and asked for my account number. I told him 'no' at first, but he said it was the least he could do. He said he wasn't good to be around, but he wanted his grandchildren and me to know that, well, he wasn't all bad. So, I gave him the information, and money appeared in my account."

"How much, if I can ask?"

"Seven thousand. Every month like clockwork." She bit her lip again. "He…he didn't steal it, did he?" she asked. The fear in her eyes made Tory's heart constrict just a bit.

"Not that we know of. The money is yours to keep." The words came out of Tory's mouth before she could stop them.

She wasn't sure that was true, but she'd do her damnedest to make it happen.

Mrs. Hollister's shoulder sagged in relief. "Oh, thank goodness. With me not working, the money makes a huge difference. We're saving up for a bigger house and for the kids' college fund." Then she frowned. "I supposed the money will stop now."

"I have no idea what will happen with the money," Tory answered honestly. "But can I see one of your bank statements?"

The frown deepened. "Why?"

"I want to see where the money came from. It might help us to track down your father's address."

She dutifully rose and disappeared down the hallway and came back a minute later with a bank statement in one hand and a card in the other. She sat back down. "Here's the statement, and here, this is the card he sent for my son Brian's birthday. I thought you might want to see it. I don't know why."

Tory gave the woman a kind smile and took the card. She opened it up and read the note of birthday wishes for a grandson. She blinked. ME. Miles Eckert. On the note, It had been Eckert's initials. He wrote the note. The handwriting was the same. Then she stretched out the card to Finn. He stepped over and took it, reading the inside. He looked up at her when he was finished, gave her a small nod, and handed the card back.

"The card is lovely." She looked at the bank statement and then took a quick picture of it. She stood up. "Mrs. Hollister, thank you so much for your time and, again, I am so sorry for your loss."

Mrs. Hollister stood as well. "What did he do?" she asked. "My father? You're searching for some information about him. What did he do? How did he die? Was he in trouble again?"

Tory offered her another smile. "Your father was killed by some very bad people, but he did a good thing before he died. I'm sorry, but I can't share details." She paused. "I think maybe he was a better man than he gave himself credit for." She smiled again and then went out the front door.

She and Finn got into the SUV and pulled away from the curb a minute later.

"That was a nice thing you did for her," Finn said. "Making her believe her father was a good guy."

"Maybe he was. Axe said it could be a redemption story, but I shot him down. Maybe I was wrong."

Finn gave her a look.

"Okay, maybe 'good' is a bit relative. But he had to be the one who left the note in the towel dispenser. His initials were on it so let's just say he wasn't all bad. Now we just have to figure out what the hell this all means."

Finn didn't respond. She glanced over at him, but he was looking in his rearview mirror. "Is there a problem?" she asked. She glanced at her own side mirror. The dark-colored SUV behind them made a right.

"No, I guess not." Finn gave her a quick smile.

"I like the way you tried to put Mrs. Hollister at ease while finding out who was in the house."

He gave a nod. "I didn't want her to panic, but I also didn't want to be surprised by another adult."

"Why didn't you search the house if you were worried?"

"That would have just upset her more. I figured her husband wasn't home yet. She pulls all the way to the right in their driveway so he can put his car on the left. If he didn't have a car, she would have parked in the middle. No one knew we were coming, so the chances of someone there waiting for us were slim."

"Which is why I could have gone on my own." Tory sighed to herself. She really did need to take charge and stop letting Nick run the team. On the other hand, so far it had worked out and maybe she was earning a little more acceptance.

"I said slim, not none. There is always the chance that someone knows you're coming. We could have walked into all kinds of trouble. Better to have backup than go it alone."

She could argue the point, going alone drew less attention, but it wasn't worth it. Currently, she was enjoying Finn's company under the guise of business, and she didn't want to do anything to jeopardize that for now. Her mind went back to the interview. "What do you think changed his mind?"

"Who? Eckert?" He shrugged. "He might have been ill, or maybe it was the birth of his grandkids."

"You think grandkids can change a man like Eckert?"

"I have no idea. I didn't see the file. I only know what you said about him on the drive. Broke a lot of laws and was a gun for hire. He could have wanted to reconnect with his daughter and her family, or at least be a better person."

Tory snorted. "Maybe. He worked for Silverstone up until eight months ago."

Finn turned to stare at her for a second. "You seem to be going back and forth on this guy. You want to believe it's a redemption thing, but in the end, you just can't bring yourself to it. Here's a tip, it doesn't really matter. What matters is he left us that message. Now we just have to figure out what it means."

Tory glanced out the window. Finn was right. It didn't matter what Eckert's motivation was, just that he was leaving clues. The handwriting was a dead giveaway. He was the note writer.

It was dark by the time they'd gotten off the highway. The road they were driving on was heavily wooded. She leaned back in her seat. Even though she'd napped a couple of times that day, she was still tired. It was relaxing being in the truck with Finn. His presence seemed to be a balm for her nerves. There was so much to do, but at this moment, she couldn't really do any of it, so she just had to sit back and take it easy. Not something she did all that often.

A huge jolt from behind and the accompanying loud crash had her upright in a fraction of a second. "What the hell?" Her heart hammered against her rib cage.

"We're being hit from behind," Finn said as he fought with the steering wheel. "Take my cell and call Nick. Tell him where we are and what's going on!"

"Who's doing it? Can you see anything?" She glanced in the side mirror. The shadow of an SUV was there, gaining on them. Its headlights were off so she couldn't see enough in the darkness to tell make and model. Probably the point. That, and so they could sneak up on them.

She fumbled with the phone before hitting the button to call Nick. They were smashed from behind again. She shot forward and was pulled back by her seatbelt. She'd be lucky if she didn't have whiplash. Hell, she'd be lucky if they survived.

"Taggert," Nick's voice filled the SUV.

"Nick," Finn yelled, "we're being hit from behind." There was a crash as the SUV ran into them again. "Fuck!" Finn fought to keep the SUV from sliding.

"Where are you?" he said to Finn and then yelled, "Gear up. Finn and Tory are in trouble!"

Tory started to relay their general location, but Finn cut in, "Track my cell for location. These guys are pushing us toward somewhere. The hits aren't enough to send us off the road, but I missed the turnoff to get back to you guys. I'm guessing there'll be a sniper up ahead, otherwise they would have put us off the road by now."

"Roger that. Tracking you now. On the way." The call dropped.

Tory braced for the next impact. "The kid!"

"What? What kid?" Finn fought to keep the SUV steady.

"The tech who came to pick up the boots at the airport. He went off the road and died. They couldn't find the boots. Said they must have been thrown from the vehicle. It was these assholes. They killed the tech." Tory's stomach rolled. She closed her eyes and saw the kid's face. He'd been so young. Her eyes popped open. "Fucking animals."

"Change in plans." Finn glanced at Tory. "You have your seat belt on?"

"Yes, but what plans?" She stared at him as she put an arm on the dash to brace for the next hit.

"I'm gonna take us off-road before we get to their sniper, who is probably just beyond that curve."

"What? Why?" she yelled. Her stomach did another flip and sweat trickled down her back. She looked out the window. To her right was a rock face with trees on top, and to the left was a steep embankment with trees at the bottom. There was nowhere to go.

"Because we don't have a chance against a sniper, and we have better cover in the trees. Hang on!" Finn went left and purposefully drove off the road. They went down the embankment half sideways, Tory thought for sure they were going to roll, but the SUV stayed upright until it hit the bottom and then it barreled toward the trees. A huge Douglas fir filled the windscreen before everything went black.

CHAPTER FIFTEEN

"Tory," Finn said her name in a hushed voice. "Tory," he said again. He leaned over and eased her back from the airbag. She was out cold. Damn. He immediately turned off the engine and the headlights. He glanced in the mirrors, but he couldn't see the top of the embankment. It wouldn't take long for whoever the hell these guys were to get down here. He and Tory needed to be gone when that happened.

"Tory," he called softly again and squeezed her shoulder.

She groaned. She was waking up. *Thank God.* He'd been worried. He still was. He reached over and touched her face. "Tory, honey, we have to move." He undid his seatbelt and then undid hers. "I'm going to get out and then come around and get you, okay?" No response. "Tory, honey, you have to wake up now."

He opened his door as quietly as possible and slid out of the truck. Then he closed it with a soft click. Something dripped into his eye. He wiped at it with his hand. It came away wet. Blood. He must have banged his head on something.

As he moved around the front of the SUV and the tree

that was now a hood ornament, the darkness was suddenly lit up by high-powered flashlights. He crouched down behind the tree.

The flashlight beams danced all over the SUV, and the low hum of conversation reached him. He couldn't make out their words, but there were three of them up there looking for a way down. The flashlights went over to his right. They must have spotted an easier route than the one he'd taken with the truck. It was almost a sheer drop. He'd been fucking lucky as hell the SUV hadn't rolled the whole way.

Moving swiftly, he opened the passenger door as soundlessly as possible. The three men were making noise coming down the embankment so he doubted they heard him. He reached in and grabbed Tory's shoulder, giving her a gentle shake. "Tory, wake up." She moaned again. He needed her awake *now*. They had to move. He leaned in and kissed her hard on the mouth. It was that or smack her, and he wasn't interested in hitting a woman no matter what the circumstances.

Her eyes flew open and she gasped. "What?"

He pressed his hand to her lips to quiet her. "Shh. The men who are after us are coming down the embankment. Do you think you can walk?"

Slightly bewildered, she looked around, but nodded. She shifted and slid out of the truck. Her knees buckled, but he caught her and held her against his chest. "Are you sure you're okay to walk?" he whispered into her ear. He couldn't see her well enough in the darkness to know for sure, but she didn't seem hurt.

"Yeah, fine. I'm…I'm good now. Let's go," she whispered back.

He released her but reached into the foot well to grab his phone and then pocketed it. He took her hand. "Keep low."

He moved toward the front of the SUV again. "We're going deeper into the trees."

She nodded and pulled a gun out of her pants' side pocket. That made one of them with a gun. He hadn't taken his to his doctor's appointment and he hadn't grabbed it before he left. *Fucking rookie mistake.*

They stayed low and moved deeper into the woods. He was conscious of the fact they were leaving a trail, but he didn't think they had much of a choice. It was hard going in the dark. The moonlight only penetrated the tree canopy in spots. Maybe the guys tracking them would have a hard time finding their trail in the dark. He prayed that wasn't wishful thinking. "Tory, turn on your cell phone flashlight."

She did as he asked and it gave them some light to work with. It seemed overly bright to him but they needed to be able to see. They also needed a game plan. Nick and the team would be here soon, but maybe not soon enough.

There was a yell. The men had reached the truck. Finn watched the beams of light bounce around the inside of the SUV. He turned back toward the woods Ahead of them was a tree that had half fallen over. It was large and lay at a forty-five-degree angle.

He turned to Tory. "Can you climb a tree?"

She blinked. "Yeah. It's been a while, but yeah."

He nodded, took the phone and grabbed her non-gun hand. He led the way to the tree. It was almost like they could walk up it because of the angle. He went first and seconds later she joined him. They walked up the trunk, navigating their way around the branches. He stopped her when they were about halfway up.

"See where that other tree branch intersects this one?" When she nodded, he said, "Good. We're gonna switch trees. You go first. You walk from this tree to the branch of that one and then start climbing straight up."

"Are you sure it will hold me? It looks a little flimsy."

"It will hold you," he whispered in her ear. She nodded once and went to the branch. She put one foot on it and then reached up and grabbed the overhead branches to haul herself up. He gave her a few seconds to get moving and then he turned off the cell phone flashlight, waited for his eyes to adjust and followed suit.

The flashlights were getting closer. These guys were smart enough to keep their sounds to a minimum so Finn and Tory had to be quiet as well. They climbed higher as the men came closer. There was more moonlight up here. Finn touched Tory's foot. When she looked down at him, he gave her the signal to stop. She nodded once.

He moved over so he was no longer directly under her and then climbed up so they were at the same height. He leaned over and spoke into her ear, "Are you okay to stay up here?"

She nodded once, but then her knees gave out. Finn grabbed her around the waist and brought her against him. It was his bad arm, but it couldn't be helped. He had to hold on to the tree with his good one.

"I'm okay," she whispered. He nodded but didn't let her go. She might have a concussion, and he didn't want her falling out of the tree. Chances were good she'd break her neck on the way down.

The sound of the men moving through the forest below reached them. They were getting closer. Tory froze. Finn held her crushed against his chest.

Tory wrapped her left arm around Finn's neck and lifted her right to aim her gun. She had it trained on the three men or at least where their flashlight beams were. It was hard to make out anything more than shapes in the darkness.

"If the flashlights shine upward, do not hesitate," he whispered in her ear. She nodded once and kept the gun steady. Finn wasn't thrilled that she was going to have to do the shooting. Not that he thought she couldn't shoot, but he was worried her vision might be blurry since she'd passed out. He almost said something but stopped himself. It wasn't like they could switch now anyway. The men were almost directly below them.

Tory leaned into him a bit more, but her gun hand was rock-steady. Finn was conscious of Tory holding her breath. "Breathe," he whispered, his lips touching her ear lobe. He felt her chest rise against his. He was aware of her closeness: the smell of her hair, the sound of the air leaving her lungs, the feel of her breasts pushed against his chest. He had the insane urge to kiss her. Stupid, he knew, but that's what happened whenever he was in dangerous situations. A holdover from his childhood. His brain would distract him with random things so he wouldn't be so terrified of his father's wrath.

"We don't have much time." The voice reached Finn. It was the guy behind the first two who spoke. He was holding a phone and checking something on the screen. "They'll be here in less than ten."

"Shit," the first guy said. He waved his flashlight around. Finn couldn't see any details of any of the men. The darkness was too thick. The first guy was the tallest of the group, if he had to guess, or at least he held his flashlight up higher.

"This isn't working," said the second man. "We're not going to find them in less than ten minutes. He was smarter than I anticipated. He drove off the road on purpose. He must have figured out Paul would be waiting for them. That's on me. Let's go."

The taller guy said, "We could go back and set up to take out the rest of them. That would eliminate the majority of the problem."

The second man, who Finn figured for the leader, said,

"That would only eliminate part of the problem and draw a lot more attention to the situation. No. We leave. This was a serious fuckup. The boss is not going to be happy."

The third guy checked his screen again. "Seven minutes."

"Let's go." The leader turned and started walking.

The tall man swore. "How can this asshole be that hard to kill? He's in the fucking Coast Guard!"

"Everybody gets lucky once in a while," the man with the phone said before urging them to go faster. The three men disappeared back through the trees. A few minutes later, Finn heard several vehicles start and drive away.

"Are you alright?" he whispered.

Tory nodded. "That was…terrifying."

"Yeah. It sucked."

She started to laugh. "You do have a way with words, Finn." She put the gun back in her side pocket and looked up at him. "So, any ideas on what we do now?"

He looked down at her. Just then, the moon came out from behind the clouds. In the ambient light, he saw a flicker in her eyes. Desire. He was sure of it. Yeah, he had a lot of ideas on what they should do now, and not one of them was business related. He lowered his head and captured her lips in a swift kiss. When she opened her mouth, he deepened the kiss. Her other arm snaked around his neck, and she shifted her weight so her entire body was solidly pressed against him.

He desperately wanted to cup her ass so he could bring her closer, but he also didn't want them to fall out of the tree. But then she shifted again and rubbed against his hard-on. He let out a soft groan, and she responded by sinking her hands into his hair.

A few seconds later, he broke off the kiss. "We are gonna fall out of this tree if you don't stop. I've only got one arm holding both of us."

"Oh, my god!" she breathed. "Is it your bad arm?"

"No, but we need to get down." Suddenly, he started to laugh and so did she. The stress of the situation had been intense and laughing was such a release. They laughed like fools for a full minute before they heard vehicles pulling to a stop on the road.

Tory turned toward the sound. "I guess we should make our way down now. That will be the cavalry."

Finn smiled. "Yeah, and not a moment too soon." He pulled out the cell phone and turned on the flashlight again.

Tory moved over to another branch and then started lowering herself down the tree. "See you at the bottom."

Finn took a moment to relax his sore arm. He had used it to hold her in place, and although the strain wasn't great, it hurt like a son of a bitch. The doctor had said there wouldn't be permanent damage *if* he took things easy and didn't overdo it. Finn had neglected to mention that part to the others. He couldn't cope with being benched. Not now. Not when he'd found his Lady X again. Not when someone was selling government secrets.

He took a breath and started down the tree. Nick called to him when he was almost at the bottom. "You guys okay?"

Finn jumped down from the last branch. "Yeah. A few bumps and bruises, but okay. Tory needs her head examined." He glanced over at her, and the two of them laughed again.

"In more ways than one," she said as the laughter died out.

Finn grinned. "What I meant was, she was knocked unconscious during the crash. She should at least have some EMTs look at her."

Nick nodded. He and the guys were at the base of the tree, fully decked out in tactical gear, assault weapons at the ready. Finn rolled his shoulder. "You guys can stand down.

They're gone." The guys relaxed and turned on more lights so they could see.

"Axe, call 911," Nick directed. "Let's get an ambulance out here to look at both of you."

Tory held up her hands. "I don't need an ambulance. I'm fine."

"It's faster this way. If you won't see them, then you're going to have to go to emergency, and that's likely to take all night. Your choice."

"Fine, call the ambulance," Tory said, her voice filled with resignation. "That means the cops are going to come as well. There's going to be an official report. I'm not sure we want all that."

"Yeah, we do," Finn said. "We gotta talk. Let's get to the top of the embankment, and I'll tell you what's going on.

Ten minutes later, Tory was seated in the back of an ambulance and the EMT was checking her over. The EMT had already checked Finn over and put a small bandage over the cut on his forehead. He'd been given the all-clear. He was leaning on the back of a police cruiser with the guys all around him.

"You want to tell me why we're over here and not in one of the SUVs?" Nick asked as he leaned next to Finn.

"When we were up the tree, we overheard the guys that were trying to kill us talking. One of them had what looked like a phone in his hand that he kept checking. There wasn't any light so it could have been some other sort of electronic device, don't know for sure, but the important thing is he kept announcing how far away you all were."

"Wait, are you saying we were being tracked?" Nick asked.

Finn nodded.

Axe frowned. "How would they track us? The SUVs?"

"Yeah. And I don't want to say anything by them because they could be bugged as well." Finn shrugged. "Anything is possible."

"They knew where we were to put trackers on the SUVs," Elias pointed out. "That means there's a leak. No one is supposed to have our location."

"I think it's worse than that." Finn crossed his arms over his chest. "I think the vehicles were delivered to us with the trackers already in place."

"Son of a bitch," Axe bellowed.

"Yeah," Nick agreed. "Someone knew we were coming. The whole setup could be compromised."

Cain shifted his weapon across his chest. "You wanted this circus out here," he said, pointing to the cop car, "because you're afraid DHS will let us be killed and it will all be swept under the rug."

Finn nodded. "Yes. That's exactly what I'm afraid of." His gut had been in knots since the reality of what he'd heard hit home. "Someone on the inside is trying to get rid of us."

Cain nodded once. "It makes the most sense. They tracked you, so they know where you were and who you were talking to."

Axe nudged Nick. "Do you think we should warn Eckert's daughter? Do you think they'll go after her?"

"I already did," Tory said as she approached the group. She wedged herself in between Elias and Cain.

"How's the head?" Finn asked, letting his eyes roam over her whole body, looking for damage now that they were in an area with enough light.

"Fine. Little sore. Slight concussion, but I'll live." She gave him a quick smile. "I called Mrs. Hollister and advised that she grab her kids and her husband and get out of town for a little while. She's going to stay with her in-laws down in South Carolina. Not ideal, but better than staying put."

Nick turned to Tory. "Can you shed any light on the situation?"

She shook her head and winced. "I have no fucking clue. I assume you all have come to the same conclusion I have. Someone inside the government is working for the other side and they want us to stop poking around." Her eyes glinted with anger.

Finn nodded. "Do you have any thoughts as to who?"

Tory sighed. "No, but now isn't the time to discuss it. The cops here are going to leave soon. We need a plan. By the way, I do think you calling them was a good idea. Call attention to the incident so it can't be swept under the carpet. The only thing is… now the world knows where we are, or at least they will once the reports get filed. We need to get to a new location quick-time."

Nick nodded. "She's right. We have to figure out a game plan. I think we can start by taking the SUVs back to the office and leave them there. I think we leave our stuff, too. It's bound to be tagged at this point. We need to start fresh somewhere else."

"Agreed," Tory said. "The thing is, we can't use any DHS safe houses, including those the Coast Guard has. We have to go off-grid. I'm open to suggestions."

Cain spoke up. "I think we can arrange something." He glanced over at Nick. "Captain's?"

Nick nodded. "Yeah, probably the best bet."

Cain lifted his chin in agreement. "But I do think we have to take the guns and other equipment with us. We can leave the computers, but we need the explosives and ammo."

Nick nodded. "We take the weapons, but that's it."

"First, we need vehicles," Nick counted off on his fingers.

"On it," Axe said as he pulled his phone out and moved out of the circle.

"Second, we need supplies, laptops, that sort of thing."

Elias tapped Nick's arm. "Got that covered."

"Third, we need places to stay tonight. We'll regroup at the new location tomorrow. Can you have it set up by then, Cain?"

Cain nodded. "It's all ready to go. I'll text everyone the address, but first, we all need new burner phones."

"I have some to hand out," Nick said. "Back to places to stay. I say we do *the usual*. Finn, you take Tory with you. We'll meet again at Captain's."

Tory had remained silent until now. "Can you explain 'the usual' to those of us who are new?"

Nick turned to her. "Sorry, Tory, I should have consulted you on this. Just habit."

"No worries. You all are doing what I would have suggested, so it's fine. Just not sure of 'the usual.'"

Finn rested his butt on the cop cruiser and crossed one leg over the other in front of him. "We separate into groups and don't communicate. We don't share locations. If we get into trouble, we can reach out, but we only meet up at a specified time and place. If there's trouble at that location, we have a signal."

"Sounds good to me."

Nick nodded once. "Okay then. Let's head back to the office." He undid his leg holster and handed it to Finn. "You're gonna need this."

Axe rejoined the circle. "All set. Someone will meet us not far from the office and drop us at a new location. There will be vehicles there waiting."

Tory squinted at Axe. "Should I ask?"

Axe grinned at her. "Probably better if you don't."

"Elias, you good?"

He gave a thumbs-up even though he was still on the phone. "Okay then," Nick said. "Let's go." They headed over and piled into the two SUVs. Elias waited until he was off his call and then got in. Finn was in with Nick and Elias. Tory had gone with Cain and Axe. He didn't like not being in the same vehicle with her.

Twenty minutes later, they were back at the office and then spent the next hour throwing out random theories for whoever might be listening. Finally, they declared it time to sleep and proceeded to quietly exit the building through a window in the back. They all helped Nick and Cain get the equipment and loaded it into a minivan that Axe's contact had left in a parking lot three buildings over. Nick handed out burner phones, and then he and Cain left.

Axe turned to Finn. "Change in plan. You take these keys. Your car is two parking lots over to the left."

Finn looked down at the keys. "A Tesla? Seriously?"

Axe grinned. "Beggars can't be choosers."

Finn shook his head. He turned to Tory. "Ready?" She looked a bit surprised. "Er, sorry. I just assumed you were coming with me."

"Sure. Not a problem." She gave him a nod. "But I'm driving. I don't trust you to keep it on the road."

Axe laughed softly. "I like her. She's fun."

Finn shot him a dark look, but Axe ignored him. "Be safe," Axe told them.

"You, too." Finn headed for the other parking lot with Tory two steps behind. They reached the Tesla, and Tory slipped into the driver's seat. Finn sat in the passenger seat, trying to appear relaxed, but he was on edge. "Where are we going if you don't mind me asking?"

"We're heading into D.C."

"Er, why?" Finn frowned. Being in the middle of the city where people wanted them dead did not seem like the best plan to him.

"Because I have a place we can stay there. I made a call earlier, and before you lecture me that we can't go someplace attached to my name, I will tell you no one knows I use this place and it's not in my name." She shot him a glance. "I did work for the CIA. I'm not a total newbie at this shit."

Finn put his hands up. "I didn't say a thing."

"But you were thinking it."

She had him there, but he wasn't going to admit it.

An hour later, they pulled into an alley.

"Is this a hotel?" Finn asked her.

"Yes. It's one of the best in D.C., and a friend owns it. He's letting us stay in one of his best suites. It has a private entrance. The hotel has top-notch security. We should be fine for one night."

"Okaaay, I guess. A wee bit unorthodox, but let's give it a shot."

She snorted. "Thanks for your trust."

Fuck. That wasn't what he meant at all. "I just—that is—I'm not used to—"

"Save it. I'm too tired to sit here and listen to you try and pry open your mouth to remove your foot." She got out of the car and went up the steps to a loading dock. Finn followed her. They crossed the open area and stopped in front of a small door. Tory pulled it open to reveal a stairwell. She started up.

"How many floors?" Finn asked.

"What? Are you going to complain about that, too?" Her voice had a bite in it.

"Ouch. No, I was just wondering." He was going to end up paying for his big mouth all night. He grimaced. At least he was going to sleep in a real bed. That was a definite bonus.

Tory put a hand up to her head and grimaced. It had to be pounding by now. He jogged up beside her. "You okay?" he asked and pointed to her head.

"Fine," she said through clenched teeth.

He let out a long breath but remained silent for the rest of the climb. It was only eight floors, but after the day they'd had, he was done for. Tory stopped on a landing in front of a door and keyed in a code. The door made a quiet click and then slid open. Tory entered, and Finn followed.

To the right was a kitchenette area. They walked through it and a dining area to the main living space. The whole wall was windows offering an incredible view of the mall. The room was decked out in soft grays and creams. The carpet was thick so his shoes didn't make a sound.

A glass coffee table in front of a light gray sofa held a platter of cheese and crackers as well as fruit and a small chocolate cake. His stomach growled.

The TV that was across from the sofa was massive, and state-of-the-art by the looks of things. He'd noticed a smaller one in the dining area as well. The winding staircase on the right side of the room must lead to the bedrooms. "This place is amazing."

"The bedrooms are upstairs," Tory said as she went over and grabbed a chocolate-covered strawberry from the tray of snacks.

"You stay here a lot?"

"No. A couple of times, but not recently. The room just underwent renovations."

Finn walked over and popped a piece of cheese with a cracker in his mouth. Delicious. He swallowed. "What hotel did you say this was?"

Tory nibbled on a piece of cheese. "The Jasmine Door."

"Who owns it? Who's your friend?" Finn's gut tightened at the thought of Tory staying here with some other man. He clamped his jaw together.

"Jameson Drake. His girlfriend used to be at DHS with me. We've stayed in touch."

The level of relief that flowed through Finn at the mention of a girlfriend was enough to make his knees weak. He sat down on the sofa and popped another cheese and cracker into his mouth to stop himself from saying something about who she had stayed here with. It was none of his business, and he needed to remember that.

CHAPTER SIXTEEN

Tory ate another strawberry. She was hungrier than she thought and not just for food. Finn looked tired and beat up but, damn, if he didn't look sexy as hell, too. Those blue eyes of his always made her feel so seen, which was the sexiest thing ever.

She sighed. The massive headache she had required pain medication and hours of sleep, but she also just needed… Finn. She wanted him like she wanted water to drink, but right now she needed him more like she needed air to breathe. It was crazy, but his presence was just so calming somehow, like nothing could hurt her if he was there, which obviously wasn't true since they'd driven over a cliff earlier, but still, he made her feel safe and that was something that hadn't happened in a very long time.

"I'm going to go to bed. I told Drake we were in a tough spot at the moment so he said he would supply toiletries and the like. He also said he would have clothing sent up in the morning."

"That's…great." Finn blinked but said no more.

She cursed silently. She'd gotten her arse in the air earlier over his comment and had been a bit bitchy, not that he didn't deserve it, but now he was choosing his words carefully and she didn't like that. "Look, Finn… I…" She hesitated. This was the thing she still struggled with. Speaking her mind at work or to friends was no big deal, but telling a man that she liked exactly what she wanted or what she thought had always been a struggle. It was a holdover from her father's abusive ways.

Finn stood. "I should apologize for my comment earlier. I know you know what the fuck you're doing. I shouldn't be second-guessing you. You're a professional in the field. You don't need me mansplaining anything to you. So please ignore my comment. It won't happen again."

Tory frowned. "No."

Finn blinked. "Er, no? You won't accept my apology?"

"No, no. No, I don't want you to watch what you say. You have every right to ask questions about where we're going and if it's a good idea. I would do the same to you, no question. If we start watching what we're saying, then maybe we'll miss something. Maybe something falls through the cracks because we're afraid the other will think they are being criticized. Does that make sense?"

He nodded. "I get what you're saying, and I agree. I just meant that I could have said it better. I'm tired, and my brain isn't working so well. My arm is killing me, truth be told." He smiled at her sheepishly. "I think we both just need some sleep."

She nodded. "I think you're right." But that was a lie.

Disappointment rolled through her. She wanted to spend time with him. Sleep beside him. Screw his brains out, really, but there was no way her headache was going to let that happen. She just wanted to be with him. She knew she wouldn't sleep if he wasn't in the room. It wasn't that she was scared. It was more she needed to know backup was close by.

That she could relax or at least get some rest without being in a panic that someone might hurt her while she slept. This insane urge was a holdover from Afghanistan. She never felt she could sleep over there because anything could happen at any moment. Sleeping next to Finn meant there was someone to keep an eye out for her. It was stupid, but there it was.

Finn walked to the stairs and started heading up. "Do you have a preference of bedroom?"

"I want the one you're going to be in." The words came out before she could stop them.

He froze on the stairs. Then he turned and looked at her. She met his gaze defiantly. "I know what I said before about keeping it professional, and I meant it. Then. Now I just really want to sleep in the same room as you. Neither one of us is up for anything more, but I know I won't sleep if you're not nearby."

There, she'd said it aloud.

Finn continued staring at her, his blue eyes peering through to her soul. He cleared his throat. "Do you want the right side or the left side of the bed?"

She smiled as relief washed through her. "It doesn't matter."

He nodded and continued up the stairs. She popped another strawberry in her mouth and grinned. That hadn't been so hard, and he hadn't freaked out so maybe they were making some sort of progress. She swallowed the berry and then went up the stairs.

The main bedroom was off to the right and the second bedroom was off the landing to the left. She turned right and walked through the sitting room area. The hallway leading into the bedroom was actually the closet. She moved into the bedroom. The bathroom door on the left was open. She frowned. Did he go to the smaller bedroom?

Then it dawned on her. He was letting her get organized and in bed before he came back to the room. Solved the whole getting undressed issue. She took a moment to appreciate Finn all over again as she walked into the bathroom.

Ten minutes later, she walked into the bedroom and got undressed. She pulled her gun out of her pocket and put it under the pillow on the left side of the king-sized bed. She left her T-shirt on but took off her bra and cargo pants. Then she crawled under the cream-colored duvet and put her head gently down on the pillow.

The bed felt like heaven after the day she'd had. Now, if the ibuprofen she'd taken in the bathroom would just kick in, she would be good to sleep. But her mind wouldn't stop racing. So many unanswered questions. This whole situation was so fucked up. Who would want to sell America's secrets? Really, who *wouldn't* was an easier question to answer. It was all so convoluted, the politics of the world. Nothing was ever black and white, always shades of gray.

Her eyes flicked open, and she looked around the room. It was decorated in earth tones. Soothing colors that were easy to look at. The bed was huge and the mattress divine. Everything a traveler could want. If only her brain would calm down.

The sound of someone walking down the hallway reached her ears. Her heart gave a mighty thump. Logically, she knew it was Finn, but she moved her hand underneath the pillow and gripped her gun.

Finn came around the corner and stopped dead. He raised his hands. "Are you okay?"

She nodded and immediately felt like an idiot. "I'm sorry. Just being stupid, I guess."

"Being smart. You didn't know who it was for sure. I assume your gun is under there, which is a good thing. We're not on vacation. This is work, and our work is dangerous. You never have to apologize for being prepared."

She gave him a quick smile and closed her eyes. She didn't want him to see the tears that were threatening to fall. A kind word from him, and suddenly she was a mess. What the hell was wrong with her? Maybe the hit on the head had done more damage than she thought.

She opened her eyes slightly with the hope of watching Finn undress, but he was too smart for her. He turned out the light and then came over to the bed. She heard rustling and then he climbed into bed beside her. "Just so you know, my gun is under my pillow as well," he said.

She smiled into the darkness. "Thanks for sharing."

"No problem." The smile in his voice relaxed the lingering tension in her shoulders. Now, if only her brain would stop buzzing.

Ten minutes later, she was fast asleep.

Finn opened one eye slowly. *Hotel room. Tory.* He immediately turned to look, but she was gone. He put a hand on her side of the bed. It was still warm. He heard a sound and realized she was in the bathroom. He relaxed.

She'd fallen asleep almost immediately last night. It had taken him longer. He was worried. The fact that the SUVs had been tagged before they arrived in D.C. made a huge difference. There was no way it had been done in the office parking lot. There were cameras all over the place. That meant that someone knew they were coming. Someone knew what they were planning. Someone had advance warning about their playbook.

The bathroom door opened, and all thoughts of work flew out of Finn's mind.

Tory stood in the doorway with her long blond hair falling over her shoulders. Her gray T-shirt was stretched tight across her breasts, showcasing her nipples. The T-shirt only fell to her hips so he could see she was wearing black lace underwear. It would be a thong if he remembered correctly, and there were some things he just didn't forget.

He cleared his throat. "How's the head?"

She smiled. "Much better." When she stretched her arms above her head, he couldn't help but stare at her chest. She climbed back into bed. "We have lots of time before we have to be…wherever we're going, so we can lounge for a bit."

He made an affirmative noise in the back of his throat. Watching her had stirred up all kinds of feelings, and body parts, too. He was trying to decide if it was better to get up and get dressed to hide it or lie in bed longer and hope for some kind of miracle. He was trying to abide by her wishes. Keeping this work only, or some semblance of it, but she was making it damn hard in oh-so many ways.

He had started to move when she turned on her side and placed her hand on his stomach. "How's your shoulder?"

"Fine," he mumbled. "I should get up." He went to remove the covers, but she put pressure on his stomach, keeping him there.

"You should not get up." Her voice was low and sexy.

He turned to meet her gaze. Her gray eyes were full of mischief and desire. "Tory," he growled.

"Finn," she said in a teasing voice as she ran her hand over his chest.

"You said you wanted this to be strictly business. You feeling me up like this is not business."

"No, you're right. It's not. A woman is allowed to change her mind though, isn't she?" Tory moved closer and skimmed her hand lower so it touched the waistband of his underwear.

"Tory," Finn growled again. "I'm not in the mood to be teased. You said you didn't want this."

She shook her head. "No, I never said I didn't want you. I said work had to come first. And it does but, currently, we're stuck in a hotel room together with a bit of time on our hands."

Finn was already hard as a rock, but he waited to give her every out possible. She needed to tell him she wanted this. Mixing personal shit and work together the way they seemed to be heading might be a colossal mistake. Her hand went lower until she cupped him through his underwear.

He clenched his jaw. "Tory, are you sure?"

She looked up at him, and their gazes locked. "Yes." She moved so she was lying next to him and then she leaned over and brushed one soft kiss across his lips, then another. He knew he should stop her. He knew with every fiber of his being that this was going to blow up in his face, but he wanted her like he'd never wanted anything else in his life.

He wrapped his arms around her and brought her against him as he swooped in and captured her lips in a scorching kiss. She tasted of toothpaste. This was planned. That thought made his heart sing. She'd planned on seducing him. He plunged his tongue into her mouth, rolling and dancing with hers.

His skin seemed to come alive under her touch. He could feel her everywhere, and he wanted more. She ran her hands over his chest as he kissed the hollow of her neck. He lifted her on top of him, and she groaned as he cupped her ass.

He rocked her across his erection until the fire that was building was almost too much. She kissed him hard and shifted so her legs were over his hips. He rolled her onto her back, and she wrapped her legs around him.

She moaned as he moved against her. With one hand he pushed her thong down over her hips. Dropping her feet to the bed, she wriggled out of the scrap of lace and tossed it onto the floor. Then she pulled her T-shirt over her head. He lowered himself back down on top of her and kissed the hollow of her throat. She moaned again and arched her hips up to his.

Groaning, he dropped his mouth to her nipple and tugged the taut peak with his teeth. He stopped and looked at the bruise across her shoulder from the seatbelt. "Does it hurt?" he asked as he dropped soft kisses along the edge of the bruise.

"Not when you do that."

He went back to teasing her nipple. "Tory, you are so damn beautiful," he whispered. He swirled his tongue around one nipple while he ran his thumb back and forth over the other. This was even better than he remembered. They'd been so frantic before, in a rush. Now, he was taking his time, enjoying every touch, every taste.

When Tory pushed her breasts forward, he took her nipple deeper into his mouth. She pulled his head away to reclaim his lips, her tongue rolling with his in a deep kiss. He broke off the kiss and went back to her breasts. He lowered his head and tugged on her nipple with his teeth.

"Finn," she whispered as she reached for his underwear. He groaned when her fingers ran the length of him. He kissed her again, burying his hands deep in her hair. She ran her hand up and down his shaft. He couldn't stand it. If she kept touching him, he was going to lose it.

Growling, he grabbed her hand and held it above her head. She wrapped her legs around his hips and moved against him.

"Fuck, Tory, if you keep doing that, it's going to be over before we've even started," he panted. "You are so fucking hot, you're killing me." He loved the feel of her underneath him. She arched her hips up and locked her ankles behind his back, rubbing her too-hot center against the length of his cock.

He groaned as he rolled away and pulled off his underwear. As soon as he settled back on top of her, she rubbed against him again. "Finn," she breathed, "I want you inside me."

Being with Tory was exhilarating and excruciating all at the same time. He gripped her ass and tugged her closer. She angled her hips so he could slide inside of her, but he pulled back.

"What's wrong?"

"Not yet. I want to taste you." Their gazes locked, and her eyes turned stormy. She bit her lip before she kissed him hard. She wanted him, and that made him feel invincible. He shifted his weight until his head was between her thighs. He blew on her hot center, and her hips jerked in response. He captured her with his mouth. While he swirled his tongue around her clit, and moaned. And he teased her sensitive flesh until she was panting.

He put one finger inside her and moved slowly. Her hips strained upward to his mouth, telling him it wasn't enough.

"More," she demanded, fisting the sheets.

He alternated between licking and sucking while thrusting his fingers deep inside her. She yelled his name as her thighs tightened and her body clamped around his fingers. She threw her head back as her orgasm exploded through her. She was so beautiful and wild it made his breath catch. If she only knew the effect she had on him, it was crazy. She only had to ask, and it was hers, whatever she wanted.

Tory caught her breath while he lay back down next to her. Her gaze locked with his. "My turn," she sat up. She rolled him over and climbed until she straddled his waist.

The sensation of her body on his was intense, like his skin was on fire.

She kissed his neck and worked her way down his chest. He groaned when she played with his nipples. "Turnabout is fair play," she said and then captured one nipple in her teeth and gave it a tug. He had to clamp his jaws together to keep from yelling out.

Tory worked her way down his chest and across his stomach, dropping little butterfly kisses on his skin. She bit his hips and drew her tongue across his skin until her mouth was level with his cock. Her tongue touched the tip, then slowly, she drew more and more of him into her mouth, sucking and twisting her tongue around his shaft as she went.

His growl deepened and rumbled out of his chest. His voice was rough when he said, "You're killing me."

His hips started to move. He couldn't help it. He grabbed her and pulled her back up. "I want to come inside you."

"I like the sound of that." She smiled, and he captured her mouth with another scorching kiss. She moved until her core was hovering above his hard cock. Seconds later, she lowered herself down slowly on top of him. Just a little bit, and then she lifted again. She teased him, taking him into her a little bit at a time until he couldn't take it anymore and grabbed her hips.

"Stop! You're driving me insane."

Tory grinned. "Like I said, turnabout is fair play."

"I'll give you fair play." He whirled her around so she was on her back and then lowered himself on top of her. He kissed her hard, his tongue demanding and hers answering in kind. She wrapped her legs around his waist, and he buried himself inside her.

She tilted her pelvis and started moving. He thrust into her again and again, building the torment for both of them. "Finn, God, deeper, harder. You feel so damn good." She angled her hips to allow him to go deeper. She was so damn sexy he couldn't stand it. She felt like heaven, and he plunged as deep as he could inside of her.

Her breath was coming in small gasps. She moaned his name and urged him on, her hips rushing to meet his rhythm, her fingernails raking across his chest as he pounded into her. Nothing had ever felt this good, this right. He buried himself inside of her again and again. She bit her lip, and he lost it. He thrust deep inside her and growled her name as he came. She let out a moan and gripped his shoulders as her own orgasm hit.

He rolled off her and wrapped both arms around her while they caught their breath. "Tory, you are going to kill me if we keep this up. God, you're amazing."

"I'm not the only one." When she smiled at him, his heart gave a small flutter. She stretched her arms above her head. "I don't know about you, but I'm starving. I think I'll grab a shower and then work on breakfast. She kissed him again and rolled out of bed. As he watched her go, he knew he was in trouble. This wasn't just sex. This was so much more, and he was powerless to stop it.

CHAPTER SEVENTEEN

Tory let the hot spray run down over her shoulders. She was sorer than she'd anticipated from yesterday's excursions, or maybe it was the activities from this morning. Finn was amazing. She found herself grinning. Sex with him was so freakin' unbelievable. She hummed to herself as she glanced down at the bruise that was forming from her shoulder down across her chest. The seatbelt had saved her life but left behind some ugly reminders.

She grabbed the shampoo bottle. Back to reality. As much as she'd enjoyed her moment with Finn this morning, life had to go on, and work was her top priority. Maybe they could steal away for a weekend when all this was over. He lived in Miami and she lived in D.C. Not really conducive to a relationship. Besides, work and fun should not cross. Disappointment lodged in her chest, but she shook it off. Finn was awesome, but work was work.

She'd crossed the business and personal before in her life, and it had never ended well. Hargate flitted through her head. Admittedly, that was a little different. They didn't actually work together but they were in the same field.

Josh Hargate was just a big ol' mistake by any measure. There was no denying it. She could offer herself a million excuses, but she knew the truth. She'd been out of control after Walli died, and he'd sensed it. They'd dated for about three months before she realized that he was a conniving, underhanded slimeball who was using her to get to her father.

He had some new venture with a partner he wanted funding for, and he thought her father would be a great fit. Or that's what he'd said. She hadn't bitten, but he managed to speak to her father one day when he was at her apartment and her phone rang while she was in the shower. He'd charmed her father into a lunch meeting.

When she found out, she'd lost it. Totally flipped out. Now, she realized it was because Josh's actions felt controlling, and stirred up hard, raw feelings about her dad. Back then, she just knew she was out of control, so she found Doctor Fleming and got help. Dumped Josh immediately.

The bitterness of that experience was definitely still with her. Unfortunately, she'd agreed to marry Josh six weeks into their relationship, when he'd asked her on the spur of the moment. She shuddered at the thought. What a nightmare that would have turned into.

Not that Finn would do that but it was just better to find someone totally different from her line of work. She frowned. She didn't like the hollow feeling that bloomed in her chest when she thought about dating other men.

Giving herself a mental shake, she rinsed her hair and picked up the soap. It smelled divine, citrusy with a hint of some spice. When she imagined using the soap on Finn, warmth spread between her thighs. Not helpful. She was supposed to stay away from Finn. She snickered, a little late for that. But, she reminded herself, he had violent tendencies. He'd damn near killed his commanding officer. She smoothed the bar of soap thoughtfully over her shoulders. The longer she was around Finn, the more she thought there had to be more to the story. Regardless, now was not the time for a relationship. Especially with someone who was technically a subordinate. Still, maybe a booty call now and then wouldn't be so bad, would it?

Her cell rang, and she quickly rinsed off the soap and then turned off the spray. She grabbed the phone off the sink. "Yes?"

"Tory," Stephen said, "I have some details about the banking info you sent over."

"Go on," she instructed as she wrapped herself in a towel.

"We traced the money that Eckert sent to his daughter back to a Swiss bank account."

Tory frowned. "That's…odd."

"I agree. You would think a man like Eckert would know we could trace it. We made a deal with the Swiss quite a while ago now. He had to be aware."

She closed the lid of the toilet and sat down. "Maybe he wanted us to know. He did write the note. If all this didn't sit well with him, then maybe he was leaving breadcrumbs for us to follow. He probably couldn't outright say anything without being killed, but he could do small things so that if someone was looking, they could find clues."

Steve agreed. "That does make some sense. Hopefully, he left some more crumbs because we need to catch a break on this one."

"So where did the money originate? Who did Eckert work for?"

"Greyscale Industries."

Tory's lungs froze, cutting off her breath. She shivered violently, as if her body were suddenly encased in ice. *Josh Hargate owned Greyscale*, or at least he was a partner in it. This just couldn't be happening.

"Tory, are you still there?" She tried to make a sound, but only a small squeak came out. "Tory!" Steve said more sharply.

"Y-yes." She finally managed to get her lungs working again. "I'm h-here."

"Are you okay? You sound weird."

She swallowed. She was so far from okay she was on the other side of the planet. "Um, you know how these burner phones are. I'm fine."

"So Greyscale is the company. I've got people digging around as we speak."

"Stop!" Tory's heart thudded wildly against her ribs. "Don't assign anyone… No one should do anything with this information."

"I don't understand. Why not?" Steve's voice was full of confusion.

Tory took a deep breath. "Because someone told Greyscale where to find us yesterday. They knew where we were going to be. Someone on the inside had to share that information. If you tell people at DHS to look into Greyscale, then they'll know we're on to them."

Steve swore. "You think there's a mole at DHS?"

"I told you that last night after the accident," Tory said in an accusing tone.

"Yeah, but I thought you meant like one of the tech guys who set up the site or one of the guys that dropped off the vehicles. You think it's someone much closer to home."

He had no idea just how close.

She bit her lip. "I think it makes more sense if they have a mole who has access to a lot of information. Low-level techs don't know shit, really."

Steve was silent for a moment. "You're right. I wasn't thinking. I told two people here. I will go round them up and put the fear of God into them. They'll stop working on this, but how are we going to figure this out if we can't use our resources?"

Her mind was already leaping all over the place. "We'll have to use different resources. Leave it with me. I'll use the Coast Guard guys to help. We'll figure it out."

"Okay, but stay in touch. I know you're off radar, but don't disappear completely without telling me. I…don't want to start a full-blown panic over here if I can't reach you only to find out you're fine just lying low."

"Agreed. I have to go. I'll be in touch." She clicked off the call and sat staring blankly at the wall in front of her. It just couldn't be happening. There was just no way it could be real. Tory jumped at a knock on the door.

"Brunch is here, and it's gonna get cold." Finn's voice was muffled by the closed door.

"I'll be down in a minute," Tory called back. She stood slowly and placed her phone on the vanity. She turned and looked at her reflection. Her gray eyes had turned the color of steel. Her skin looked chalky white. Shock. That's what she was seeing in her reflection.

She closed her eyes and gripped the sink with both hands. *Get it together.* She took one deep breath and then another. There was no way around it; this was a shit show. She needed to tell the team what was going on. She also needed to find a way to distance herself from the mess, but she'd have to worry about that part later. It was more important to stop Greyscale at this point.

Shit. Finn. She really needed to keep him at arm's length. She was going to be tainted by this, no question, but she didn't want him to go down with her. Hargate was bad enough, but this, this was career suicide. She'd be lucky if DHS didn't get the CIA to throw her in a black hole and forget she ever existed.

Tory finished drying herself off and then toweled the

excess moisture out of her hair. She combed her long hair out with the brush that had been supplied by the hotel and secured it in a bun. She pulled on her bathrobe and went down the hall to the bedroom.

She reached for the underwear and clothing Drake had sent up. A navy lace underwear set with a pair of faded jeans and a light gray-blue sweater that made her eyes look the same color.

She quickly went downstairs and found Finn fully showered and dressed and putting out breakfast. He heard her come in and glanced up. "You said you were hungry so I over-ordered. I thought it might be a while before we get good food again. Might as well take advantage while we can."

Tory stared at the table. It was a wonder it didn't collapse under the weight of the food. There were pancakes, scrambled eggs, bacon, smoked salmon, bagels, and a whole dish of pastries. Not to mention a huge pot of coffee with two mugs. She felt ill just looking at it. She wasn't sure she could eat, but she knew she had to make an effort.

She gave Finn a quick smile and then grabbed one of the coffee mugs and filled it. Her hand shook a bit, and she could only hope Finn hadn't noticed. She walked around the table and took a seat on the back side facing out. She needed some space. Being close to Finn was sling-shotting her between wanting to reach out to him for comfort and being horrified that he was going to find out the truth.

"You okay?" he asked, his wet hair falling over his forehead. His blue eyes, bluer from the sweater he wore, looked concerned.

"Yeah, I, um…I'm fine." She tried to smile but just couldn't pull it off so she picked up a plate and put some food on it.

Finn sat down at the head of the table and watched her. "What's going on? You're not fine."

She glanced at him and then glanced away. "I… It's fine. I just need to eat something."

He studied her and had opened his mouth to say something when her cell rang. She reached down and immediately answered it. *Saved by the bell.* Just a reprieve actually, not saved. "Stanhope," she said into the phone. There were only a couple of people who had the number so she was puzzled.

"Ms. Stanhope, this is Mr. Yazley, head of security for the hotel. Mr. Drake asked me to inform you should there be any…difficulties."

She immediately captured Finn's gaze. "Ye, Mr. Yazley." She mouthed to Finn. *Head of Security.* "Our staff has noted that there are some men watching the hotel. This in itself is not unheard of, but Mr. Drake did request that we inform you if such a thing occurred."

"Men are watching the hotel," she informed Finn. Her heartbeat ticked up. She asked Yazley, "Would you by chance be able to send me a picture or video clip of these men?"

Finn nodded at her. He picked up his cell and got up from the table.

"Of course." Tory provided the email address and thanked Yazley. "Please let me know if there is any change. If the men move or if they leave."

"Of course, Ms. Stanhope. Rest assured, they will not be allowed to enter the hotel."

"Thank you, Mr. Yazley." She hung up and immediately looked at her email. Finn came over and stood beside her. The icy fingers gripping her heart eased slightly. Hargate wasn't one of the men. It didn't mean he wasn't involved. She knew he was, but at least he wasn't sitting outside watching for her. Not that he would. That was beneath him.

"I don't recognize these men but that doesn't mean much. Let me send them to Steve and see if he can come up with names to go with the faces." Tory forwarded the email immediately.

Finn nodded. "I called Nick. He says to sit tight here until we know more."

"Yazley says they won't let the men into the building but honestly how does he know one of them isn't already inside as a customer? Maybe they even booked a room."

"It's true. He can't know for sure. I think we're safe enough in the suite but we need to be prepared anyway." He checked his weapon and tucked it back in the waistband of his jeans.

Tory didn't bother doing the same. She knew her gun was ready to go. She refilled her coffee mug and took a sip of the hot, strong brew. Food was out of the question now but coffee was always welcome

He reached out and grabbed her hand. "Tory, what's going on?"

"Nothing." She tried to move her hand away, but he held it in place.

"Tory." His voice held a warning and yet warmth all at the same time.

It made her want to throw herself into his arms and pour out her biggest secret and her biggest fear. She clamped her lips together and waited for the urge to pass.

Finally, she extracted her hand and lifted her face to Finn's. "I am just a bit upset with myself. We never should have slept together. It was"—*fantastic, amazing, mind-blowing*—"stupid at best. At worst, some sort of HR nightmare."

His face went completely and utterly still as if a mask had slid into place. A dull ache started in her chest. His eyes, those beautiful, expressive eyes, had flickered from the pain that her words caused before turning into chips of ice.

She went on. She needed to make sure there was real

distance between them because when the truth came out if he was anywhere close to her, his career could be over. "Finn, yesterday was a lot with the accident and…everything. I appreciate you staying with me and offering me comfort, but it was a bad call on my part, and it really can't happen again. I'm sure you understand." She pushed back her chair and stood. "I'll go get my things together. We should leave shortly." She started walking out of the dining area.

"Tory." His voice was so cold she got a chill. Her knees went weak, so she grabbed the wall as she turned to look at him. He stood. "I warned you about this. I asked repeatedly if you were sure. You said 'yes'. What changed? I deserve an answer."

He was right. He did, but she wasn't prepared to give it at the moment. "I just…wised up."

He took two steps toward her. "You're lying. I don't know what kind of game you're playing, but you won't get the opportunity to play me again no matter how much you try to seduce me. We're finished."

"Understood," she said in a soft voice. Her gut churned, threatening to spew out the coffee she'd managed to drink. Turning away from Finn, she slowly went across the room and up the stairs. This had turned into her biggest nightmare, and all she wanted to do was ask the man downstairs for his help, but what she needed to do was keep him as far away as possible. It was a hopeless situation.

Her cell rang. "Steve," she answered.

"I just got a call from some guy named Ronin Conroy. He said he's a former colleague of yours from the CIA. He's in their Morocco office and wants you to call him. He doesn't have your new cell number, and I wasn't about to give it to him. He wouldn't tell me what's up, but he says it's important."

"Got it. Thanks, Steve." She clicked off the call and

dialed Ronin's number. "Ronin," she said when the other man answered, "what have you got for me?"

"I'm good, Tory. Thanks for asking."

She sighed and stood up. "Ronin, how are you? I hope you're doing well. How are Carla and the kids? Now, I assume you've got something to tell me and I don't have a lot of time."

Ronin snorted. "None of us have a lot of time the way the world is going, but I'll get to the point." For the next five minutes, Ronin outlined Tory's worst fear.

She closed her eyes and swore a blue streak in her head. Her stomach was in her shoes and her heart had stopped beating. It was the stuff of nightmares. "Are you sure?" she croaked.

"Yeah. It's gonna get ugly, Tory."

She put a hand on her forehead and closed her eyes. This was all bad. "And your friend had no idea on timing?"

"No."

"Great. Have you told your bosses yet?"

Ronin hesitated. "Not yet, but I'm pretty sure I'm not the only one with this information, so they must know by now. I'll call them when I get off the phone with you."

She bit her lip. "Do me a favor, Ronin, and let me know if you hear anything else. And I mean anything."

He sighed. "Will do." He was silent for a second. "This could be it, Tory. The big one. The thing we were always afraid of."

She swallowed. "Fuck, I hope not Ronin." She bit her lip. "Keep me in the loop. Okay?"

"Yeah, okay."

"Ronin?" she said, trying to catch him before he hung up. "Be safe. You're still fighting the good fight. Don't forget that."

"Thanks for the reminder," he said, and she knew he

meant it. She hung up and turned around to Finn leaning on the door jamb behind her.

"What's going on?" his voice was flat.

"Maybe we should wait for the others."

"Stop stalling," Finn growled.

Her shoulders slumped. This was all just too fucking much. "I have bad news. I just spoke with a contact in the CIA. He spoke to people in Libya, Tunisia, and Algeria. They said that there's going to be an auction. Highest bidder gets the highly classified U.S. information. Someone is selling our military and government secrets to whoever has the deepest pockets."

"Fucking hell," Finn growled. "This is unbelievable. Does he know the timing on this?"

She shook her head. "No. They didn't know but predict it will be sooner rather than later. They aren't major players, so the auction is above their pay grade. My source thinks these countries were originally approached with the idea of bidding together as a block of countries for the data, but they don't get on well enough to do that. No one trusts the other to share all the information. Plus, my contact says the African nations are worried about American retaliation. They couldn't withstand that."

"But not everyone is afraid, I take it," Finn stated.

Tory shook her head. "No. My contact says there's going to be a lot of interested bidders from Europe and the Middle East, not to mention Asia."

"Shit." Finn rubbed his face with both hands.

"Yes. It's going to get ugly." Tory ran a hand over her hair which she had up in a tight bun. "If any one of a few countries gets their hands on some of this information, it's game over for us. The American people do not want to know the truth about all of our deals with foreign powers. They don't want to know the ins and outs of how the game is played.

They just want the U.S. to win and be on top. They have no idea of the cost."

"Let me guess," Finn started, "Russia and China are at the head of the line."

She shrugged. "That's a reasonable guess."

"Does your contact know where this is going to take place?"

"No. His sources don't have enough money to be in the bidding so they don't have any more details."

"So someone out there is trying to make millions by auctioning off our secrets..." Finn shook his head. "Don't they know what giving out that kind of information will do to us?"

Tory put a hand to her head. It was starting to ache. "Oh, I think he knows. I just don't think he cares."

Finn leaned forward. "Who is 'he'?"

She looked up and met his gaze. "What?"

His eyes were still icy. "You said 'he.' Who is 'he'?"

She bit her lip. Figures he would pick up on her slip. This was it. Time to come clean, but how much did she tell him? It was a hard call. "Josh Hargate."

Finn frowned. "Who is Josh Hargate, and why do you think he's involved?"

"Steve called me this morning to tell me that they'd tracked the money Eckert sent his daughter back to a bank in Switzerland."

"One, I thought we agreed not to give out our numbers to anyone since we think there's a mole." Finn raised his eyebrows as if demanding answers. When she remained silent, he forced out a breath and continued. "And two, why would Eckert have a Swiss account? He had to know we'd track it."

"One"—she looked directly at Finn as she spoke—"your commanding officer might let you have all the leeway in the world, but my boss expects me to be reachable twenty-four hours a day, seven days a week. That's sort of my job. So there is no way he is not kept in the loop.

"And two"—she held up two fingers—"I think Eckert knew we'd be able to track him. I think he was having doubts about this whole project. As a U.S. soldier, it would be pretty tough to sell out your own country after fighting for it for so long. It must have rankled him. He left a trail of breadcrumbs so if anyone came looking, they could figure it out. Just enough to appease his conscience, but not enough to be ratting out his colleagues."

"Makes sense," Finn agreed grudgingly. "He left the note and he let us track the money. Do you think there are other breadcrumbs?"

"Maybe," she said. "We'll just have to be on the lookout for them."

"Can we go back to Josh Hargate? What's he got to do with this?"

Tory frowned. "Eckert was getting paid by Greyscale, which is Hargate's company. It's a security company that does contract work in all the war-torn countries. Eckert worked for Hargate."

"So you think this Hargate is the man behind the scenes? The one who is auctioning off this information?"

"It would not surprise me," Tory said.

"Why do you say that? How well do you know him?"

This was the million-dollar question. "Well, enough to say this would be his type of thing. Josh is a crook and a slimeball of the highest order."

"And how do you know that?" Finn asked.

"Because I dated him for three months. We were engaged."

CHAPTER EIGHTEEN

The air hissed out of Finn's lungs. *She was engaged to a traitor?* The man who was selling U.S. government secrets to the highest bidder? She'd had sex with him. Finn straightened up. He felt ill. He wanted out of this mess. It was all too confusing. This morning when he woke up, he was happier than he'd been in months…years even. Now, he was trying to figure out how he could have slept with a woman who'd dated a traitor.

He clenched his jaws. That wasn't fair. He could have dated twenty mass murderers by now and just didn't know it. His head was spinning. This was all just so fucked up. "I need more coffee." He turned and went back down the stairs and into the dining room. Tory came down behind him. He refilled his cup but didn't bother to offer her any. He just didn't have it in him at the moment.

He collapsed into a chair and drank deeply. He desperately needed the caffeine hit. Tory took up pacing the length of the dining room. His mug clattered on the table as he set it aside. He needed more information. "When were you engaged to this bastard?"

She didn't pause in her pacing but took up twisting her hands together. "Last year. It didn't last long. He, as I said, is a slimeball. A social-climbing, money-grubbing asshole with delusions of grandeur and a love of power."

Tell me how you really feel. "I see."

Tory shot him a glance but continued to pace.

Finn took a beat. "Okay, so what else can you tell us about him and his company? What did you call it? Greyscale?"

Tory nodded once. "Greyscale does government-sanctioned contract work in countries with 'conflicts.' Josh always wanted to be the next Blackwater, the top security firm in the business. The thing is, he was never that good. He had some former military personnel working for him, but they certainly weren't the most reliable crew. They were bottom feeders who couldn't get a job anywhere else. Eckert would be a prime example of that."

"And how do you know this?"

Tory met his gaze. "I did a background check on him right after we broke up and learned all kinds of things. I wish I'd done it before we'd gone out."

Finn's stomach hollowed out. "What else did you learn?"

She glanced at him, and her eyes narrowed slightly. "Greyscale has a reputation of going where others won't. He sells his teams as tougher and stronger, but the reality is, they have no moral compass and they're willing to do what others aren't."

Finn drummed the table with his fingers. "What does all this mean?"

Tory sighed. "Good question. I think it means that we know who is auctioning off the information, but we don't know the how or the where."

"So what *do* we know?

"Eckert worked for Josh Hargate."

Finn cut in. "But do we know he was working for Hargate at the time of his death?"

"Good point," Tory nodded. "He was paid by Greyscale about two weeks before his death so I think we can assume yes."

Finn sat back and watched her pace. He was still livid over her little speech this morning. She had begged him to sleep with her so she felt safe, and then she initiated sex that morning but changed her mind after it was over. He pushed his coffee away and swallowed hard, crushing the bile rising in his gullet. It wasn't fair. She got what she wanted, but what about him?

His brain was all over the place. He was angry about this morning, and he was not going to be able to work with Tory if he didn't figure this shit out. He needed to occupy his hands and get himself under control. Otherwise, the rage that lived in his soul might come out, and that would not be good. He got up, walked into the other room, and grabbed a pad of paper from the desk, then came back and sat down. He carefully tore a strip off the page to reduce it to the square he needed.

He slowed his breathing, focusing on his hands. He folded the paper again and again. Bending it, twisting it. Soon, he had an origami moose.

Finn started on the next piece of paper. Tory got what she needed. Did he? Yes and no. Yes, he wanted her so badly it hurt and, yes, the sex was just as amazing this time as it was before. And it would be amazing again. But was it what he needed? No. He needed more. He needed someone who would be there when he needed it, not just when she did. He needed someone to rely on. Someone who didn't frustrate him so much that he was reduced to making origami animals during an important strategic meeting.

He and Tory were done.

He glanced up. *What had they been saying?* Finn set the crane he'd just made next to the moose. "Assuming Hargate's people were behind the tapping of the fiber lines, does that mean he has the information and he's running the auction, or is someone else calling the shots on this thing? Would Hargate have the skill to pull off the tap or the money to pay for it? Not only expensive but the logistics and manpower of the operation would have been colossal."

Tory's face paled slightly. Her eyes flashed something before she looked away from Finn and did an abrupt turn, walking away from him. She was hiding something. Something she was feeling guilty about because that flash was guilt.

He decided to test the waters. "Since you know Hargate, if he is behind this, where would he hide out?"

Tory turned to meet his gaze. The guilt was still present. "I don't know where he'd hide out. But I don't think Hargate is smart enough to do this on his own. He has the muscle and the lack of morals to do it, but not the brain power to come up with a plan, and he probably would have needed some financial backing as well." She glanced down and untangled her clutched fingers, shaking the blood back into them. "I'm going to reach out to one of my CIA contacts. I bet they have a file on him. I didn't do it before because"—she took a deep breath—"I was afraid of what I would find." She seized a Sharpie from the table and started twirling it, like she needed something to do with her hands to avoid spewing out the truth.

"Okay," he said but he captured her gaze and wouldn't let it go. She had to tell him what was going on. A lot was riding on this. She had to share her secret. She owed him, and his team, at least that. "You have an idea of who is behind all this." It was a statement of fact. He knew it in his bones.

"Would you mind sharing your thoughts?" he asked in a soft voice.

Tory swallowed and then nodded, as if she'd come to some decision. She took a deep breath. "I think Senator Jeffry James MacAllister is behind this."

Finn stared at her. She was accusing a United States senator of subverting the U.S. government. *Of treason.* This was no small thing. Hell, even suggesting it could be a death sentence, at least for her career. It took a lot of guts to say that out loud. He admired her for it. But she was still hiding something. She knew more about it. This wasn't a random thought or a guess. The way her gaze flitted around the room and her fingers played with the marker. There was definitely more here.

"That's a hell of an accusation. Want to tell me how you came to that conclusion?"

Tory eyed him and bit her lip. She gave a little shrug and then started speaking again. "Last year, just before we started dating, Josh mentioned that he was bringing on a partner of sorts. He was excited because now he had the financial foundation he wanted, but he also needed an 'in' with the government to legitimize his business. He reached out to Senator MacAllister, and my understanding is that they came to some sort of agreement."

"And you know this because…?" Finn asked.

"For a short while, MacAllister used Hargate's guys as extra security, and then he stopped suddenly. I reached out to Hargate to ask about it, and he made up some story about MacAllister not needing his assistance anymore, but I saw them together a few months later and they were pretty chummy."

He shook his head. "Based on the fact that MacAllister used some of Hargate's security people for a private event, and a few months later they looked chummy, you think

MacAllister is committing treason? 'Think' is an understatement."

"MacAllister is a very vocal opponent of the current administration on just about every front. Depending on the secrets he's trying to sell, he can swing the next election in the direction he wants. He wants to be President but polls say he's too old to win. If he can't be king, he'll settle for being king-maker. And Vice President."

Finn raised his eyebrows. "Those are some pretty big leaps you're making. What aren't you telling me?" He wasn't letting her off the hook. She was going to have to share whatever secret she was holding close to her chest.

Tory looked at him but her gaze skittered away again. "I know this is true because Senator Jeffry James MacAllister is my father."

The bottom of Finn's logical world fell away. Of all the things he thought she would say, that wasn't in the top fifty. Finn stared at the paper on the table. That changed everything "I'm sorry. Are you accusing your father of treason?"

"Yes," she said simply. "He wants to be President, but polling numbers show he won't be elected so he wants to own the election. He'll take Vice President as long as whoever he chooses for President does his bidding. Auctioning off the right information can make that happen. He can buy loyalty and get support with all the money he'll make and, by releasing select details to the public, he can poison voters on certain policies and people."

Finn stared at Tory. "And you think your father is capable of being involved in this type of operation?"

Lips seamed together tightly, she simply nodded.

"But you don't have the same last name," He pointed out. He just couldn't get over the shock. Not only was she MacAllister's daughter but she was accusing him of treason.

"I took my mother's maiden name. I didn't want to ride

his coattails in my own career. To get back to your other question, I think he and a few close, like-minded political animals are the brains behind it. Think about it," she said as she came forward, dropped the marker, and placed her hands flat on the table. "They make money auctioning off information, but really there's a pile of back-channel deals. They go to Russia and say, 'If you help us get elected, we'll tell you what the U.S. plans are to counteract Belarus' involvement in the Ukraine war. You know damned well communication about that has gone back and forth to Europe."

Finn cocked his head. "So you're saying the auction is not the big-ticket event, but these backroom deals are?"

"I'm saying I think it's both. I think they need money and support from outside sources, so they'll auction some information, but they'll also make deals. I think the little bits they shared with certain countries so far was just to whet people's appetite."

"What proof do you have?" he demanded. "I'm not saying I don't believe you, but we need evidence that he's involved."

She let out a long breath. "I know. I don't have any. Yet. There's got to be a way to find some because I know the relationship between my father and Hargate exists."

Finn leaned back in his chair. Her revelations were a lot to process, and it wasn't even his father. Jesus, what she must be going through. Was this why she shut him down this morning? He rubbed his face. The way his mind was spinning right now was too overwhelming. He grabbed another piece of paper and started folding. He needed to settle his brain.

Tory's cell went off. "Steve," she said. There was a long silence. "Okay. I'll check the email and get back to you." Another silence and then, "Thanks." She ended the call. "The guys watching us are Hargate's."

"Shit." Finn grabbed his phone and called Nick. "It's confirmed," he said as soon as Nick answered.

"Fuck," Nick growled. "We're all here. None of the rest of us were followed. We have to come up with a plan to get you two out sight unseen."

"Yeah, but first we have to figure out how they found us." He looked over at Tory. "I'll call you back." He clicked off the call. "The guys are close by but we need an escape plan."

"Agreed. I'm sure Yazley can help us." Tory stopped and leaned against the dining room wall.

"The bigger question is, how did they find us?" Finn stared at Tory, waiting for some kind of answer. "The rest of the team wasn't followed. So how come we were?"

She shrugged. "I have no idea. We didn't bring anything with us from the office except for weapons and the clothes on our backs. We have new cell phones."

Her eyes darted all over the room, her wheels evidently turning. She didn't know any more than he did. Relief washed over him. He had to know for sure that she wasn't involved with Hargate and her father. There was no guilt this time. She was in the clear.

"Were our clothes tagged? The guns? What?" she asked.

Finn pointed out, "It couldn't have been our clothes unless one of us installed the tracker. We've had our clothing with us the whole time. It can't be the guns because we'd have noticed them, and we changed the bags out last night. Any other ideas?"

Tory glanced down at her watch. "Time," she murmured. "It's me. It's my watch. It was my best friend's. She died, and I always wear it to remember her."

A dead best friend? Fucking hell. Finn blinked. He really didn't know this woman at all.

"The only time I take it off is at the pool when I swim. Six weeks ago, my father came to the pool. He must have put the bug in it then." She unstrapped the offending timepiece from her wrist and threw it on the table.

Finn picked it up and then pried the back off. He turned it so she could see. There was a small device inside. She'd been right. Her father had bugged her watch. Jesus Christ.

He started to lift the bug out, but she held up a hand to stop him.

She scowled. "Leave it. The watch will need to stay here so they can't fucking track us anymore. I'll pick it up later."

He snapped the back plate into place and dropped the watch on the table.

This was all so fucked up.

Tory grabbed her phone and pounded in a number. "Mr. Yazley," she said a moment later. "Those men are watching us. We need to get out of the building without being seen. We assume the exits are covered. Do you have any ideas?"

Finn took a sip of his cold coffee. This situation was so far beyond anything he'd been a part of he couldn't get his brain around it. He could make all the origami animals in the world and still not be able to process all the shit.

Tory hung up. "Yazley said to go down the back staircase and meet him at the bottom. He'll get us out from there."

"Let's do it." Finn stood and followed Tory through the dining room, passed the kitchen into the hallway. She touched a spot in the wall and a panel slid back to reveal a keypad. She typed in the code and a portion of the wall in front of them retracted, revealing a staircase. "That's handy. Your friend Drake has an interesting hotel."

"Drake is an interesting man."

A small jolt of jealousy burst through Finn's system before he could squash it. She wasn't his, as she'd so coldly pointed out that morning. He was just a passing fancy.

They came to the bottom of the stairs and a man was waiting for them. He was tall and thin with greying hair at the temples. His brown eyes were on full alert. "Ms. Stanhope," he said and offered her his hand.

"Mr. Yazley." She shook with him. "This is Mr…" she paused.

"No need for names." He smiled at her and nodded at Finn. "Come with me." He opened the door to the staircase, and they followed him out to a loading dock. He pointed to a large laundry bin. "If you please."

Finn blinked. "You want us to get into the bin?"

Yazley nodded. "The truck," he pointed to the one backed up to the loading bay with its rear door already up, "will take you wherever you wish to go."

"That works. Let me make a call." Finn walked away and made a quick call to Nick. Then he came back and told Yazley that they wanted to be dropped a couple of blocks away.

Yazley nodded. "Mr. Drake wishes you luck and please let him know if there is any other way he can be of assistance."

Tory smiled. "Tell him thank you for me."

She started towards the bin but Finn stopped her. "Let me get in first."

He climbed into the bin and got settled. Tory climbed in after him, essentially sitting curled up in his lap. He gave Yazley a thumbs up and the man threw bedsheets over them, effectively hiding them. Damn, he felt like a bad actor in a B movie, making a quick getaway in the most obvious manner.

With a quiet chuckle, Finn tightened his arms around Tory. The bin jostled and rattled as it was rolled along the dock. There was a sharp bump as they were pushed onto the truck. Someone then secured the wheels and left. The door was pulled down and they were in total darkness.

"Sorry if my elbow is digging into you," Tory said as she shifted her weight.

It wasn't her elbow he was worried about. She was moving in his lap with her ass against his crotch. He was getting hard. She'd made her thoughts on that subject perfectly clear but there wasn't a damn thing he could do about his physical reaction to her. She shifted again.

"Stop fucking moving, Tory," he growled.

"Um, sorry, I was just trying to—"

"I don't care what you were trying to do. Your ass is rubbing against my dick. Even if you aren't interested in sex with me anymore, it would take a better man than I am not to get hard. So just. Stop. Moving."

Tory froze. They spent the next ten minutes in total darkness with Tory sitting utterly motionless in his lap. Finn had to laugh because if he didn't, he might actually cry. He'd thought he had the world by the tail this morning, but now it had him and it was swinging for the fences.

CHAPTER NINETEEN

Twenty minutes later Tory sat huddled in the corner of the back seat of the minivan with darkly tinted windows. Finn was beside her in the last row of seats. This was going to be one of the longest car rides of her life. The temperature in the car was beyond frosty. It was a fucking deep freeze. Well, what did she expect? She'd hurt him. Deeply by the look of things.

But she was hurting, too, so much more than he knew.

She tried to sort it out in her head. Her father had bugged her watch a month and a half ago. At that point, she had just started to poke around. Who had she spoken to? Who could have told her father she was investigating? Then another thought hit her so hard she actually jerked.

"What?" Finn demanded in a quiet voice.

Elias was behind the wheel and Nick rode shotgun. Axe and Cain were in the middle seat ahead of Tory and Finn.

She glanced at him. "Nothing."

He stared at her. She was struggling as it was. She didn't want to tell him her latest thought. She'd been so turned on in the laundry cart that she'd been moving so she could get away from him. All she really wanted to do was screw his brains out then and there. That was too embarrassing to admit. Too painful. She shook her head. She couldn't even look at him. If she did, she was likely to throw herself into his arms and beg forgiveness. He'd already told her that wasn't going to happen, so chances were good she'd go down in the hall of fame of embarrassing moments.

She stared at the back of Cain's head. Would they trust her now? Would they blame her for being found? Worse, would they think she did it on purpose? She frowned.

Nick turned in his seat to face the rest of the team. "I have some news. The Navy, with the help of the *Walton*, found where the cables have been tapped."

Tory let out a long breath. "Well, that's good news. How long will it take them to kill the wiretap?"

"A day or two at the most. They've already told Washington, and they've got experts flying in to help ASAP."

She allowed herself a small smile. "Well, that's a step in the right direction. Anything else?"

"Eckert was injured in an IED explosion. The Army wanted to kick him out on disability because of a plate in his leg. He fought them. When it became obvious it wasn't going to go his way, he stole some weaponry. Nothing major, but enough to get busted and go to military prison. They were going to court-martial him, but it was all swept under the rug. There were some irregularities in the investigation. It seems Eckert's lawyer was drunk most days at his trial, and the judge let it all happen anyway. So, they sprung Eckert and gave him a discharge."

"He had a grudge against the military then," Finn said. "I've seen it a few times. For some guys, it's all the family they really have, and being kicked out makes them bitter as hell."

"That goes to motivation I guess." Tory glanced at Finn.

A desire burned in her to confess all of her sins to this man and beg him to take her back. She was sure it wouldn't work, but maybe if she told the truth now, if nothing else it might buy back a little self-respect. "I have news as well." She went on to tell them all about Hargate and her father. It wasn't a fun confession and she didn't feel better at the end of it but at least now her entire team knew.

"That's just so…unbelievable," Elias said.

She nodded. "I should also tell you I think this was a setup from the very beginning."

"What do you mean?" Finn asked, his voice hard.

"I think my father was the one who asked to have me assigned to this project. I made the initial report and someone high up, the Director or Assistant Director, probably mentioned it to him. He would have pushed to keep me on it." She knew it in her very marrow. It was the type of thing he would enjoy doing.

Finn cocked his head. "What makes you think that?"

"Because he bugged my watch about six weeks ago, right after I got back from the conference in Brussels and informed my bosses about what I'd learned. He had to know I was poking around, and what better way to be kept in the loop than have your daughter's boss report her progress to you. He could track my every move. The mole at DHS is very high up the chain of command. My father knew when we landed in Virginia and where we were the whole time. Otherwise, why do it? Why bother bugging my watch?"

"It's a theory." Finn tapped his fingers on his thigh. "So what's our play here? Do we just hand this mess off to you guys at DHS and let you take care of it? Does the FBI take over? How do we move forward?"

She hesitated. "That's the rub. MacAllister and his friends have contacts everywhere, and they themselves have a very high level of clearance. He called me when we landed in Virginia to see what I knew."

"That was your father?" Finn demanded. His face went hard.

"Um, yes. He knew we'd just landed." She kept her voice level, but it was costing her. She peered out the tinted window, blinking back angry tears, and doing her best to keep her hands from shaking.

Elias whistled. "That means that your father tried to have you killed."

"No way." Axe shook his head. "What kind of parent would do that?"

Finn cleared his throat. "Follow the logic. Tory said the SUVs were tagged before we came, and she was right. We would have seen them on camera if they'd done it after we arrived at the office building. Presumably, they wanted to know what we're doing. They might even have had the office bugged or very likely got the same information we did as we got it. Then, when we went to see Eckert's daughter, they decided to eliminate us because we were learning too much.

Nick looked at Tory with sympathy. "It appears your father did try to have you killed. What a bastard."

Tory glanced down at her hands in her lap and then back up at him. "We're not what you'd call close. Anyway"—her hands were shaking and there was a tremor in her voice, but she gamely carried on—"My father has friends at DHS and just about everywhere else. I'm not sure who we hand this off to, to be honest. I trust my direct boss, but I wouldn't go higher than him. I don't know anyone at the FBI that would be high enough up the ladder to get things done, but not at the top where my father has influence. The CIA is not allowed to be involved in anything inside the US, but I suppose we could talk to them."

"We need to call Bertrand," Finn stated.

"You're right," Nick said. "Bertrand needs to know. He'll know some people to talk to. We can't do this alone."

Tory frowned. "I like the idea of Bertrand. I think you're right. We can trust him but we need to be very careful. I would like to speak with him in person. How do we make it happen?"

Nick turned to face the front. "I have an idea." He spoke quietly to Elias.

Exhausted, Tory sunk further into the corner of the seat. Surreptitiously glancing at Finn, she knew that as much as she wanted him, she'd be better off to stay away. Looking out the window, she realized they were heading toward Central D.C. Once the truth came out about her father, her life would be over, but if things went well, at least she would have taken him down with her. That was alright with her. Maybe she'd move to Europe. Start over in Brussels. She could get a job with a non-government organization at the UN.

"Your father abused you." It was a statement.

She met Finn's gaze and nodded once. There was nothing more to say. It happened, and it was over, or at least she had thought it was over, but she now saw how wrong she'd been. He merely had retreated into the background, but he was still manipulating her, getting her to do what he wanted. He was just cagier about it.

"How do we find proof of the connection?" Finn asked.

Nick glanced back. "What do you mean?"

"This is all well and good. It's a semi-plausible theory but there's no proof."

Silence settled in the van. It was true. She knew it was true but without proof, there was nothing she could do to get people to believe her.

Finn leaned forward. "We could do what we did in the Suez."

Nick frowned. "What do you mean?"

"With the phones. If we can trace Hargate's number and see where he's been and what phones he's been around, then do the same with the senator, if they connect up, we know they're at least friends."

"'Friends' doesn't get us to treason, but I hear what you're saying. It's not exactly legal." Nick rubbed his jaw.

"Neither is treason," Finn pointed out.

"There's that," Nick agreed. "I'll call the Callahans and see what they can do." He grabbed his cell and started the call.

"Currently, we have bigger issues," Axe pointed out.

"Such as?" Finn asked.

"We need a place to hole up. We need to solve that issue before we deal with the bigger problems."

"Agreed," said Nick. "Elias, take the back streets. Drive at the speed limit. No sudden moves. Avoid any kind of area that might have cameras. Residential is best. Even if they have those doorbell cameras, someone has to know our general whereabouts to start looking at the footage."

Everyone stayed silent.

"Fiancé?" Finn asked, his voice a whisper.

She glanced at him and nodded once. "I was…out of control. It was stupid and I regretted it immediately. It took me another six weeks to do anything about it."

It was obvious that Finn was slowly going through everything she'd said and processing it. It was a lot to take in. She knew it. She was still struggling with her failed engagement to Hargate. How could he be any different?

Twenty minutes later, they rolled into an upscale neighborhood on the outskirts of D.C.

"Park here." Nick gestured to the curb.

When Elias pulled over, Nick told him, "Okay, I'm going to get out. When you see that garage door go up"—he pointed to a large white house with black shutters—"drive in. I'll close the door behind you."

Elias nodded. Nick got out of the minivan and walked along the sidewalk and up the driveway. A few moments later, the garage door went up. Elias pulled away from the curb and then turned into the driveway. After he came to a stop in the garage, the door closed behind them.

"Is this another one of your safe houses?" Tory asked.

"No," Finn said bluntly.

Elias opened his door and then the back door of the minivan, and they all filed out. Nick opened the door to the house and ushered them in.

Tory walked into a lovely bright kitchen. It was painted a jaunty yellow and had beautiful white cabinets with marble countertops. She suffered a pang of envy at the sight of the huge high-end stove, and she barely cooked. The counter running the length of the room had a sink under a window that overlooked a pool in the backyard. A black granite countertop anchored a large central island and four stools. The fridge was on the left surrounded by more cabinets. Pendant lights hung over the island.

And in the middle of it all stood a petit woman dressed for a game of tennis. Tory guessed her age around sixty but the woman looked a decade younger. Her blond hair was bobbed, and her sparkling blue eyes were framed with deep smile lines.

"Well," she said, "come in, come in. Let me get you some coffee." She hustled around the kitchen and in no time they were all sipping a hot beverage and eating homemade cookies.

"I called George and told him he had to come home immediately. He wasn't too pleased, and he's goin' to grumble somethin' awful when he sees you here, but don't you worry, he'll get over it. He'll just be happy y'all are okay."

Her soft southern accent reminded Tory of her long dead mother.

"Victory? Is that you?" the woman asked Tory.

Tory blinked. "Um…yes."

"I bet you don't remember me. We met years ago at a school play. My daughter Ashley went to the same school as you. You were pretty as a picture in that play. I was so sorry to hear of your mom's passing."

"Er, thanks."

"You know, Victory, Ashley's room is just upstairs. She has her own bathroom why don't I take you and let you freshen up."

She glanced down at herself. Was it that obvious she needed a minute or two alone? "I couldn't possibly."

"Oh, pish. Of course, you could." The woman grabbed Tory by the arm and pulled her out of the kitchen into the foyer and then up the stairs. They passed by family photos on the walls. Ashley. She recognized the girl right away. They hadn't been friends, but they'd been friendly. Ashley Bertrand. *Holy shit!* This was the Admiral's house. He was going to have a shit fit when he got home and saw them.

"Here you go," Mrs. Bertrand said. "You take all the time you need. I'm sure you've been through a lot and being around men like these is not easy on a girl's system." She winked.

You have no idea. Mrs. Bertrand smiled and then disappeared out of the room again, closing the door behind her.

Twenty minutes later, after throwing some water on her face, Tory re-entered the kitchen. The guys were still all sitting, drinking coffee and eating cookies.

"God damn it, Marian," George Bertrand swore as he slammed the front door. "What's so damned important that I had to reschedule a meeting with the Secretary of State?" He walked into the kitchen and stopped dead.

"Taggert!" Bertrand roared. "What in the bloody hell is going on? Why are you in my kitchen?"

Rear Admiral Lower Half George Bertrand moved like a battleship as he crossed the floor. The tall man had salt and pepper hair and clear blue eyes. He was still in good shape for his age, which she would put at early sixties. It was obvious he didn't skip regular workouts.

Her team jumped to their feet and stood at attention. Tory stood by the stove and braced herself.

Bertrand came to a stop no more than a foot in front of Nick. "Taggert, I am waiting for an answer!" he demanded.

"Well, sir, the men who tried to kill Finn and Tory found us again. They came ready to kill. At least, we assume it's the same men. We think we know who is behind the tap and the selling of U.S. secrets, and it's…delicate." Nick's convulsive swallow was the only movement on his body as he remained at attention and relayed the facts. "We are out of safe places to stay in the area and our resources are limited. Logically, we thought no one would dream of looking for us here."

Bertrand's face turned a shade of reddish-purple Tory had never seen before. "Dream? You are endangering my family! I will have you court-martialed and kicked out of the Coast Guard!"

"All right, George, simmer down," Marian Bertrand said. "The neighbors will hear you, and that will defeat the purpose of all this. Your team needs your help. Yelling at them won't solve anything."

The admiral glared at his wife. Then he turned back to Nick. "In my office, all of you. Now."

The men all trooped out of the kitchen. Tory started to follow when Marian grabbed her mug and refilled it. "You're gonna need it." She winked.

Tory smiled and then scurried to catch up to the others.

The office was done in dark paneling with beige carpet.

Bertrand slammed the door after Tory entered, then stalked to a humongous wooden desk with ornately carved legs.

The admiral threw himself into a cushy-looking chair and crossed his arms over his chest. "There were far better options than coming to my home, so you had better start talking, Master Chief, and it had better be one hell of a story."

The men were all standing in front of Bertrand's desk, Nick alone out front with the others flanking him in two rows. Tory ended up standing next to Finn.

He said in a whisper, "Victory? Your name is Victory?"

She nodded once and took a sip of coffee. She wasn't having that discussion now. She squared her shoulders. This was her operation, and these men had been assigned to her. She might not have done much leading so far, but it was better late than never.

"Sir," Nick started, but Tory stepped forward.

"Admiral Bertrand, if I may," Tory interrupted. "I realize Chief Taggert and the rest of the team answer to you, however at this point, per the Director of Homeland Security, they have been assigned to me. So, let me fill you in and we can go from there."

Bertrand's lips compressed into a thin line.

Tory smiled slightly again and started her report. She covered everything from the hellish helicopter ride to the *Walton*, the sinking of the *Oceanus Explorer*, their arrival in Virginia and almost being killed, to finding out about the auction. He knew most of it, but she thought it was important to review it with him before she revealed the rest.

"As you can see, Admiral, the team has been doing great work. We have managed to find out who is behind the auction and the leaking of U.S. secrets, but as Chief Taggert said, it's delicate."

Bertrand had been studying her the entire time she'd been speaking. "Delicate? What the hell does that mean?"

"Sir, we think one of the main movers behind this disaster is Jeffry James MacAllister, my father." She relayed that fact in a strong, clear voice. She wasn't going to shy away from this, and she wanted him to know it.

"Jesus Christ! Senator MacAllister? Why in God's name would you think it was him?" Bertrand's face had turned thunderous.

Nick spoke up. "If I may, sir, we have reason to believe that Eckert worked for Hargate at Greyscale, and Hargate is a close associate of Senator MacAllister."

Bertrand growled, "Just because someone is an associate —" His face changed, and he stopped speaking. His eyes were darting around the room.

"Sir?" Nick asked.

Tory knew what was happening. Bertrand was connecting the dots. He'd seen or heard something that struck him as odd at the time, but now he had a frame of reference for it, and it made sense. His mouth went from being slack to forming a tight line.

"Son of a bitch," Bertrand mumbled. He blinked and looked around the table. Then he focused in on Tory. "Your father is also good friends with Senator Wilber Clayton, isn't he?"

Tory nodded. "He is."

"Hmm. Senator Clayton made a request less than an hour ago to *interview* my team. He claims he's heard such great things he would like to meet the men in question. He is willing to help get us more funding so we can form other special operations groups in the Coast Guard."

"Sir, permission to speak?" Finn asked. At Bertrand's nod, he said, "What is the point of that? Does he think you will pull us from a mission for a meet and greet?"

Bertrand paused before answering. "Prevailing rumors have it that money might become available shortly to help with certain projects. Senator Clayton implied to me that he could help secure some of that funding. Most would jump at the chance to get that money. I happen to not like the Senator very much and, more importantly, I don't trust him. His offer reminded me too much of a snake oil salesman. But, for him, it's worth a shot, isn't it?"

"You mean, if one of us went to this interview, Hargate's men would attempt to follow us to get to the whole team?" Finn asked.

Bertrand nodded. "That would be the smart play. It's a good plan B in case they couldn't find you lot."

"I agree, sir," Nick chimed in.

"And it might be worth considering," Finn added.

"What do you mean, Walsh?"

"Well, sir, what if we lead them to where we want them to be? Then we can grab them, and with any luck, get one of them to flip so we can find out what exactly is going on."

Bertrand cocked his head. "The idea has some merit."

Tory said nothing, but she agreed. If they didn't mind using one of the team as bait, then it would be worth a try.

However, she had reservations. "Admiral, I do have some concerns. I agree this is definitely worth a shot, but I think first we need to discover when the information auction is going to be held.

"Also, I wanted to point out that, due to the extremely high level of access these people have, we can't use any of the normal safe houses or hotels. They'll have people out searching for us using facial recognition software. They have access to everything, sir. So coming here, although unorthodox, seemed like the best solution at the time. We're all happy to leave as soon as we have a plan in place."

Bertrand nodded slowly. "I see what you mean. They know all the tricks in the play book and they have all of the tools to use as well. Going way outside the lines was the smart move. I can't say I like that you picked my damn house, but I understand it." He rubbed a hand down his face. "Back to the auction. Do we have any ideas on location?"

"No, sir," Nick said.

Cain cocked his head. "Where is the best place to hold an auction like this? Online. No one has to be there in person."

Tory bit her lip. "You're right. The buyers won't be there for the auction. Not in person. We need to find Hargate before we do anything else. He will be present for the auction. He'll know all the details. There's no doubt. He wouldn't miss it."

Finn crossed his arms over his chest. "So we agree the auction will most likely be online. Assuming we can find Hargate and actually tail him, how long will we have to do that? When will the auction be held? The general consensus is it will happen soon, but how soon?"

Bertrand sighed. "I suppose I could go to Senator MacAllister's birthday party. He's invited half of Washington. I might be able to find out the latest scuttlebutt. D.C. thrives on gossip."

Tory froze. Her father's birthday. Half of Washington. "That's it. That's when the auction will be."

"What?" the Admiral asked.

"The auction will be during my father's birthday party. No better alibi. As you said, sir, half of D.C. will be there. I think the final exchange, the delivery of the secrets is the more important event. We may or may not be able to stop the auction. What we need is the information so even if we stop the auction, if my father denies the whole thing, then we don't get the information back. It will still be out there floating around unless my father confesses, which is pretty unlikely.

"No, the important thing is the small intimate gathering

for close friends down in Turks and Caicos he's having after the D.C. party. He does it most years, but he is for sure doing it this year. He invited me."

Finn frowned. "Why is that important?" He turned quickly. "Sorry, sir."

Bertrand waved his hand. "I was about to ask the same thing."

"Turks and Caicos is a major banking mecca. Even after the last hurricane, they were up and back online quick time. They have high-speed internet. It is also easily accessible via air or sea, and it's not on American soil, so it's less likely anyone is paying attention to what's going on. It's a sleepy island in a lot of ways, full of tourists looking for fun in the sun. What better place to do the exchange? Great banking and internet for the money part of things and great access by land or sea for the physical exchange of the information."

She continued. "He won't do the exchange here in the U.S. but Turks and Caicos, on the other hand, is a perfect location. So he holds the auction during his birthday gala and does the exchange during his intimate, close friends and family only, birthday weekend. And the beauty of doing the exchange then is once again it gives my father the ultimate alibi. He's at his birthday party getaway with a group of Washington elite. No one would ever suspect him of being involved, but if they did, they certainly wouldn't expect him to make the exchange while a group of top government officials are in the same house. There is no better cover. And my father's ego is such that it would appeal to him to get away with it under their noses."

Tory knew she was right. Knew it in her bones. Knew it like she knew her father was an abusive bastard. She wanted to be there, she realized. When they slapped the cuffs on him, she wanted to be there to see it. Hell, she wanted to be the one snapping the cuffs tight around his wrists. She wanted to see the moment when he realized it wasn't a joke and that he wasn't going to get away with it. When the realization dawned on him that his career was over and all he'd worked for was gone, she wanted, no *needed* to be there. He deserved prison. She fervently hoped they would throw him in a dark hole somewhere and never let him out again.

First, she had to get proof, or all this talk was for nothing.

Bertrand stared at her but remained silent. She knew he was thinking, turning it over in his head.

"I'm right," she assured him in a quiet voice.

Bertrand looked at her and nodded. "As much as I hate to think it, I agree. If, indeed, this is happening and your father is really committing treason then, yes, that whole setup would appeal to your father. He is a man with a large ego and an inflated sense of his importance. Hard not to be when you've been a power player in Washington as long as he has. I'm sorry, Ms. Stanhope. I cannot imagine how difficult this is for you."

"Not as hard as you might think. My father wants to be king. This is his way of making that a reality. But the U.S. is a republic. No kings allowed. It's time someone reminded him of that."

"What do you propose?" Bertrand asked.

"It's a hard call. We need people we can trust, but that's a difficult thing to find. My father and his cronies have a lot of friends in high places in Washington. Even people who don't agree with him won't openly go against him. As you said, he's been around a long time and has a long memory. No one wants to be on his bad side.

"We"—she indicated the team—"know we need help, but we're unsure of what agency or which people to call. I know my boss, Steve Wiseman at DHS, is trustworthy. I'm not sure who else besides you, sir, that we can bring in on this without risking exposure. I do have contacts at the CIA, but they aren't allowed to work on American soil and they would need some serious evidence to get involved with an op like this. We would have to get them involved on the Turks and Caicos end of things."

Bertrand nodded. "I know someone at the FBI I trust wholeheartedly. I can call him. We're going to have to come up with something fast. Your father's party will be this weekend."

She nodded. She knew to the bottom of her soul her father was part of this. There would be a group of them, but her father would be one of the power players, maybe even the ringleader. "If you don't take big risks, you can't get big rewards." It was his favorite saying.

"Where do you think they're storing the information?" Bertrand asked.

She blinked. "That's a very good question. I have no idea. I mean, they must have the information going to a server somewhere, but I'm not sure where. It could literally be anywhere."

Bertrand sighed. "Is there a way to track it?"

"I'm not sure, sir. None of us have that level of tech experience."

Finn spoke in a quiet voice. "The bigger question is, sir, *how* are they going to do the exchange? If you are buying the information for top dollar, or ruble or yuan, you don't want it given to your enemies, so how do you know they aren't keeping a copy and selling it multiple times?"

"That's true," Axe agreed. "They have to guarantee that no one else gets the information, otherwise their buyer turns into their enemy."

A wave of exhaustion rolled over Tory and she swayed where she stood in the middle of the floor. "I think they must offer up a server. It's the only thing that really makes sense. The server will be one of those massively encrypted ones that are portable. There are many tech companies that make them. The hard cases they're transported in look sort of like medium-sized hard-shell luggage."

Bertrand nodded once. "What about the money? Are they taking it in a cryptocurrency or just having it transferred into an account or multiple accounts?"

Finn shrugged. "They could be doing the exchange in almost any medium. Art, diamonds, NFTs. It doesn't have to be currency, and it might not be as important. I mean, if we grab the server, that's priority number one. It would be nice to know who is buying our secrets, but I think the money is less of a worry. It would be nice to have the server *and* the money, but I imagine whoever is going to pay top dollar for their information will find a way to get their money back when they don't receive the server."

Tory added. "I do know my father would never deal in cryptocurrency or NFTs. Too volatile. He likes his money to be safe."

"Well," Bertrand said, "you've all given me a lot to think about. I also have some calls to make. I need you to be out of my office."

Nick nodded. "Er, sir. Any ideas where we can go? And, once again, I want to apologize for showing up here."

Tory cut in, "My father is close with the Director and Assistant Director of the FBI. He's on various committees with other intelligence community officials. He has the ability to find us at his fingertips if we do any of the usual things, like street and highway cameras, cameras at tolls. We need to find a way out using backstreets only and then go somewhere rural and remote. We won't have access to many resources, but we should be safe if we're really careful. Facial recognition software is our enemy at this point."

Nick suggested, "We could go back to Virginia or West Virginia maybe. That's probably better."

Bertrand let out a huge sigh. "There is a pool house in the backyard. Go make yourselves at home. Do not come out. Do not let my neighbors see you. I will rustle up some food for you in a bit."

"Thank you, sir," Nick said and then turned to go.

Bertrand stopped them. "You all were right. This is delicate. We're talking about accusing some of the most powerful men in this country of treason. We need to make sure all of our ducks are in a row. Work on a plan that will save our bacon and our secrets and keep my family safe."

Nick nodded. "Yes, sir."

"Maddox," Bertrand bellowed. "Get a haircut. Ponytails in the Coast Guard are not acceptable."

"Sir," Cain said.

Finn stifled a laugh with a cough.

Tory followed the men out of the office. Bertrand was right. If they didn't manage this well, if they didn't have overwhelming proof, her father would turn the tables on them. They would find themselves being accused of treason and buried in a hole. Her father was a master at the art of manipulation. It was a damn good thing she'd been forced to study at his feet for all these years.

CHAPTER TWENTY

Finn straightened. "Are there any more blankets? I'm getting cold over here."

He was standing in the kitchenette of the pool house Bertrand had given them permission to lay low in. Unfortunately, the heat was out in the pool house. The team lounged around the room, most wrapped in blankets or beach towels that Mrs. Bertrand had supplied but Finn had been in the bathroom when they got handed out so the greedy bastards had scooped them all, as well as all the comfy seats. There were some hard wooden chairs left and that was it.

"We left you pizza. Don't complain."

Finn shook his head as he crammed the last bite of crust into his mouth and then leaned back against the counter. The pool house wasn't huge, but it was well-appointed. The kitchenette had a fridge, microwave, small stove, and dishwasher, all stainless steel.

The entry point was on Finn's left, and beyond that, the pool. Creamy-white floor tiles were covered in a couple places with colorful rugs. A big screen TV dominated one wall with a couch and coffee table strategically placed in front. Opposite the comfortably appointed bathroom was a closet with laundry machines. Tory was seated at a small dining table to Finn's right. He didn't care for the vacant look on her face as she stared into space.

Finn tore his gaze away from her and tried to figure out where the best spot to sleep might be. There wasn't a designated bedroom, so the couch was the obvious choice, but chances were good they'd all give up that spot to Tory. Or, at least, they should. Finn had noticed a hammock on his way in. Once he got his clothes back, he'd make a beeline for that. He'd steal someone's blanket before he went.

"Tory, do you want some more food?" Axe called.

Mrs. Bertrand had gotten a smattering of all kinds of different foods. There was Chinese, Italian, sushi, and pizza. Tory didn't respond. Axe shot Finn a look. Finn shrugged and crossed his arms over his chest. Axe glared and tilted his head toward Tory. Finn glared back. Axe narrowed his eyes at Finn.

Fuck. Finn walked over and sat down at the table across from Tory. When she glanced up at him, he asked, "Do you want more food?" Which was dumb since she'd barely touched the food she had.

"No, I'm not hungry." She looked away. Her arms were across her chest, and she kept rubbing her right one like she was cold.

"Do you have a chill? I can get you a blanket." Finn felt obligated to ask. He was still royally pissed at her for her turn-on-a-dime attitude, but he was starting to think there was more to it than she was just some sort of Jekyll and Hyde who got her jollies by screwing with his brain and his heart.

She offered him a ghost of a smile. "Do you have one you can give me?"

Axe snickered again. "She got you there."

Finn turned and glared at Axe. "You should offer the lady your blanket."

Axe frowned. "Uh…do you want it?"

Tory shook her head. "No, that's fine. Thanks, Axe."

A small buzz of jealousy shot through his veins. She'd smiled at Axe. *Fucking ridiculous.* He needed to get a grip. He shifted his weight as if to rise, but Axe shot him another look.

Finn cursed silently and then turned back to Tory. "You okay?" *Dumbass question.* Of course, she wasn't okay. "Sorry, that's a stupid question."

Tory shrugged. "I'm as good as can be expected under the circumstances. My father is committing treason, and I have doubts we'll be able to stop him. But even if we do, my career is tanked. Actually, it's tanked either way. I am tainted with his brush. If we are successful and people find out, then they'll assume I was in on it. If we aren't successful, my father will crush my career as revenge, and I will be lucky if that's all he does. He's already tried to kill me once…" Her voice cracked and fizzled at the end as if it took too much energy for her to get the words out.

Finn's chest constricted. Tory was suffering, and as much as she had pissed him off, he knew she'd been through hell at her father's hands, and now she was back there again. The rage that he tried to keep dormant surged through him. It was all so unfair. He could cheerfully kill her father right now with his bare hands, and it wouldn't bother him in the slightest. And that's the part that he had a hard time with. He knew he shouldn't feel that way but, goddamn it, he hated abusers. He just couldn't see their deaths as any kind of a loss.

Finn blurted out, "We'll just have to find a way to get your father quietly so the world doesn't know and you get to keep your career." *Fuck.* He might as well have offered a seat on the next shuttle to Mars. *Fucking never gonna happen.* Why had he said it? Because seeing the pain in Tory's eyes was killing him. She might have ripped his heart out and stomped on it, but that didn't mean he'd ever quit caring about her.

Nick stood and came over to the table. "Finn is right."

Finn looked at his team leader in surprise. "I am?"

"Yes. We can't make waves because, if we do, this will all get blown up in the press. Then the rest of the world will have to publicly comment on the breach they currently pretend they don't know about. We also have secrets we really don't want everyone to know. All those phone conversations, all those emails, between the Pentagon and every country for the last couple of months. No one wants that stuff out there."

Tory nodded. "Europe knows the cables have been tapped. Don't forget that means they've been tapped, too. At least their communications to us have been picked up as well. I am sure they don't want to have their secrets get out any more than we do."

Tory's burner phone went off. "Excuse me." She got up and went into the bathroom to answer it.

Finn stared after her. "CIA," he mumbled.

Ten minutes later, Tory was back. She dropped into the same chair. "That was my contact at the CIA. Hargate has been on their radar for a while. As we suspected, he's up to his eyeballs in shady security contracts in various hot spots around the world. But of late, they've heard rumblings that he's involved in something closer to home. He's approached some people, saying that he will be in a position to be a back channel to the next President, and did they want to get in ahead of the game with any requests?"

"Well, shit, that sounds suspiciously like proof," Finn said.

Axe dismissed it. "As a law enforcement officer I can tell

you that's just circumstantial. It's not a bad start, but we have to link him to MacAllister and both of them to something tangible."

Nick's phone buzzed. "Logan Callahan's calling. Cross your fingers," he said as he stood up and went into the bathroom.

Finn continued to work the problem in his head. He needed paper or something to do with his hands. Cain walked over and handed him a paper towel. "Better than nothing," was all he said. Then he tightened his ponytail and returned to his spot on the couch.

Finn nodded his thanks and started folding. A glimmer of an idea lurked in his mind. The question was how to pull it off.

Nick came back into the room. "The Callahan's came through. MacAllister has two phones. His normal number but also a cell that is always with him. Always. That cell has been in the same vicinity as Hargate's phone numerous times in the last few months. Also, there are lots of calls going back and forth between Hargate's burner phone and the burner that's always with MacAllister."

"So, they're friends." Axe shrugged. "Again, circumstantial."

"Yes," Nick agreed. "But here's the kicker. The burner that is always with Hargate has calls to the phone that was next to you guys when you were run off the road. That phone was also by the hotel. The best part? Both Hargate's burner and MacAllister's had multiple calls going to a different number a couple of months ago. When they looked back at the data, that cell phone was located at a dock in Boston. Looking at security camera footage at the time, the *Oceanus Explorer* was in port."

Finn smiled. "Circumstantial, yes, but put it all together, and it paints a picture." He turned to Tory. "I think you have what we would call a preponderance of evidence that your father is *indeed* selling U.S. secrets. It's enough to start a full-scale investigation."

"Yeah, but who investigates?" Cain asked.

"We do," Finn said. "This just covers our ass. When they look, whoever 'they' may be, the data will show we're right. Nick, Bertrand should know we're good on proof, or at least we have enough to justify our continued involvement. He's going to frown on the use of outside sources, but we'll get around that by saying we had to use different channels due to MacAllister's connections."

"Agreed," Nick stated. "Oh, and by the way, Senator Clayton also made calls to Hargate as well. He's most likely dirty as well."

Finn felt the knots in his gut ease just a bit. It wasn't rock solid, but it was a good start. And he was hoping he had just come up with a way to get rock-solid proof. "I have an idea," he announced.

"About what?" Nick asked.

"How we get MacAllister."

Nick's eyebrows went up. "Go on, then."

"We know he's going to hold the auction here but the exchange in Turks, which is a British Overseas Territory. So, not U.S. soil. We now have enough circumstantial evidence to bring in some help from the CIA. All we have to do is have the exchange take place on the water, and then we can grab him."

"I like where you're going with this," Tory said. "But one: we need to choose our CIA contacts very carefully, and two: how do we force the exchange to take place on the water? Why can't he have one of his goons drop the hard case at the airport and have the buyer pick it up there after depositing the money?"

"Because"—Finn grinned—"the airport is going to be

shut down. Typhoid fever outbreak on the island. No one in or out for a couple of days until they get it sorted. Or Ebola or whatever. It's a British Overseas Territory. MI6 has skin in this game, too. I'm willing to bet they'll play ball. Doing it on the water is safer because there will be less collateral damage and because we can be there waiting."

Cain nodded. "I like it. Makes sense. It's more controllable. And MacAllister is outside of his influence zone."

"It has merit." Nick rubbed his knuckles over his stubbled jaw. "But how will we know where and when the exchange is taking place? That's gonna be a hard one to figure out. We're gonna need to place MacAllister and all of his people under surveillance twenty-four seven."

Finn shrugged. "We'll have to manage it, but I think it will be Hargate that will make the actual exchange. It's him we'll have to watch the closest. After everything Tory has said about MacAllister, I can't imagine him at the actual exchange. He'd want to be close but not close enough to get his hands dirty."

Tory met Finn's gaze. "He's right. Hargate will conduct the exchange but I can help with keeping an eye on my father."

A surge of adrenaline went through his system and his gut cramped. Whatever was coming was a bad idea. His early warning system was going off like a five-alarm fire. He said the next words slowly. "How do you mean?"

"I can accept my father's invitation. I can be in the house on Turks."

CHAPTER TWENTY-ONE

Tory listened quietly in her seat across from his desk while the admiral finished his call. He put down the phone and looked at her over the rim of his cut-crystal glass. "How are you really, my dear?"

The question caught her off guard. "I, um, I'm okay." *Not really.*

Finn had damn near lost it when she said she would go to the party. His anger had been palpable, but that was just too damn bad. She needed her father out of her life permanently. That could be accomplished by him going to prison for treason. And if he didn't, she'd find a way to disappear. Be gone so she never had to deal with him again. She had resources and could make that happen. But that solution could rob her of time with Finn, something she'd discovered could quite possibly be soul crushing for her. She wondered what her shrink would have to say about her overwhelming need to make sure her father paid for everything he'd done. Yeah, she needed that so much it was scary.

"You can't possibly be, but the world is expecting you to hold it together and get this done." Bertrand shook his head, sloshing the amber liquid in his glass. "This is a nasty business. Your father… I remember when you and Ashley were in school together. I knew then something was off. Your father was overbearing to say the least. I suspected he was abusive. I have always carried a certain amount of guilt over that. I should have stepped in."

Confusion made Tory a bit lightheaded. She barely remembered their daughter, and here was the admiral, admitting he knew about the abuse, or if not the abuse itself, that something was not right. She cleared her throat. Part of her wanted to scream and rage at the man. How could he abandon a fifteen-year-old kid? But the reality of the situation was different. Her chest grew heavy just thinking about it.

"Sir, if you had stepped in, if you'd asked me if anything was wrong, I would have denied it. My father, the great Senator MacAllister, would have made it his mission to grind you into dust. It wouldn't have changed anything for me, and you wouldn't be where you are today. I appreciate your thoughts and your guilt, but both are misplaced. We cannot change the past, but we are in a position to change my father's future. Help me make him lose everything that has any value to him, namely his reputation and his power." They'd always meant more to him than she had. "That's a tangible goal that is worth working towards."

Bertrand sighed. "I will do everything in my power to help you make that happen. It's a debt I owe you and to myself. You have my word."

Warmth replaced any lingering upset. She appreciated his support. It had been a long time since she'd looked at any man in authority and thought of them as worth respecting. George Bertrand had just changed all that. It meant a lot.

He set aside his drink. "Taggert filled me in. You want to

go to the party. Do you think that will ring alarm bells for your father?"

"I wish I could say no with one-hundred-percent conviction, but there is a chance. Mostly, he thinks I am pathetic enough and he's so much more intelligent that it won't occur to him that I could have uncovered his secret. As long as the team watches me and we have an emergency exit strategy, it should be okay." She hoped that would be the case, anyway. There was always a chance…

The blotter on his desk muted the sound of the admiral's knuckles rapping on the surface. "I feel certain we can provide both of those. I do worry about you though. It won't be easy, and if he suspects anything, it won't go well."

"I'm aware. It's dangerous, but letting him sell our secrets to our enemies is far more dangerous."

"Agreed. Taggert filled me in on everything. I need to make a couple of calls. The FBI is out. My contact says there are too many top-level connections to your father to seek help from them. Someone would leak what's happening. He was sure of it."

"I'm not surprised. I expected as much. I have a call into some CIA contacts. As soon as we're more concrete on things, they'll be ready to go."

"Okay." Bertrand studied her for a moment. "You are doing a very tough thing. I commend you for it."

"Thank you, sir. That means a lot." It really did. She swallowed the lump that had built in her throat. "Well then, I will head back to the pool house. We'll get things moving bright and early tomorrow morning."

Bertrand nodded. "Good night, Ms. Stanhope."

"Admiral." Tory turned and walked out of the room. She crossed the hall and went through the dining room out to the backyard. It was dark so she carefully picked her way across the lawn. She took a deep breath.

She felt reasonably confident that she could get the CIA piece sorted. She was less confident that she could pull off showing up at her father's party without raising suspicions. She couldn't just show up. That would set off major alarms. She needed to come up with a good story to convince him of her need to be there.

Tory stood for a moment and peered at the stars. It was going to cost her, but if she told him of her recent brush with death and how it was making her rethink a lot of things in her life, then maybe, just maybe, he would buy it. She'd like them to start over. He was the only family she had left.

Revulsion swam up from her stomach but she choked it back. She loathed her father, but if telling him—no, selling him—that story would get him to relax and welcome her to his birthday weekend, then it was all good. Her therapist often told her revenge wasn't worth it, and maybe she was right, but bringing down her father would make her feel infinitely better.

She breathed out a long breath. She really didn't want to go back into the pool house. It was a lot being around the whole team. What would make her feel awesome at the moment would be if she could go in and curl up in Finn's arms. She had no idea what it was about that man that made her feel so safe, but she longed for the comfort that his arms gave her.

Of course, she had shot any chance of a relationship to hell when she cut him off. She shook her head at the dismal thought that in hurting him, she'd hurt herself even worse.

Tory stared at the pool. The dark water looked inviting. Hurting him hadn't been her intent; she'd tried to save him. From her. If this went bad, anyone connected to her would suffer. As it was, the admiral could run some interference, although it was questionable how helpful that would be in the long run. His career would be over as well.

She propped one hand on her hip, and wrapped the other around her throat, trying to calm her racing thoughts. This *had* to go right. Then maybe she could talk to Finn and tell him how she really felt about him. Tory frowned. She wasn't even sure what her feelings were, but she knew she wanted to spend time with him.

Niggling doubt crept out from its hiding place in the corner of her mind. He was violent. He had a temper, or so the file said. She'd seen some mild flashes of annoyance, but nothing major. Yet. The file didn't lie. She hoped it just wasn't telling the whole truth.

"Penny for your thoughts." Finn's voice carried across the yard.

She jumped. It was as if she'd manifested him out of thin air, except where was he? Then she saw movement in the hammock that was strung up between two trees next to the pool house. She walked over and stopped beside him.

"You're sleeping out here?" she said, her voice barely above a whisper. They were supposed to be hiding out. The last thing she wanted was to bring trouble to the admiral and his wife. It had been a bold move to come here in the first place, but she understood why Nick chose it. Where else could they hide away from all the cameras that monitored D.C.?

"Yeah. Kind of crowded inside." His voice was low and sort of rumbled out of his chest. A shiver swept across her skin that had nothing to do with the cold.

"Here, take the blanket." He started to pull it off, but she shook her head and put a hand on his chest to stop him. "No, I'm good. You be warm for a while." She smiled at him through the darkness.

"Did you get everything sorted?"

Tory rubbed her arms. "Mostly. Just waiting on a call from a friend at the CIA. We'll set things up from there." She wanted to say how scared she was that she was wrong or that it was all going to blow up in their faces. She would be responsible for killing so many careers.

"You're not wrong." His voice floated up to her. "Your father is behind this."

How had he known what she was thinking? Sometimes she was sure he could read her mind. "I wish I could be as positive. I know it in my bones, but having solid proof would be better. So much of our evidence is circumstantial. It's a tremendous risk for everyone to take on a few phone calls and my gut instinct."

"It's a bigger risk not to check it out. If we're wrong, then we're wrong, but we have a duty to check it out. And we're not wrong. Your father is selling secrets so he can get ahead." The hammock swayed slightly in the breeze. "I won't ask how you're doing. I imagine you're numb right now. But when you slay your dragon, it won't feel like you think."

"What?" What was Finn talking about?

"Tory," he said in his rumbling voice, "when you take your father down, it won't feel like a…victory. It will make you feel hollow. It takes a long while before it finally sinks in that the monster is gone."

"Your father?" she asked gently. It was hard to see his face in the dark, but she was sure there was a look of pain in his eyes.

"He beat me and my mother. She died of a heart attack when I was in my teens, but he hung on for another handful of years before he died. He had cancer, and it ate him up from the inside out. I thought I would feel relief, even joy, when he died, but I just felt…hollow. It wasn't until years later that I realized I was still holding my breath, waiting for him to walk in the door and hit me. It takes a while to let go. Just be prepared."

Tory wished she could see Finn's face. "Thanks for the

warning, but I've done my therapy over what he did to me and my mother. He is already dead to me." As she said it, she knew it wasn't true, but somehow, she couldn't admit to Finn that she still had days where she felt like a victim.

Finn made a sound low in his throat but said nothing.

She stared at him through the darkness. This was the man that had saved her life, but more than that, had held her close when she needed it most. Yet she still had to ask, "Finn, what happened with your old commanding officer? I read the report…"

The hammock stilled. She felt rather than saw a change come over Finn. "What does it say happened?" The rumble had turned cool.

"That you beat him half to death and he was forced to retire early because of his injuries. They were all set to court-martial you, but you got shot during the raid on that cartel-owned yacht so they stopped the proceedings and then the admiral scooped you up and added you to his team."

"What do you think happened?" His voice was flat.

She shivered. "I don't know, Finn. It sounds…scary. You almost beat a man to death."

"Scary." He made a disgusted sound deep in his throat. "I'll tell you what's scary. Chief Warrant Officer Bilkins came home drunk out of his mind and beat the shit out of his significantly younger wife who was holding their newborn baby. She and the baby ended up in the hospital, but Bilkins got away with it because his father is high up in the Navy. Strings were pulled. Sadie and baby Grace were released, and he did the same thing two weeks later. Sadie damn near died. I know because her grandmother told me. She happens to live in the same nursing home as my grandmother. So, after a training exercise, where Bilkins was being a belligerent asshole, I challenged him. He swung on me, but I swung back." Finn's words were dipped with ice.

"Why didn't they charge you?" She doubted getting shot would be enough to stop a court-martial.

"Because they knew if they took it to court, it would open them up to a lawsuit and a lot of negative publicity. You see, Sadie had gone to Bilkins' commanding officer and to the family support people, but everyone swept it under the rug. Orders from on high. All that would come out in court. The fact that he swung at me with a tire iron didn't help his case. When the investigation was through, it was deemed to be unnecessary to proceed due to my injury. They thought I was going to leave anyway. Bertrand tapped me for his team, and the rest is history."

"I see. Well I'm glad to know that—"

"That I'm not some deranged violent abuser? Did you really think I was? Deep down, Tory, did you really think I would hurt you? Have you ever been afraid of me?"

"I…" She hesitated. Had she ever been afraid of him? No. Not once. "Finn, I—"

"Forget it." He turned his head slightly and closed his eyes.

The apology died on her lips. To say she'd always believed in him, but that wasn't strictly true. She'd always *wanted* to believe in him, and she'd trusted him with her life, but she'd still had to ask.

Damn. The fact that her heart plummeted to her belly was a sure sign she'd blown it again. She had zero chances left with Finn Walsh, and that was tragic because she just realized she was in love with him.

CHAPTER TWENTY-TWO

Finn woke with a start. Pain screamed through his shoulder, and he was fucking cold. He was also getting wet. Big, fat raindrops were hitting him through the trees. *Great.* He'd thought sleeping in the hammock would be preferable to sleeping on the floor. Maybe he was wrong. On the other hand, after what Tory said, he was glad he didn't have to be in the same room as her.

He shifted his weight and rolled out of the hammock. He stood and stretched, moving his right arm to get the muscles to loosen a bit. His navy sweater clung damply to his chest. He smoothed down his dark hair and then glanced at his watch. It was later than he thought.

"Walsh."

He turned and saw the admiral waving him over to where he stood on the patio. Finn glanced around then moved quickly across the yard. It was fenced, and there were trees, so it would be hard to see in, but he didn't want to take any chances. The last thing he wanted to do was bring trouble to the door of the man who'd saved his career. Keeping his head ducked, he scooted under the tree canopy.

Finn stepped onto the patio and stood at attention in front of Bertrand. "Sir."

"At ease," Bertrand said before taking a sip of coffee.

Finn relaxed his stance and clasped his hands behind his hips. He had no idea what was coming, but he hoped it wasn't bad news. He'd only had a one-on-one with the admiral once, and that was when he was being told he was reassigned to the admiral's new team.

"Walsh, your suggestion of how to make this take-down happen is nothing short of brilliant. It's politically savvy and it keeps us in the game. It's also very risky. Not just to you and your teammates, but to me and my career."

Finn wasn't sure how he was supposed to respond. Admirals didn't speak to chief petty officers, and they certainly didn't have any kind of a casual relationship with them. Staying silent seemed like his best bet so he kept his mouth shut.

"I'd heard a lot about you before I brought you on to the team. Your senior officers all sang your praises. They said you were a smart out-of-the-box thinker who could get the job done. Even Bilkins before…the incident thought you were stellar."

Again, silence seemed like the best call. Finn wasn't sure where this was going.

Bertrand sighed. "The fact that you risked all of that and more to right a perceived wrong carried out by your superior officer was stupid beyond measure. You could have been put in prison for a good long while."

Finn ground his teeth. He knew it was stupid. He had known it at the time, but he just couldn't stop himself. Once Bilkins swung that tire iron toward him it was game on. He just happened to be a better fighter than Bilkins.

"It was also…understandable. You saw an ugly wrong, and you fixed it. Not many men would sacrifice their careers to help save a total stranger. Your strong moral compass is commendable. Most of us would have likely made a different decision in a similar circumstance and come to regret not helping.

"I believe we have a similar type of situation here. Ms. Stanhope's relationship with her father is obviously…not good. But if you remotely step out of line on this operation to protect the damsel in distress, I will have you up for court-martial so fast your head will spin. Do you understand?"

"Yes, sir." He tried not to show the shock he was feeling. He always thought of Bertrand as being hands off, but obviously he was aware enough to know that Finn would be the one who would want to put the senator "in his place," as his grandmother would say. What else did the admiral know? It didn't bear thinking about.

"In this case, you must think of your career first. You must control yourself."

"Understood, sir."

"That's all." The admiral took another sip of his coffee, then pointed toward the sliding glass doors. "I believe Mrs. Bertrand has some sort of breakfast organized. Help her with it."

"Yes, sir." Finn saluted and hurried inside.

Two hours later, after eating a solid breakfast of pancakes, eggs, and home fries, then grabbing a quick shower, the team was ready to move.

"Tory," Finn said deliberately keeping his voice cool and professional, "we're going to need a copy of the blueprints of the house. Do you know where we can get them?"

She shook her head. "They won't do you any good anyway. My father changed a lot of things in the house. I can walk you through the layout, though, for both the main house and the guest house."

"There's a guest house?" Axe perked up. "I'd love some

time in the sun. Think your Pops would mind one more visitor?"

Tory cracked up. "Pops." She laughed so hard tears sprung up in her eyes. "The day my father goes by Pops, hell will have well and truly frozen over." She wiped her eyes with the back of her hand. "Thanks, Axe. I needed a good laugh."

Finn tried not to scowl. Axe was making her laugh and smile. That should have been Finn's job. Stupid. She didn't want him. Didn't trust him. He needed to get over her.

"Okay, you can sit down with Axe and go over all of it. Include staffing details and anything else you think might be relevant." He tried not to growl but his voice sounded funny to his own ears.

"Will do."

Finn fisted his hands. He was in desperate need of some origami therapy. No, he needed to get out of this place, away from Tory. The cost of being around her constantly and not being able to be *with* her was more torturous than recovering from the gunshot wound.

He took a deep breath and tried to clear his head. "We need to figure out what he's going to want for security too. He's not going out there without Hargate and at least one team. They have to bring the hard case with the server in it. MacAllister is not stupid. We should see if we can watch the airplane, so we do know who's on it. I assume they're taking a private jet."

"Yes, my father will use a private jet to go down, but I don't think Hargate will be on the same one. My father won't be on the same plane with Hargate and the hard case. He doesn't want to get that close to it just in case it all goes wrong. He will want plausible deniability."

A sudden thought came into Finn's head. "How do we know whoever buys the information won't turn around and sell it again?"

"We don't," Tory stated flatly. "I've been thinking about it though and I think it's most likely going to be either China or Russia. Those governments have the most to gain. They're not going to share that knowledge with more people because that would make them less powerful. The other thing I am willing to bet is that my father had the data vetted. Some stuff that would have been recorded would not help *him* if it got out. I'm quite sure the information on the drive will be tailored to a certain degree."

Finn cocked his head. "You think he wouldn't, for example, let the nuclear launch codes go but he might let emails through that incriminate anyone that might run against him."

"Precisely. Any information getting out is bad for us, but my father is nothing if not pragmatic. There's no point in running a country that is powerless. He won't do anything that would hurt his cause."

"Do we know when your father is flying down?" Elias asked. "I was just checking the weather. Looks like a bad storm is heading for Turks. Not quite a hurricane, but flights will be delayed or canceled for sure. It's set to happen Friday night. Will he go down if that's going to happen? Maybe he'll just send Hargate."

Finn glanced at Tory. Her eyes were a bit wild looking and her chest was rising and falling at a rapid rate. *Fuck.* She was panicking. Her father had to go. She needed this over with now. He knew the courage it was taking her to face the man who'd abused her all her life. It didn't matter how long ago it was, or how much therapy she'd had, this was a momentous thing she was doing, and it was not easy. It took guts and backbone. Even if she didn't trust him, he didn't want to see her lose this chance. It would make all the difference in her life.

"Do we know what MacAllister's schedule is?" Finn

figured getting her focused on details instead of what-ifs would ground her a little.

"The birthday party here in D.C. is Thursday night. I'm assuming he's heading down after that."

"Can we find out when he's scheduled to fly down to Turks? That would give us a window to start setting up our surveillance. It's Tuesday. We need to go down tomorrow at the latest, but if we had his schedule, it might help."

Tory cleared her throat. "I see what you mean. I'll call his office. It's about time I called anyway if I'm going to go with him." She picked up her burner phone and dialed the number.

"Hi, Gale. It's Tory. Is my father in?" There was a pause. "Right, the party. I don't know what I was thinking." Another pause. "Actually, Gale, do you know what his schedule looks like this week? I thought maybe I'd take him out to lunch to celebrate his birthday. We haven't been close of late and…I'd like to change that."

Tory gripped the phone so hard her knuckles were white. Finn's heart thumped in solidarity for her pain. This was a hard phone call for her to make, and things were only going to get worse.

"He's going to Turks on Friday? You mean Friday night? A storm? Oh, so he's leaving early on Friday. I had no idea. Okay, well maybe I'll call him at home. Thanks, Gale." Tory hung up. "He's going down early Friday afternoon."

"So, we need to get down there pronto." Nick picked up his cell. "I'm going to call Bertrand. We're going to leave here as soon as possible."

Tory sat down on a kitchen chair. She rubbed her face with both hands. "I'm worried."

Finn met her gaze. "About what?"

Nick held his phone away from his ear. "Are you having doubts?"

"No, it's not that. I'm worried he's going to wiggle out of it somehow. He's so smooth, so charismatic. I don't want him to get away."

"He's not going to wiggle out of it. We know it's him. We're going to get him." Finn sounded more confident than he felt. He and Nick exchanged a look. They were both thinking the same thing. They were screwed if the senator managed to get away with it. It was a bit iffy. Finn said to the group, "Hargate is the key."

Nick put down the phone. "Bertrand's going to call me back. What do you mean Hargate is the key?"

To give himself time to organize his thoughts, Finn stood up and went over to the fridge. He got himself a bottle of water and offered one to everyone else. No takers. "Hargate. Look at his file. Does he strike you as a standup guy? We get Hargate cold so he has no fallback, and we have your father. I can guarantee he has some piece of insurance to prove your father's involvement. Tory, you wanted us on this initially because you wanted us to think like the bad guys. They are trained like us, with similar experiences. They just chose a different path.

"I'm telling you now, if I were in Hargate's shoes, I would have insurance that proved the senator is part of the plot. There is no way I would be out there on my own with that server, doing an exchange with whoever, and not have my ass covered in case it all goes to shit."

Cain whistled. "Finn is right. Hargate is the key. If he's faced with life in prison with no chance of ever getting out, then he'll sing like a bird to make sure he gets to see the sun again. He's no martyr for the cause. He's about money and power."

Tory studied Finn and then nodded slowly. "You're right. He will be the key to proving my father is involved. We need to find him."

"No." Finn shook his head. "We need to be down in Turks so we can see him when he arrives."

"That makes sense. It also makes sense if I am at the house, too."

"No." Finn shook his head again. "That's way too dangerous. That man tried to have you killed."

"True, but he didn't succeed. If I go there by myself, then we can have eyes and ears inside the house. That's better than watching from a distance."

"She's got a point," Cain said.

Panic rose in Finn's chest, but he crushed it down. "How do we know they won't kill her right away?" Finn demanded.

Tory frowned. "Because he's going to want to know what I know first. Like I said, my father won't think I'm smart enough to be on to him. It's better if I'm on the inside. I'll call him and arrange to go down on Saturday."

"But—" Finn started to protest.

"It's the smart move," Nick said. He pinned Finn with a hard look.

The idea of Tory in that place unprotected was terrifying. There had to be a better way. Just the thought of it made every nerve in his body scream. He bit back the rage that wanted to pour out of him. Instead, he said, "When do we leave?"

CHAPTER TWENTY-THREE

"Tory, darling, come say hello to some friends." Her father gave her a large, slightly sinister grin.

Bile rose in her throat, but she painted a false smile on her face and stepped out onto the patio. He put his arm around her waist, and she had to bite the inside of her cheek to keep from screaming. She'd been in Turks for less than three hours, and already her skin was crawling. She wasn't sure she could do this.

Her father smiled his politician's smile. All white teeth against a tan. It was only spring, so how he was tanned already was a mystery, but she had to admit it looked good on him. His dark hair had just the right amount of silver shot through it to be debonaire. His classic good looks and gray eyes made women of all ages swoon. Of course, being a Harvard graduate, and coming from a long line of blue blood stock didn't hurt either. The MacAllisters were an old money family and very well-connected. She suspected they were also a long line of abusers as well.

Tory had gotten her coloring and looks from her mother. Only her eye color came from the beast standing next to her.

It was a small thing, but it made her feel better to know that he hated that she didn't look more like him.

"Tory, darling," a voice said from over her shoulder.

She turned as a well-dressed woman approached. The woman's dyed blond hair was swept back from her perfectly made-up face. She was wearing chunky gold earrings and a matching necklace over a green Lilly Pulitzer dress and matching heels. The green made her eyes pop more than usual. "Minerva, how nice to see you."

Her father's girlfriend of many years gave her air kisses on each cheek. "I'm so glad you could make it this year. Your father said you're having a bit of a tough time at work. Fresh air and sunshine are just what the doctor ordered."

"Yes. Turks has always been one of my favorite places. I was just lucky I could get away this year."

Minerva took her around and introduced her to the rest of the guests. There were two other senators and their spouses, one of whom was Senator Clayton. He had brought his wife, Jennifer. There was also Chris Horner and his wife, Judy. He was a junior Congressman from somewhere in the middle of the country. Rumor was he was an up-and-comer for the senate. She was not surprised to see him at her father's party. Not in the least.

Tory made small talk with various people and tried to relax. Extra security around the place made that an almost impossible dream, but she knew better than to comment on it. Her dad wouldn't appreciate her drawing attention to something most of his guests might take for granted. She was walking on eggshells, and she hated it.

"A runaway digger is what I heard," Chris said. "It went across the runway, dragging the bucket, and broke up all the asphalt. Apparently, the repairs will take a couple of days, or possibly longer. Something to do with the drainage system the city is installing next to the airport. Anyway, we're stuck here for a while longer than planned." He smiled. "Nice to be stuck in paradise, although it does point out the issue with only having one main runway."

Tory smiled at him. "Yes, it's an unexpected perk."

Her father walked over and slid his arm around her waist. "Pardon me, Chris. I want to chat with my beautiful daughter for a moment."

Her father kept his arm solidly around her as they walked back into the house. She pasted a serene look on her face but inwardly seethed. She could do this, just be patient. This would all be over soon. He walked her right into his office and closed the door.

"You look uptight, Victory. Not a good look, I'd say. People don't want to see you looking so tense." His words were as staccato as the beat of his heels on the terrazzo floor as he crossed to the bar. The back wall was all glass and looked out over the turquoise water.

"Sorry, Father—" She brought herself up short. It was amazing how quickly she fell right back into the patterns from long ago. She glanced up and saw the gleam in her father's eye. He knew it, the bastard. He was enjoying the hell out of this.

He came across the room and offered her a glass of Scotch. She took it but didn't drink any. She hated the spirit mostly because it was what he drank. She crossed the room and sat down on one of the chairs across from his desk. He'd been heading to the sofa in front of the windows, but she refused to sit anywhere he could sit directly next to her.

"Work is a bit difficult at the moment, as I said." She turned to face him so that the tiny camera hidden in the brooch she was wearing could record everything going on. The camera had been a gamble, but one she was willing to take. She was sure he didn't suspect her of being on to him.

She sighed. "It's this investigation. We keep hitting brick wall after brick wall. I've never been so frustrated."

"If you want to tell me about it, perhaps I can help." Her father's tone became soothing. She knew he was just waiting to pounce.

"There's nothing to tell. We're not getting anywhere." She glanced up at him again as he went behind his desk and sat down. The desk was done in mahogany, and the setting sun created an annoying glare on the surface.

"Come now, I'm sure you've made some progress," he cajoled.

The bastard wanted details. "Not so you'd notice. We just can't get a grip on the thing. Not one loose thread to pull." She shrugged. "Something will come. If we wait long enough, dig deep enough, something will turn up. I'm just finding it hard to be patient."

"You always were an impatient child. It's one of your least charming qualities." He took a sip of Scotch. "I appreciate you coming for my birthday, but you need to get back. It won't look good, you taking time off when you're working on something this important. You don't want to sabotage your career, do you? You already did that once at the CIA. If you'd listened to me in the first place, you never would have been in Afghanistan. Stupid of you."

Tory kept her face neutral and her hands relaxed around the glass even though she wanted to throw it at his head. "Well, I'm listening now. I came down to get career advice. I feel like I might be topping out at DHS. The old boys club at the top do not seem keen to let me in."

"Ah, I see the truth comes out." The gleam in his eye was back. "I knew there was a reason you came. You never come to my birthday weekend. I should have known you would want something from me." He sighed and put his drink down on his desk with a thunk. He played like he was annoyed, but the gleam in his eyes told her he was loving it.

Of course he was. She was groveling, and he loved it when people groveled at his feet. "I just want your advice, Father." She tried very hard not to sound annoyed. In reality, she'd stopped listening to his advice as soon as she graduated from college and joined the CIA.

"After all these years, you want my advice. Other children would have loved to have me as their father, used my name to establish themselves. But not you. You thought you were better than that. You had to do it on your own. The CIA. Stupid. You should have gone to law school and then started up on the Hill. You could have been a junior congresswoman by now. Such a waste."

She'd heard this speech a million times over the years. It took everything she had not to tell him to fuck off and simply get up and walk out. It would drive him over the edge. He'd lose his shit and start throwing things if she did that. It would almost be worth it. Almost.

She was here because she had a job to do. They knew Hargate was on the Providenciales, the third largest island of the Turks and Caicos archipelago. Finn and Elias had clocked his arrival by private jet yesterday just before the storm. He had the hard case with him. They said that he was in the guest house, but she hadn't seen him yet. Just his goons walking around.

"Well, Father, I understand if you don't wish to give me any advice. I was planning on flying back tomorrow, but the whole mess with the runway means I'll have to extend my stay. Sorry, but you're stuck with me for a few more days."

"Yes, that screwup at the airport. It has made things difficult. Plans had to be changed." He was looking out the window as he took a sip of his drink.

"I'm sorry it ruined your plans."

He looked sharply at her as if trying to see if she meant anything by the comment, but she kept her face placid as she'd learned to do all those years ago.

"It's fine." He waved his hand as if to dismiss her comment.

She stood.

"I thought you wanted my advice?"

There was a sound behind her. Tory turned to see her father's righthand man, Louis, coming up behind her. *Great.* He was not her favorite person.

Louis, who looked like someone had shoehorned him into his summer suit, smiled an oily smile that didn't make it to his beady brown eyes. "Tory! How lovely to see you." He leaned in for a kiss, and she stuck out her hand. "Oh," he said as he grasped it in both of his.

Her father snickered behind her.

She offered a faint smile. "Louis. I didn't realize you were here."

"Yes, working hard. Your father has so much going on."

"Lovely," she said. "I will leave you both to it." She handed Louis her untouched drink and walked out of the office, straight down the hall to the bathroom.

Once inside, she locked the door and leaned against it. She wanted to scream and cry and throw up all at the same time. This was harder than she thought it would be. "Okay, Tory," she said out loud and then remembered the guys could hear her. She couldn't hear them, but they could see and hear everything she did. She sure as hell wasn't using the bathroom now. Instead, she splashed some water on her face and adjusted her clothing. She could do this.

Tory left the bathroom determined to stay away from her father for the rest of the evening. There were plenty of other guests. She didn't think it would be too hard. The plan was for her to eat dinner and then say she had a headache. She would go to her room and see if the team had sent anything new. She was hoping they had an idea about the exchange because she sure as hell didn't.

Two hours later, she was coming down the hall after having changed for dinner. She was wearing a dark purple sun dress that made her gray eyes shine. She had added diamond stud earrings and gray pumps to complete the dress. She pulled out a different brooch camera. This one was a blue flower. Hopefully, someone would say something helpful.

She was lost in thought and didn't notice until too late that her father had come up next to her. She'd forgotten he liked to stalk her. He loved popping out of nowhere and scaring her. Of course, he yelled at her if she startled or jumped or made a sound.

"Father, you look nice this evening." He was wearing a white button-down with the sleeves rolled up and a pair of summer-weight light-gray pinstripe pants. It was his casual at home look.

"Thank you." He turned to her. "You look…passable." He touched her hair, which she'd fastened in a knot at the nape of her neck.

They rounded the corner into the dining room where the other guests were assembled. She didn't say anything to her father but tried to put some distance between them as he greeted the guests. No such luck. He held her hand on his elbow so there was no escape. Her heart plummeted to her feet. This was a mistake. She couldn't do this. She wanted to run from the dining room screaming. She wanted Finn to hold her and tell her everything was going to be okay. She wanted to be anywhere but here with this man.

"Tory," Minerva said, "why don't you sit next to Mr. Childers? He's with transportation. I'm sure you two have lots in common."

Tony Childers was pushing eighty if he was a day. He was a large donor to her father's campaigns, and he was also the biggest letch around. Tory smiled at Minerva and moved forward to the other end of the table where Childers sat.

When Minerva had first shown up in her father's life, Tory thought maybe, just maybe, she'd found an ally, but it soon became apparent that Minerva resented her. To this day, even though she was mostly absent from her father's life, Minerva viewed her as a threat.

Tory said hello to Childers and Chris, the man from earlier. Then she swung around and took the last seat on the left side of the table next to Salome Jones, a federal judge. Salome was bucking for the supreme court, and she made no secret of it. Tory respected that. She might not agree with some of Salome's more conservative leanings, but the woman was intelligent and articulate and always fun at dinner.

"That was a fine escape, young lady." Salome winked at her.

"I didn't want to spend the next two hours pushing his hand off my knee. You would think in this day and age we wouldn't have to deal with crap like that."

Salome laughed. "Oh, sugar, it's never going away. Don't kid yourself."

"Well, that's a happy thought." Tory used sarcasm to cover the disappointment stabbing her.

Salome laughed again. She was an attractive woman with short black hair clipped to frame her face. Her deep brown eyes and warm smile often hid the fact that she was tough as nails, and everyone knew it. Her husband, Noah, had died unexpectedly a few years ago, and Salome had poured all her grief into her work. An amazing woman and role model to be sure. Tory had always admired and looked up to her. It was nice to find a friendly face at the table.

Someone sat at the foot of the table, and Tory turned to see Hargate sitting next to her.

She blinked. "Josh?"

The surprise in her voice was genuine. She hadn't expected Hargate to be at dinner. It seemed out of character for her father to invite the help to sit at his dinner table. She turned and glanced in her father's direction. Thunder clouds were across his face. *Interesting.* He wasn't expecting Hargate for dinner either.

"Josh," Minerva cooed. "I'm so glad you could join us. I know you're always on the clock, but you do have to eat."

Hargate smiled and flashed his dimples at Minerva. "You were so kind to invite me." He immediately turned to Tory. "I didn't expect to see you here."

"Likewise," was all she said.

Hargate's attention was immediately captured by Chris on his right. They got into a conversation about the war in Ukraine.

The salad course was served, and Tory studied Hargate under her lashes. How had she ever fallen for those boyish looks? His dark blond hair was cropped close, and he was also sporting a tan. His blue eyes were pale and not remotely as captivating as Finn's. He was shorter than Finn, too. Not as well built. *Great.* Now she was comparing the two. Was she going to end up comparing every man she met to Finn?

Tory managed to make it through dinner without screaming her frustration. As the guests made their way outside for nightcaps by the pool, she made her excuses. Walking back to her room, she made sure her father wasn't lurking this time. She entered the bedroom and leaned on the closed door. The night had taken more out of her than she'd anticipated.

She glanced around the room. It was beautifully decorated in creams and greens. The king-size bed with its colorful duvet added just the right pop of color to offset the cream walls and tile floor. A balcony overlooked the garden, and down the hill was the guest cottage. Her room was at the back of the house, of course. The guests got the best views. She was just family.

Tory sighed and took off her brooch, leaving it on the dresser. Did it turn off or just keep going until the battery ran out? She'd forgotten to ask. She had three of them and kept them in a little box on her dresser.

She switched off the overhead light but the light from the bathroom was enough to see where she was going. After pouring a glass of water she walked onto the balcony and dropped onto a comfy chair. For a while she was motionless, letting the cool night air settle around her. She knew she should be on the other side of the house, drinking coffee or a nightcap with the other guests, pumping them for any information she could get, but she just didn't have it in her. Being around her father was so much tougher than she had anticipated. This tiny reprieve couldn't be called a setback. Or even dereliction of duty. Allowing herself a half hour in her room would make going back to mingle easier. She knew from past experience the guests would be drinking and chatting for hours yet.

She sat in the chair for a while and just let her body relax. She needed a real vacation after this. She did love Turks and Caicos. Maybe she'd come back and stay on the other side of the island in one of the big hotels.

"I know what you're saying, but I still have questions." Senator Clayton's voice floated up to her. She glanced over the railing. Three figures strolled toward the guesthouse. Other than Clayton, she couldn't make out who they were. Wait! Her father was there too but it was too dark, and their voices were too low now that they were farther away from her to figure out who the third person was.

She stared after them and made a decision. She got up, grabbed her brooch, put it on, and eased out of her room. The stairwell was on her right and she hurried down, then headed out the side door. Tory stuck to the shadows, making her way across the lawn toward the guesthouse. She moved around to the far side so she was hidden from view of the main house. It was also where the living area was located, so with any luck maybe she could get a peek at what was going on.

She moved silently to the window. The shade was down, but it was open just a crack as though someone hadn't shut it properly.

Her father's voice reached her ears. "I know you have concerns, Wilber, but we are moving forward as planned. The auction has already taken place. We can't go back on our word now. That would be catastrophic."

"But North Korea? I really don't like the idea of giving them this type of information," Senator Clayton whined.

"I agree, it's not ideal. It was…shortsighted of me not to realize they would be in the running." Her father never admitted mistakes, so this was huge. He continued, "However, I do think we can turn it to our advantage. You know North Korea is going to share with China. I think we can work with the Chinese president to utilize the information to his advantage within his country and get his help on some trade issues in ours. Don't worry, Wilber. It will be a win for us."

Someone else spoke, but she couldn't make out the words. The person must have been on the other side of the room. Then, they all seemed to have moved because the voices faded.

Not wanting to be caught out there, she made her way back around to the front corner. No one was around so she slipped into the shadows of the palm trees and made her way back toward the house. She was almost there when a hand reached out and grabbed her arm. She whirled and started to slam her fist into her attacker only to have it caught.

"Don't you remember? I taught you that move," Hargate's voice whispered in her ear.

He hadn't taught her anything. She'd learned it all in the CIA, but she'd let him take credit when they were dating. "Is there a reason you needed to scare me?"

He let out a soft laugh. "It was always fun sneaking up on you."

"A riot of laughs."

"I saw you," Hargate said in a soft, menacing voice.

She froze. *Shit.* Had he seen her listening at the window? She knew her father had more security around, but had he installed more cameras, too? She cursed herself silently for her stupidity. She might have just blown the whole thing. "What do you mean?"

"There's no need to play coy. I know you were over at the guesthouse. You came looking for me. And here's me gone looking for you."

She immediately relaxed. The asshole thought she wanted a booty call. *Fucking idiot.* "I was just out for a walk," she said lamely.

He pulled her close, crushing her against his chest. "A walk. You're an adult. You can admit the truth. You came to find me to get your fix." He let go of her arm and wrapped both of his around her. He tried to kiss her, but she immediately tromped on his foot with her heel and wrenched free.

"I went for a walk," she snarled. There were voices behind her. She whirled to see who it was, but the group went the opposite way.

"I see," Hargate said. "Still afraid of Daddy. Well, don't worry. After tomorrow night, we can get off this island. I have a boat, and we can spend some real time together. Far away from your father." He swooped down and kissed her hard before taking off along the tree line.

Tory wiped her mouth with the back of her hand. She wanted to hurl. The thought of Hargate touching her again was enough to make her lose her dinner. She scurried back in the side door and up to her room.

That had been stupid and risky. She shouldn't have done it, but at least now she knew the auction was done and her father, along with Clayton and two others, were selling secrets to North Korea. She picked up her cell phone and typed out a text, holding it in front of the brooch.

Auction happened already as we thought. North Korea was the highest bidder. Exchange is tomorrow night.

She deleted the unsent text and put her phone back. She took off the brooch and put it in the box. She kind of hoped Finn hadn't been watching that last exchange. She didn't want him to get the wrong idea.

Who was she kidding? He'd made himself perfectly clear. They were through. Still, she could hope, couldn't she? She needed some ray of sunshine to cling to. Her father was selling state secrets to one of their country's biggest enemies.

How the hell was she supposed to deal with that?

CHAPTER TWENTY-FOUR

Finn couldn't sleep. That whole scene between Tory and her father, and Tory and Hargate, played on an infinite loop in his mind. She'd been stupid to go out there on her own. His heart had been in his mouth the entire time she was sneaking around the guesthouse. When Hargate assaulted her, Finn had almost lost it. There weren't enough origami animals in the world to squelch that rage. He'd had to leave the control room once Tory was back safely in hers.

This whole thing was killing him. She was suffering. There had to be a better way. That's what his heart thought. Logically, he knew Tory being at her father's was the best possible chance they had for getting information. And it had worked. They knew about the auction and North Korea, but at what cost to Tory?

To him?

It wasn't just Josh Fucking Hargate. Watching her be insulted and berated by her father, his entire body had screamed at him to do something. Anything. Her father was even more of a nightmare than Finn had imagined. It must have been so hard for her to sit through that conversation with the arrogant bastard. After the man had belittled Tory, Finn envisioned folding the bastard like an origami animal and then crushing him under his boot.

The prick's language and tone hadn't come across as offensive. But knowing what he knew from Tory, the man was being a manipulative son of a bitch, giving it his all to undermine her confidence. Finn had bit his lip hard enough to draw blood while listening to that conversation.

He had forced himself to stay for the whole thing, but once it was over and she was out of there, he had to release his energy. He'd taken a long swim off the yacht they were on. Even the pain in his shoulder with each overhead crawl stroke hadn't distracted him. When he'd come back on board, he'd made a whole fucking zoo of origami animals and he still wanted to punch someone.

"If you're going to think that loudly and be pissed off, go out on deck. I need sleep," Axe grumbled from the bunk above his.

Shit. "Sorry, man."

"You gotta let it go. There's not a damn thing you can do right now."

Finn froze. "What are you talking about?"

"Tory. You can't do anything to help her at the moment. We all just have to do our jobs, and it will all fall into place."

Finn didn't know how to respond. Did they all know about him and Tory? "I… How…?"

"It's freaking obvious, man. The way you two look at each other. She only really responds to you when she's upset. And you get pissed off with her at the slightest thing. Dude, you need to chill. Everyone knows. If anyone even talks to her, you get all tense. You got it bad. Take it from someone who knows."

Finn was shocked. "I didn't realize it was that obvious."

Axe snorted. "You're an idiot." He yawned. "And you're keeping me up."

"Sorry." Finn apologized again. Maybe Axe was right. Maybe being on deck would help.

"I know how much it sucks that Tory is in there with those people who could hurt her, and you're stuck out here with us. I really do understand. It's the hardest thing in the world. The best you can do is get some sleep so when it comes time, you're on your A-game and you can help Tory."

Finn didn't say anything, but he did appreciate Axe's words. Axe did know what he was going through. His girlfriend, Sloan, had been in trouble not long ago. It had almost killed Axe not to be able to get to her immediately. He had seen it in the other man's eyes. Is that what his eyes looked like? Haunted?

Finn threw an arm over his face and tried to relax. Axe was right. He needed to rest so he could be on top of his game. There was no way he was going to let anything happen to Tory. He wouldn't forgive himself if she didn't come out of this unscathed.

The sun hit Finn full in the face as he surfaced. He'd been diving again. The swimming was helping him with his arm and his anger. Tory's morning seemed quiet from what they'd seen on camera. She was supposed to spend the afternoon shopping with Salome, so he'd thought it was a good time for him to take a break. The guys were being good about it. No one was pushing. He appreciated it more than he could say.

He got out of the water and went below to have a shower. Twenty minutes later, he entered the galley and started making lunch. They'd gotten conch from some local fisherman earlier in the day, so he was making conch chowder with biscuits and a salad. He'd learned to cook because he didn't want to starve, but over time, he realized he enjoyed it. It relaxed him so he took an interest. And today he needed all the help he could get with relaxing. He'd managed a few hours of sleep last night, but not much. He was too tied in knots about Tory and her father and Hargate.

"Something smells good," Axe said with a grin. "How long 'til lunch?"

"About five minutes. Tell Nick." Finn put the finishing touches on the salad and started taking up the chowder. He put three bowls on the table.

Finn pulled the biscuits out of the small oven and put them on a plate and then set them on the table. He added butter to the table as well as bottles of water. Axe and Nick entered and sat on the left side of the table. Finn perched on a chair across from them.

"This is good, Finn. You need to cook more often," Axe proclaimed as he dug into the chowder. "Cain and Elias are really missing out."

Finn laughed. "You just don't want to make dinner."

Axe grinned. "That may or may not be true, but this is still good."

They ate in silence for the next few minutes until the spoons started scraping the bottom of the bowls.

"Anyone want seconds?" Finn asked.

Axe and Nick both took some more. Nick cleared his throat and took a swig of water. "Bertrand called while you were swimming, Finn. Nothing so far on anyone suspicious arriving in Turks before the airport closed. He's working with a friend at the FBI to find out from other nearby islands but, honestly, it's a needle in a haystack. They are probably traveling on fake passports, so I don't think we're going to find them. At least not that way."

"Any clue on where the meeting is tonight?" Finn asked. "We still think it's on the water, right?"

Nick shrugged. "We have no clarification on that yet but with no jets allowed in, there is no other way onto the island, or off. Chances are excellent they'll do the exchange on the water because it makes the most sense. Fewer prying eyes to watch the exchange happen and a lot less law enforcement around. It's the smart play.

"Elias and Cain reported in that Hargate hasn't left the guest house all day. The cook is even bringing over food. He just comes out to the balcony occasionally and then goes back inside. But the yacht was brought around so it's in front of the house. It looks like we're right about the water exchange and that it's supposed to happen tonight."

Senator MacAllister's house was on a bluff, facing the ocean. It was a huge place done in a pale pink with white accents. It was surrounded by gardens in the back and had a pool on the ocean side. There was a deep-water anchorage right out front where the MacAllister yacht was now waiting.

The timer went off on the oven. Axe looked at Finn. "Did you make dessert?"

Finn shook his head. "There's some Oreos if you're looking for something sweet." He got up from the table and went over to the oven. He turned off the timer and pulled on oven mitts. He opened the door and pulled out a large pan of lasagna. "I made dinner while I was making lunch." He placed the lasagna on top of the stove to cool.

Axe grinned. "Yes!"

"Don't get too excited. You're on clean-up duty since I did your chore."

"No worries, Finn. I'm on it." He got up from the table and started sorting the dishes.

Nick also got up and started down the stairs.

Finn called after him, "I'll bring coffee." He poured two

mugs and went down below. He walked down the hallway until he came to the end room. It was usually used as a bedroom, but they'd set up their laptops and screens so they could watch what was going on at the house. They were across the bay from the Senator's house with a group of other boats. Nothing to draw attention to them. Hargate's people hadn't taken any notice of them, at least nothing that stood out.

"Thanks," Nick said as Finn put the coffee down on the desk in front of him. "How are you holding up?"

Finn shrugged. "Hanging in there."

"It will be over soon."

"God, I hope so." He glanced at the screen. Tory was back in her room. Her phone rang. It was the burner cell. She pulled it out. "Hey." The view from the brooch was of the balcony and the water. Tory must have gone outside because now all they could see was the water in front of her father's house. "Uh-huh." There was more silence. "I see. Okay. Thanks for the call. See you soon." The cell phone appeared in her hands again.

They'd decided she wouldn't speak to them through the camera unless she absolutely had to. It was a safe assumption that her room was bugged. Tory went back into the room and dropped the burner cell into her purse. Then she pulled out her normal cell. She held the phone up and started typing a text message.

CIA are on the island. Will reach out to you shortly.

She waited about five seconds and then erased the message and put her phone away. There was a knock at her door. She answered it. It was Salome. "Ready to go for a swim?"

"All set." Tory closed the room door, and the guys watched them walk out to the pool area and settle into some chairs.

"We need to plan the exchange. Once the CIA gets here, we'll figure it out." Nick clapped Finn on the back. "This is the hard part. It gets easier after this."

Finn frowned. "What gets easier?"

"Tory. Once this is over, you can go tell her you're sorry for whatever stupid shit you did, and you two can get back together."

"What makes you think it was me that did something stupid?" Finn demanded.

Nick gave him a pitying look. "Wasn't it?"

"No. I…" Was it his fault? No, she'd dumped him right after their night together. Right after the phone call. The one where she knew it was Hargate and her father selling secrets. The one where she'd figured her career was over. The one where she didn't want to bring him down with her.

"Ah, fuck." Finn ran his hands over his face.

"You figured out how you screwed up. Good. That's step one on the road to recovery. It gets easier, man."

The radio chirped. Axe's voice came through. "We've got company."

Nick responded, and the two of them headed topside. Even though leaving the surveillance monitors without cover gnawed his ass, Finn knew Elias and Cain were watching the house. If Tory was in trouble, they'd let Nick know.

A small powerboat drew up alongside their yacht. Two men dressed in tropical shirts were on board. The driver cut the engine and stood. Finn, alert for any trouble, assessed him as an adversary. Average height, slicked-back blond hair and aviator sunglasses. His red shirt had some wimpy floral design that reminded Finn of *Magnum P.I.,* the show from the eighties. If he had to guess, he'd say the guy was in his forties, but it was hard to tell.

Finn caught the rope the other passenger threw, and then quickly secured it around a cleat.

The second man was shorter and stockier. His shirt was mostly yellow, and the sun created a glare on his bald head. He looked to be closer to fifty. Of the two, Finn judged the driver to be a more worthy opponent in whatever kind of fight went down.

"Ahoy," the driver said. "We're friends of the winner."

Finn glanced at Nick and cocked a wry eyebrow. *Ahoy?* The rest was the code they'd worked out earlier.

"Hey," was all Nick said. The yacht rocked in the waves as the two men boarded. The taller of the two, the guy in the red shirt, stuck out his hand. "Bob Smith, and this is my partner, Dan Brown."

Nick shook his hand. "Mr. Smith, Mr. Brown. I'm Pete. That's Joe," he said, pointing to Axe, "and that's Jay," he said indicating Finn. Finn bit back a snort at the uninspired fake names. *Who comes up with this shit?*

Nick swept a hand toward the cabin. "Now that we're all introduced, do you want some coffee?"

"I wouldn't say no." Bob smiled. They all went through the salon to the galley kitchen. Bob and Dan sat at the table and Nick and Finn leaned against the counter. Axe went back up to the flybridge to keep an eye out. It was always good to know what was going on around them.

Finn poured two mugs of black coffee and set them down in front of Mr. Smith and Mr. Brown.

Nick gave them a minute to take a sip and then asked, "What can we do for you?"

"That's a good question." Bob nodded. He seemed like the guy in charge. "We have word that the North Koreans have rented a yacht out of Grand Turk. They brought their own captain. He got charts and maps for the area. So it looks like the meeting will be held not too far away. That's good. We have several boats at the ready to scoop them up."

"Wait, you want to scoop up the North Koreans? That wasn't part of the deal."

"If we have the opportunity to scoop up North Korean spies who are trying to buy our country's secrets, oh, hell yes, we're wrapping that net so tight around their necks—"

"On what grounds will you hold them without causing some sort of international incident? The whole point was to keep this thing quiet," Finn demanded.

Yellow-shirted Dan put his mug down. "We can't discuss that aspect of this operation."

Finn thought he might explode. How the hell had Tory ever worked for these people? "But—"

"Don't worry. That has nothing to do with the other," Bob said. "We will make sure our mutual friend is safe and we'll get the hard case."

"What about arresting the senator and his cronies?" Nick asked.

Bob flicked a glance at Dan, who shook his head ever so slightly. Finn turned to Dan. That little exchange proved that he was the real leader. "You're not picking up the Senator and his cronies because you're going to make them do your bidding. Sonofabitch! So, you are offering up 'our mutual friend' on a platter because that's what's going to happen when you don't grab the senator and friends. You're actually offering all of us up, including Admiral Bertrand."

Dan's face remained impassive. "You must understand. There are bigger things at play."

Finn damn near went across the kitchen at him. Nick grabbed his shoulder and held him back. "My colleague is right. You're screwing us over." He flexed his fingers into Finn's shoulder right where he knew it would grab his attention. Finn stood down but continued to seethe inside.

Dan nodded his head. "I can see how you feel that way,

but we did come here to tell you of our plans. That's the best we can do under the circumstances."

Finn spoke through clenched teeth. "So, you're going to move in and sweep up the North Koreans and the server but leave the traitors behind so they can continue to be powerful and do what you want. Meanwhile, they destroy the careers and possibly the lives of the rest of us."

Dan stared at Finn. "Welcome to the big leagues."

Finn fisted his hands. He was going to lose his shit. This was beyond anything he could have imagined. It was just fucking crazy. Nick dug his fingers into Finn's shoulder again and turned to the men at the table. "Get the fuck out before he kills both of you and we throw your bodies overboard to feed the fish."

Dan blinked and started to smile and then quickly realized Nick wasn't joking.

"I'd hustle," Nick said. "He's really fucking strong. I can't hold him for long."

Dan and Bob both got up and left the galley. Nick kept a hold of Finn's shoulder until the engines of the other boat revved to life.

As it faded into the distance, Axe came down to the kitchen. "What the fuck? They left in one hell of a hurry."

Finn opened his mouth, but Nick shook his head. He went over to the table and looked underneath. He pulled out a listening device. Finn saw red. He needed to scream and rage. It was so fucking ridiculous.

Nick turned to Axe and mouthed, "*Do a sweep.*"

Wordlessly, Axe nodded.

He grabbed Finn and took him out on deck and then up to the flybridge. He pulled up the anchor.

"What are you doing?" Finn asked.

"Moving. I don't want those fuckers to know where we

are. Go down and search the deck. See if they left a tracker when they tied up."

Finn clenched his jaw. He needed something to do, or he was going to put his fist through something. They were fucking sacrificing all of them to have powerful allies they could manipulate. MacAllister would make sure they all lost their jobs at the very least and the CIA would let him because it didn't matter to them one way or the other. Tory had called these people because she thought she could trust them. That had been an obvious mistake.

He searched the deck but found nothing. He peered over the side and found a small tracker hooked on the side of the yacht. "Fuckers," he swore.

He started to throw the thing in the water and then changed his mind. He went up to Nick and told him the idea he'd just had. Nick smiled and agreed. They pulled up by a buoy not far from where they'd been. Finn reached out and stuck the tracker on the thing. Then they pulled away.

Thirty minutes later, they dropped anchor on the other side of the bay. They were out of sight of the house but in the opposite direction. Axe had done a thorough sweep and found one more listening device out on the deck.

They reconvened on the flybridge. "What the fuck are we going to do?" Finn demanded. "Tory is a sitting duck. We're all fucked, including Bertrand. You know the CIA will let MacAllister have his revenge. We don't matter to them. And MacAllister is a bastard. We'll be lucky to get out with our lives."

Nick nodded.

"Wait? What the hell happened?" Axe asked. Nick filled him in. Axe massaged the back of his neck. "Well, shit. Now what do we do?"

Nick picked up the binoculars and did a three-hundred-and-sixty-degree turn. "We're clear." He put the field glasses down. "I will call Bertrand, but it would be best to pull Tory out of her father's place."

"You want me to text her the code?" Finn asked. He wanted her out of there pronto. It was going on dinner, and if it didn't happen soon, it would be time for the meeting. They couldn't be in two places at once.

"Yeah. This's what I'm thinking," Nick said and laid out a plan. Finn nodded, but he felt sick to his stomach. "It's not the best, but it will have to do. It won't stop the fallout, but maybe we can spin it so Bertrand gets to keep his job and we get to keep ours. Tory is not going to survive it, though. Her father will crush her." His heart hurt. She was going to be destroyed.

Nick nodded. "Yeah, but I can't think of any other way to make this work."

Finn grabbed his phone and sent a text to Tory. She had to get out of there as quickly as possible. He needed her to be safe, at least physically. Her world was about to come crashing down, and there would be no safe corner of the earth left for her once this was through.

CHAPTER TWENTY-FIVE

Tory glanced at her phone and read the message twice. It was their emergency abort message. She couldn't believe it. Why were they aborting? What was going on? They were so close. She stared at the phone. She'd just finished getting ready for dinner. She couldn't leave now if she wanted to. Her father would throw a shit fit. She needed to wait until after dinner and then make her excuses. Was the airport open? If not, what excuse could she make?

There was a knock at the door. "Tory?" It was Salome.

"Coming." Tory put her phone back in her purse and put the blue flower camera brooch on the shoulder strap of the light blue sun dress she was wearing. She put on a pair of white low-heeled sandals. They were easier to run in. It might be a necessity at this point.

She opened the door. "Salome, you look lovely." She was wearing a plum-colored lightweight pantsuit.

"Thank you. I thought we could walk down to dinner together. Make it easier to avoid Childers. That man creeps me out." She shook her head and laughed.

"I know what you mean. Yuck." Tory didn't need to fake

a shudder rippling through her. She closed the bedroom door behind her. Didn't matter what Finn had texted. For now, leaving would have to wait.

Dinner was a lively affair. Everyone, including her father, was in a good mood. Tory swore she could feel the undercurrent of excitement running through the group. She tried to discern who the third co-conspirator was but was drawing a blank.

It couldn't be Childers. He was the alibi. His reputation as a senator was pristine other than him being a letch of course. He was the one her father would trot out as his escape route if anyone asked any questions. That left Chris the Congressman. She watched him over dinner. Young enough to think he knew it all but smart enough to realize an opportunity when he saw it. He could be the future of the party. If they ran him for President with her father as Vice President, they would definitely have a solid shot.

The dessert was finished, and people started getting up from the table. This was her chance. If she was going to go, it had to be now while she was in a room full of people so her father couldn't contradict her too much. He hated scenes. He preferred to do his abusing in private.

"Father," she said, "I'm going to have to head out. I have a meeting I have to be at first thing in the morning."

Her father's gaze swung in her direction. His blue eyes were chips of ice. "But tomorrow is Sunday."

"I know." She gusted out a fake sigh. "I don't have a choice though."

Chris asked, "Is the airport open?"

Shit. Forgot about that. Tory indulged in some quick thinking. "Not sure. I'm going to take a ferry to Grand Turk and catch a flight from there. Just makes more sense to go tonight. It was lovely spending time with you all. I do hope I see you again soon." She turned to her father. "Happy birthday, Senator." She gave him a false smile and then made a beeline for the exit. Whatever was going on, she had to trust the team. If they said go, she needed to blow on out of here.

She hurried to her room, yanked open her suitcase and threw in her clothes. The clothes would be wrinkled, but time was of the essence. She scanned the room one last time, making sure she had everything before grabbing her bag and heading out of the room. She came face to face with her father in the hallway.

"Victory, I am not pleased." More than that, he was livid. She'd embarrassed him by leaving and doing it in front of people.

"I'm sorry, Father, but I do have a meeting to get to."

She tried to move around him, but he grabbed her arm and squeezed. Tory was certain that soon there'd be finger-shaped bruises on her bicep.

"The ferries don't run at this time of night," he hissed, a tiny bit of spittle landing on her cheek.

Her stomach cramped and sweat trickled down her spine. "I'll have to rent a boat, I guess. I really do have to be at the meeting."

He squeezed her arm harder, his fingers biting into the tender flesh on the inside of her arm. He spoke through clenched teeth, "You will be on the yacht with me. I'm taking it out. I will drop you on Grand Turk when I'm good and ready to do so. Do you understand me?" When he shook her hard, her teeth clattered together.

She wanted to throw up. That was her normal response. The one that had developed over years of abuse. But after the wave receded, it was followed by a new sensation. Rage. Full-blown rage. Ice filled every crevice inside of her body. They'd lied when they'd said a person saw red when filled with this sort of anger. Rage wasn't red. It was cold. It was blue. She was going to kill her father. She was going to beat him senseless. Hands curled into fists, she decided she wasn't going to put up with his shit anymore. She ripped her arm from his grasp and reeled on him.

"Jeffry?" Minerva called as she came around the corner. "There you are." It only took a second for her to realize something was wrong. Her eyes went to Tory's arm and then to her partner's face. She tried to back up, to turn away, but she wasn't fast enough. He was on her in a second.

"Minerva," he said as he put one arm around her shoulders, "Tory is coming with me for our little cruise, and I will drop her off on Grand Turk afterward."

Tory was about to protest when her father moved his arm so that his hand was on the back of Minerva's neck. He spread his fingers out and squeezed. Minerva didn't make a sound, but her eyes were the size of golf balls. Her mouth drew down at the corners, as if in pain. Tory had been wrong. Her father had been abusing Minerva all these years. Anyone else would be fighting and crying out in pain, but those who'd suffered abuse at the hands of Jeffry James MacAllister knew that if you did any of those things, the abuse was prolonged.

Tory met her father's eyes. He would continue to hurt Minerva until Tory said yes. She wanted to fight him, but she just couldn't do that to the other woman.

"Fine. You win." She would give in, but she wasn't going to dress up their relationship anymore. She was done hiding his shit. He was an abusive son of a bitch and she would yell it far and wide the moment she had the opportunity. *If* she ever had the chance.

His eyes gleamed with his presumed superiority. "Come along, Minerva. Come see us off." He walked Minerva right by Tory, keeping his hand on her neck. He was going to keep it that way until Tory was on board the yacht. There was no escape.

She turned and watched them disappear down the stairs. She quickly dug out her cell phone and sent a text saying she was stuck. Then she moved her gun to the front pocket of her bag. She didn't have a holster to wear it with, and the dress didn't have pockets. If she was lucky, her father would overlook searching her bag.

She picked up her luggage and went down the stairs. She walked around the side of the house and headed toward the dock. She finally understood Finn's rage. She got it. It wasn't something that was directed at the world. He didn't want to hurt everyone. Just the one person who deserved it.

It wasn't healthy. Her shrink would have a field day with it, but she got it. As the fear receded, icy rage rode in. She could only hope this ugliness would recede in time as well. But for now, it was the one thing that was keeping her going.

She walked onto the dock. Her father was waiting there with Minerva. He gestured for her to go up the walkway first. Tory glanced at Minerva, who refused to meet her gaze. Amazingly, Tory felt sympathy for the woman. She'd thought Minerva should have been able to help her when she was younger. She should have stood up to her father for Tory, but Tory realized now that Minerva was too weak and even at the beginning was probably in the same boat Tory was in. It took a lot of courage to speak out against an abuser. It was Tory who was going to have to be the one to take on her father. She'd find that courage, come hell or high water.

She walked onto the yacht with her head held high. She wasn't going down without a fight. *Bring it on.*

CHAPTER TWENTY-SIX

"They're pulling away now," Axe said into the radio. Nick responded and so did the radio operator on the *Robert Walton*. He set the radio down and fired up the yacht's engines.

Finn shook his head in disbelief. "I can't believe Bertrand brought the *Walton* down here."

"Gerhart volunteered. He wants a part in the takedown of whoever killed all those men on the *Explorer*."

"I don't blame him for that. Hargate should be drawn and quartered. You know he had them all killed just to make sure no one was left alive to turn on him."

Nick watched as the sixty-foot yacht Hargate had rented left the bay adjacent to MacAllister's house. It headed out to sea. "I don't think we're going far." Hargate's yacht pulled away from the dock. "MacAllister needs to be back for his guests."

Finn grunted. "Tory's message said she was stuck, meaning she didn't have a choice. I think he threatened that woman beside him. Did you see the way he held her by the neck?" Finn was doing his best not to freak out, but it was hard. The rage was gone, but now abject fear roiled in the pit of his stomach. What if something happened to Tory? What if her father tried to kill her again?

They'd moved their yacht closer so they could keep both boats in view at all times. The MacAllister yacht had just left. It was slower than Hargate's. Obviously, he wasn't going to meet up with Hargate on the water, but MacAllister didn't trust him to be out there on his own.

"What's to stop him from heading for the next island after the exchange?" Finn asked.

"You mean Hargate? Greed and the need for power would be my guess. Even if he had access to the money. Access to the power comes from MacAllister." Nick glanced over at him. "Finn, I have to ask. Are you going to be able to do this? Can you do your part? I understand completely if you can't. Tory being at risk puts this whole thing in a different light."

Finn didn't blame Nick for asking. "Tag, I know you and Axe and Elias know what this feels like. You've all been here. I… I've got this. I can do it. It's my job. You are my team. She is my woman. I won't fail."

Nick nodded once. "Axe is back with Cain and Elias."

Finn went down and helped them tie up. "Sorry, man," Elias said as he came on board. He lifted his hand for a fist bump. Finn tapped his knuckles against his friend's.

Axe came and stood beside him. "She'll be fine. We'll get her back."

"I know," he said, and he did. He knew it in his bones just like he knew she was his for life. He was in love with her, and he wasn't about to lose her now.

Cain came to a stop directly in front of Finn. "She's CIA trained. She knows how to take care of herself. Don't second guess her. She'll be fine."

It was true. Cain was right. He had to trust in Tory. She

could take care of herself. The way his heart clenched told him that trusting his gut and Tory's abilities was easier said than done.

Nick called down for them, and they all went up to the flybridge. "Go get your gear on. Axe, you and Cain take the tender to the *Walton*. Once there, switch to a RHIB to facilitate boarding Hargate's yacht."

"Finn, Elias and I will stay here with the other tender. You all know the rest of the plan. Let's make this happen. Watch each other's six."

The guys went down to the cabins below and got changed into full tactical gear. Axe and Cain left to head over to the *Walton,* which was following Hargate via radar.

Finn sat down in the room to monitor the video feed. He wasn't sure how long it would last, but he was so thankful that she was still wearing the brooch. "It won't be long now, Tory." He spoke softly. She couldn't hear him, but he needed her to know he was there with her. This was going to suck for her. They had no way of telling her the plan and no way for her to know why it had changed. He just hoped she had enough faith and trust in them to roll with it.

"How's it going?" Nick asked. He'd changed into full tactical gear.

"Fine by the looks of things. She is still standing on deck."

He nodded.

"How far out do you think they'll go?" Finn asked.

"Not far. Hargate will go maybe a quarter to a half a mile further than MacAllister. He'll set up for the exchange, and MacAllister will watch from a distance. He'll be on standby in case anything goes wrong with the money transfer."

Finn bounced his knee up and down. He would normally be making origami animals, but he couldn't take his eyes off the screen long enough to make the folds necessary.

The radio sounded again. "Hargate is slowing down."

"Roger that," Nick responded. "Won't be long now." He put his hand on Finn's shoulder and squeezed.

Finn just stared at the screen, willing Tory to know that they were coming for her. She was not alone.

CHAPTER TWENTY-SEVEN

Tory's teeth had begun to chatter. Either from cold or fear. She couldn't tell which. Maybe a lethal combination of both. She'd have to go inside soon but was holding out to be sure the team, especially Finn, knew where she was and that she was okay. The rocking of the yacht in the gentle waves was enough to kickstart a bout of seasickness, and on top of shivering, her gut churned, a double whammy of misery. She said a silent prayer that the team had gotten the message. With a gulp of salty air, she turned and pulled her luggage into the lounge.

"Look who finally decided to join us?" her father's voice boomed out. He was playing the jovial host.

She wasn't having it. She sat down in a wingback chair in the right corner of the salon that offered a view of the whole room. She hoped the brooch still recorded and maybe her father would say something to implicate himself. She could only hope.

Her father was behind the bar on the left side of the room, pouring Scotch. "Would you like one?"

"No. I hate Scotch."

"News to me." There was derision in his voice, as if he'd chomped down on something nasty.

"There are a lot of things about me that would be news to you."

Voices reached her ears. People were coming up from below. Finally, she would find out who the co-conspirators were. Wilber Clayton entered the salon and took the proffered Scotch. Then Salome Jones sashayed into the room.

It was a damn good thing she was sitting down because Tory wasn't sure her knees would hold her at the moment. Salome? Why on earth would she commit treason? The misery rolling in her belly intensified.

Salome saw her in the corner and turned to MacAllister. "What is she doing here?"

"My daughter seems to be in a rush to leave us this evening. I thought it was only fitting I offered her a lift."

"She knows." Salome glared at Tory. "I told you she knew something. This sudden rush to go. There's something going on."

Her father snorted. "Don't overreact, Salome. She doesn't know a damn thing. They've been flailing around in the dark for ages. It's fine. After tonight, it won't matter anymore."

Tory watched them all in shock. Then she snapped out of it. Did the camera still work? She had a couple of options. They weren't far offshore and she knew Finn wouldn't be far away. Should she take the gamble? At this point, what did she have to lose?

"I know what you're up to. I just didn't know who was involved. Now I do." Tory made her voice as cold as possible.

"Oh, my God, Salome, you were right." Wilber Clayton downed his drink in one gulp. "We're screwed. Jeff, how are we going to get out of this one?"

"Relax, Wilber. It's fine. She's bluffing." Her father arched one eyebrow and tipped his head toward her. Close enough she wanted to head-butt him.

She could almost feel him willing her to break under his scrutiny. She merely put on the blank face she had perfected all those years ago, but she added a cold little smile.

"She's not bluffing," Salome said. "She knows. We need to radio the other boat. We need to stop the exchange."

"We can't stop the exchange." Her father's voice boomed as he swept an arm out, spilling some of his Scotch on the plush carpet. "Hargate is already in position. We can't walk away from the deal now. This is an easy fix. My daughter will tell us what she knows and who else knows it and then we'll do clean up. Don't panic. Billions of dollars will buy a lot of cleaning materials." He sipped his Scotch.

Tory stared at her father. He actually believed what he was saying, and he would come out of all this smelling like a rose. It was amazing to her that he was still that confident. Well, he wouldn't be so arrogant when he was in a dark hole somewhere.

Salome came over and stood in front of Tory. "So, what do you know? What is the plan? Who is helping you?"

Tory looked up into the face of the woman she'd enjoyed spending time with and resisted the urge to hurl on the judge's designer sandals. She swallowed down the rising sick. "I admired you. I thought you were a person of character, of quality. You were someone who stood out to me as a leader. You were a shoo-in for being a supreme court justice. How could you be a traitor? Why?"

Salome snorted. "Easy. Money. I'll still be on the Supreme Court. Now I'll just do it with money in my pocket. I'm tired of being broke. I have a lot of people in my corner. I have a voice to promote important causes, but I don't have any money. My husband was a degenerate and a gambler. He lost everything, so I lost him. Now I want what's rightfully mine. I am not going back to being poor."

Tory's mouth dropped open. *Money*? All this over money? She killed her husband? Tory closed her eyes for a brief second. Her judgment of people's character was obviously way off. When she should have trusted Finn above all others, she'd doubted. Finn, who was head and shoulders above this woman, and yet she had believed in the false front that this monster had put forth.

"Well, it's all for nothing. I know all about your deal with the North Koreans. It's not going to happen so you're not going to get your money." Tory watched as her words sunk in.

Salome's face drained of color. She staggered a step and then started to lunge toward Tory.

"This is the United States Coast Guard hailing the *Wanderlust*. Prepare to be boarded."

"Holy shit!" Clayton's mouth kept opening and closing like a fish. "That's Hargate's boat. That's Hargate's boat. We're sunk. Oh, my God. We're going to prison. It's over. We're dead." He collapsed onto the matching wingback chair opposite Tory's.

Salome whirled around. "Jeffry, you said it would be fine. You said"—she was pointing her finger now—"not to worry. I told you your daughter knew too much. I told you to get rid of her."

"I did try," he said calmly as he glared at Tory. "She is hard to kill, apparently. Hargate's people couldn't seem to manage it." His admission that he's ordered her death numbed Tory. After one last sneer at her, he turned to Salome. "You need to calm down. This means nothing."

"Nothing?" she screeched. "It means everything. We're finished."

"We are *not* finished." Her father calmly took a sip of his drink. "They have nothing on us. We are not on that ship. We were not part of the auction, nor did we know what was going on. But we suspected, which is why I called my friend, Ted, the director of the FBI and reported everything to him. Hargate will, of course, blame us, but since Ted knew of our scheme to help him catch the culprit who tapped into the fiber optic cables, he knows the truth."

Tory's stomach rolled. She braced herself for what was coming. He'd outthought her, out-planned her once again. He *was* going to get away with this.

"Ted, of course, called his friend, Joe, the head of the CIA and told him about the whole plot. They are part of the whole thing. I imagine right now they are over on the *Wanderlust* arresting Hargate and his people. They'll be thrown in cells in a federal prison and the key will be tossed away. The North Koreans will be taken in for use at a later date. Spy exchange, I would imagine. And the money that they transferred into the accounts, it will go to fund special operations at the CIA and the FBI for the foreseeable future. Minus a nice cut for the three of us." He took another sip of his drink. "So, you see, we are in fine shape. The only issue is my daughter."

Tory steadily met her father's glare. He looked triumphant. He'd beaten her again, and he knew it. She wanted to scream and cry and rage, but she just sat there as the boat continued to rock in the waves. This was supposed to be the time when she came out on top. How the fuck had he won again?

"So, I will ask once more. Who did you tell? I know you were working with a Coast Guard team. I understand Admiral Bertrand has been making discrete inquiries. If that's it, if that's your whole team, then that is easily handled." His triumphant chuckle chilled her to the bone. "You thought you could win against me. You thought you could actually take me down." He laughed. "You're not smart enough. You don't have the ability to see past the end of your shoes. You are weak and pathetic." He picked up the Scotch bottle and refilled his glass. "You know, I'm trying to decide whether I should kill you or have you committed to a mental institution. I know of a few that would be happy to keep you for the rest of your days, for a small fee of course."

Wilber Clayton came over to the bar and refilled his own glass. "You might have mentioned all of this. I almost had a heart attack." He gulped the contents of his glass.

Salome went over to the bar as well. "How much? How much are we getting?"

"Eight figures each." Her father continued staring at Tory.

She couldn't believe it. She just hadn't seen that far ahead. Her father was so much more devious than even she thought. Hargate was the only loose end, and her father had his cronies taking care of that for him. Unbelievable. She was numb.

"Eight figures. I can live on that," Salome said.

"I wouldn't count your money just yet," Finn said as he entered the salon. He was in full tactical gear and holding an assault rifle at the ready. "Things aren't as rosy as you seem to think."

"Who the hell are you?" Salome yelled.

"Chief Petty Officer Finn Walsh, United States Coast Guard."

Tory's eyes welled up at the sight of him. She'd destroyed his career and the rest of the team. Oh, God, and Bertrand. They'd all be buried because she hadn't outthought her father. She didn't even want to meet Finn's gaze.

"You okay?" he asked her.

She nodded, unable to get any words out. She needed to tell him that it wasn't going to work. Their plan was no good.

Nick and Elias also came into the salon with their own guns aimed at the yacht's captain and the first officer. "Good evening, Senator MacAllister," Nick said. "We'll be taking your crew with us for questioning." With that, he and Elias led them out the back of the salon.

With barely a beat of his eyelashes, her father asked, "Mr. Walsh, what can I do for you?"

"Oh, Senator, it's not what you can do for us, but what we can do for you." Finn smiled a cold smile. "You see, currently, Hargate is in custody, and he is spilling his guts, implicating you in a treasonous plan to sell secrets to the North Koreans."

"I think you're mistaken. As I told my good friend, the director of the FBI, and our other good friend, the director of the CIA, I was aware of Hargate's activities, and I was monitoring the situation for them. They are aware of my limited participation in the matter and are thankful for my support."

"I see," Finn said. "Well, sir, it seems that since you aren't good friends with the director of Homeland Security, he felt you should be brought in for questioning. Anyone involved in treason does not get a pass. We have a tender waiting to take you to the Coast Guard cutter, the *Robert Walton,* where you will be questioned by several top officials from DHS. They are eager to hear your version of things. Hargate's has been very interesting so far."

Tory's heart hammered painfully. Was it true? She glanced at Finn, but he kept his gaze steadfastly trained on her father.

"I don't think you understand. Ted Caveller, head of the FBI, knows all about this, as does Joseph Sanders of the CIA. They can vouch for me."

Finn nodded. "I am sure that's true, sir. However, I don't

answer to either one of those men. My boss wants your ass on board the *Walton,* so you need to move."

"You need to speak to me with respect. I'm a United States senator."

"What you are is a traitor. You don't deserve my respect. Now move." Finn waved his assault rifle at MacAllister, then addressed Clayton and Salome, "You two are also coming along. Move!"

Tory watched in fascination as her father still believed he was going to get his way. He reached into his pocket.

"Hands! Let me see your hands!" Finn said and aimed his weapon squarely at her father's chest.

Nick returned to the salon and lifted his gun in the senator's direction.

MacAllister held up his right hand and reached into his pocket with his left. "I'm getting my cell phone. I'm going to call Ted." He pulled out his cell and hit a button. He put his phone to his ear. Tory heard a recorded greeting from across the room. The call had gone straight to voicemail. Her father glared at Finn as he tried another number. Again, it went straight to voicemail.

"If you're finished," Finn snarled, "it's time to go."

"I'm most certainly not finished. I will have your head for this," her father raged.

Finn smiled. "Highly unlikely. You see this flower?" He indicated the brooch pinned to Tory's dress with the butt of his gun. "It's a camera. It has recorded your entire exchange this evening. My boss, the head of Homeland, then streamed the feed to the head of the CIA and the FBI. Maybe that's why they aren't taking your calls." His smile grew. "Your ass is grass. Your daughter outplayed you. You are finished."

Elias returned. "Dammit, I miss all the best moments. If I'd been betting on this outcome, I'd have won large!"

Tory couldn't believe her ears. It had worked. The camera

worked. Her bid to get them talking had paid off. She wanted to jump into Finn's arms and scream with joy. She stood up. "I think you will also be charged with accessory to commit murder. Oh, and Salome murdered her husband so that needs to be addressed as well."

Finn nodded. "Yes, ma'am. I'm sure it will all be looked into."

Nick came around Finn and grabbed a hold of Salome's arm. He pulled her out of the salon. Elias took Senator Clayton, who had aged twenty years in the last ten minutes.

Finn jerked the muzzle of his weapon upward. "Senator MacAllister, you need to move. If I have to come get you, it will not go well for you."

Tory was elated. She couldn't believe what was happening. It was a fucking miracle. But when she glanced over at her father, her stomach instantly knotted. She knew that look. *She knew.* The senator's hand was beneath the bar. She reached for her gun.

"Hands!" Finn yelled, but Tory knew it was too late. There was a loud boom, and Finn flew backward onto the floor.

Her father looked at her and smiled. She pulled the trigger once, twice, three times. She hit him center mass. He stared at her disbelieving. He couldn't believe she'd shot him. It was written all over his face as he slid down behind the bar.

Believe it.

"Finn!" she yelled. "Finn!" She crouched down beside him and touched his face. He'd taken a shotgun blast to his chest. "Oh, my God, Finn. Please be alive. I love you. Please be okay."

But he remained motionless.

CHAPTER TWENTY-EIGHT

"Can you hand me that beer?" Finn asked as he lay in a beach chair.

"You are just milking this for all it's worth," Tory said as she reached over and grabbed the beer off the table in the sand and gave it to him.

Finn grinned. "Well, it's not every day a man gets shot in the chest and lives to tell."

"It hit your vest. You're just bruised."

"Badly bruised is what the doctor said." Finn took a sip of beer. "I need rest and relaxation."

"Uh-huh." Tory shook her head. "Did you hear what happened to Clayton?" she asked.

"No."

"He apparently couldn't take the stress. He had a stroke. Now he can't speak. He's in some sort of long-term care facility."

"What about Jones?"

"Salome? She is under indictment for her husband's murder. The trial will be lengthy and ugly, and it will be held in her former courtroom."

"Well, that's a nice piece of justice."

Finn closed his eyes and relaxed in the warmth of the sun. He'd been treading softly around Tory. It had been six weeks since she'd shot her father, and this was the first moment they'd had a chance to spend time together. There'd been way too many debriefings by every organization under the sun. It had been another level of crazy. He was just glad it was over.

"So…" He opened his eyes and looked at Tory. "Why did you invite me here?" Not that he was complaining. Turks and Caicos was beautiful. The hotel was amazing. And Tory in a tiny purple string bikini was absolutely stunning. He couldn't look at her too often or he was gonna have an issue.

"You want to do this now?" she said. "You've been here all of an hour."

"I like to get things over with. Rip the Band-Aid off quickly."

She sat up and turned to face him. They were alone on a stretch of beach. Most people were already in the water, so it was the ideal time to chat as far as he was concerned. He didn't want to get too comfortable if she was going to ditch him again. She'd invited him so he thought that was a good sign, but who the hell knew?

He'd prepared for the worst but prayed fervently for the best.

"Finn, first I want to say thank you for saving me."

"You were the one who saved me, if memory serves."

"No." She shook her head. "I thought my father had beaten me. Us. I should have known you guys would figure something out."

"You figured it out. You got him talking. All we did was make sure the right people saw it."

"No, what you did was save me. My whole world was imploding. I thought he'd never have to pay for everything he's done. I went numb inside. It wasn't until you walked in the door that I realized it didn't matter. That he couldn't beat me because I wasn't going to play the game anymore."

She took a moment her throat constricting as if swallowing hard before she continued. "I thought I had gotten him out of my life, but in the end, I was still playing his game by his rules. It wasn't until you that I realized I didn't have to play. And you were right. Killing him… It wasn't the relief I thought it would be. I'm still processing it. I'm not sure how I feel. The world is definitely a better place without him in it, but I'm not sure how I feel about him."

"It will take a while. You'll get there eventually."

"So my shrink says." She laughed.

"But what I do know is how I feel about you." She met his gaze again. "I'm sorry I hurt you when I asked about the incident with your commanding officer. You were right. I should have trusted my gut. I should have trusted you."

Finn's heart lurched as hope swarmed up his chest. "I shouldn't have gotten so angry so quickly. You had a right to ask with everything you'd been through."

"Finn, I know you said we'd never get back together after that night in the hotel, but I was hoping you'd change your mind. I can't promise I won't piss you off again, but I can promise that I will love you."

He swallowed. Hard. He sat up in the chair. "Tory, I have loved you from the moment I saw you in that bar. There is no other woman on earth for me." He leaned over and kissed her.

She laughed. "I thought you were in pain."

"Not that much pain," he said and then scooped her off the chair and brought her into his lap where he kissed her like their lives depended on it.

SNEAK PEAK: TERMINATED

Coast Guard RECON Book 5
　Here's a first look at Cain Maddox's story from Terminated, Book 5 in the Coast Guard RECON series

TERMINATED

2007 Iraq

"Are you sure this is the right call?" The soldier glanced nervously down the tunnel. Roman Vance didn't normally question his superior officer but this…this was different.

Lieutenant Asher Foley's eyes were black as night and his face was burnt from the Iraqi sun. His dark hair was badly in need of a cut, and he was in desperate need of a shave. Foley was in excellent shape as any Army Ranger should be, but he was covered in a layer of dirt that made him look more like he lived on the street rather than in uniform.

He glared at Vance. "It's not like we can just waltz this out of Iraq at the moment. It should be fine here for a while. Once things calm down, we'll move it. Remember," he leaned forward so he was mere inches from Vance's face, "this is not a sprint but a marathon. This is the beginning for us, not the end. In a few months when we get out, we're gonna build a business and this is going to help us. So don't worry and more important, don't fuck this up."

Foley walked over to check on the other men who were

rearranging the pallets in the tunnel. Vance slouched against the tunnel wall. He didn't want to be here. They had it all within their grasp but his superior officer and soon to be boss when he mustered out, was willing to put it off. How long? When would it cool down enough to move their prize?

Vance wasn't known for his patience, and he respected Foley, but the truth was, burying the whole mess was making him nervous. If it was found, they would lose their entire future. If it wasn't found, but they couldn't get it out of the country, they would lose their future plans as well. He was trying to be calm but all he kept thinking was if he died before they got it out, he would miss out. He hated missing out.

Foley came back. "They're finished. Everything is in place. You know what to do." He nodded at Vance and walked over to the rope ladder. He climbed out of the tunnel without a backward glance confident that his subordinate would carry out his orders.

Vance waited until Foley was gone as he was instructed to do. Then he went over to the four Iraqi men they'd hired to move the pallets into the tunnel. They were resting and drinking bottles of water. It was hot, tiring, work. They deserved a break.

Vance brought up his machine gun and with a loud burst of fire, shot every single man. Then he turned around and went over to the rope ladder. He glanced over at the pallets. It was killing him that he had to leave all of this behind. He was even tempted to take some of the cargo with him, but he knew if Foley ever found out, he would be a dead man.

He ground his teeth and climbed out of the tunnel. It would only be a couple of months. He could hang on for that long, couldn't he?

ALSO BY LORI MATTHEWS
CALLAHAN SECURITY

Break and Enter

Smash And Grab

Hit And Run

Evade and Capture

Catch and Release

Cease And Desist

Coast Guard Recon

Diverted

Incinerated

Conflicted

Subverted

Terminated

Coast Guard Hawai'i

A Lethal Betrayal

Brotherhood Protectors World

Justified Misfortune

Justified Burden

Justified Vengeance

Free with Newsletter Sign Up

Falling For The Witness

Risk Assessment

Visit my website to sign up for my newsletter

ABOUT LORI MATTHEWS

I grew up in a house filled with books and readers. Some of my fondest memories are of reading in the same room with my mother and sisters, arguing about whose turn it was to make tea. No one wanted to put their book down!

I was introduced to romance because of my mom's habit of leaving books all over the house. One day I picked one up. I still remember the cover. It was a Harlequin by Janet Daily. Little did I know at the time that it would set the stage for my future. I went on to discover mystery novels. Agatha Christie was my favorite. And then suspense with Wilber Smith and Ian Fleming.

I loved the thought of combining my favorite genres, and during high school, I attempted to write my first romantic suspense novel. I wrote the first four chapters and then exams happened and that was the end of that. I desperately hope that book died a quiet death somewhere in a computer recycling facility.

A few years later, (okay, quite a few) after two degrees, a husband and two kids, I attended a workshop in Tuscany that lit that spark for writing again. I have been pounding the keyboard ever since here in New Jersey, where I live with my children—who are thrilled with my writing as it means they get to eat more pizza—and my very supportive husband.

Please visit my webpage at https://lorimatthewsbooks.com to keep up on my news.

Made in United States
Orlando, FL
01 May 2024

46390218R00181